'You will o̶b̶e̶y̶ ̶m̶y̶ ̶c̶o̶m̶m̶a̶n̶d̶s̶,'
Edwin sai̶d̶

Their eyes m̶e̶t̶ ̶ ̶ ̶ ̶ ̶ ̶ ̶ ̶ ̶ ̶ ̶ ̶ear?'
he added.

'Perfectly,' Madselin replied.

Edwin turned to leave but checked himself. 'It would give me the greatest of pleasure to hear you refer to me as an Angle rather than a Saxon. Nor,' he added with a faint smile, 'do I come from peasant stock.'

He strode from the room, leaving Madselin staring silently after him. 'Insufferable man,' she hissed. 'I will enjoy teaching him some manners.'

Elizabeth Henshall is married with two young sons and lives in Cheshire. Following a degree in French and German, she had a variety of jobs before deciding to give up office life. A year in Germany teaching English convinced her that this was certainly more exhausting! She now teaches French and German at a local secondary school and finds her life is indeed very busy. Fascinated in particular by local history, Elizabeth enjoys writing and researching with wine at hand.

Recent titles by the same author:

BETRAYED HEARTS

MADSELIN'S CHOICE

Elizabeth Henshall

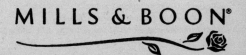

MILLS & BOON®

*MILLS & BOON and MILLS & BOON with the Rose Device
are registered trademarks of the publisher.*

*First published in Great Britain 1997
Harlequin Mills & Boon Limited,
Eton House, 18-24 Paradise Road, Richmond, Surrey, TW9 1SR*

© Elizabeth Henshall 1997

ISBN 0 263 80080 6

*Set in 10 on 11 pt. Linotron Times
04-9707-86031*

*Typeset in Great Britain by CentraCet, Cambridge
Printed and bound in Great Britain by
Caledonian International Book Manufacturing Ltd, Glasgow*

Chapter One

'Seize him!'

Madselin was surprised at how harsh her words sounded as they rang out across the copse. No doubt years of living under Alice's pitiless regime had taken its toll on her in more ways than one. Drawing her thick coney-lined cloak about her against the raw gusts of October wind, she turned to her guards.

'Well?' she uttered with rising indignation. 'Don't just stand there. Take him.'

Her Norman guards did not wait to be told a second time and hurried to do her bidding. Much to her surprise the poacher remained where he was, lowering his bow with what seemed like faint irritation. He made no attempt to escape, merely watching her approach with a bold stare.

Slightly ruffled by his arrogant manners, Madselin pursed her lips and returned his appraisal. Tall as she was for a woman, her head barely reached the man's broad shoulders. Long, unkempt fair hair framed a lean, weatherbeaten face, which was covered in stubble. Cold as the winter grey skies, the peasant's eyes glared down at her with unmistakable annoyance as the guards took hold of his arms.

'Take the Saxon peasant with us to the bailey. Sir Richard will deal with him.'

As the man opened his mouth in protest, Madselin raised her hand to halt his words. 'Hold your tongue. I have neither the means nor inclination to understand your guttural gibberish. Sir Richard may have that pleasure.'

The man's eyes glittered almost silver under the fast-darkening afternoon sky, but Madselin was glad that he made no further attempt to speak. If all the peasants in this wet, cold, godforsaken land were as surly and as ill-mannered as this, no wonder her kinsman was forever quelling insurrections.

A few streaks of rain across her face reminded her that she still had some way to go before reaching the safety of Sir Richard's bailey. The deep, wild Forest of Bowland was no place for a traveller after nightfall. Wolves roamed freely in this isolated northern outpost of William Rufus's kingdom. Madselin shuddered. She would be glad to be gone from this barbaric land.

'We must hurry.' Her words were addressed to the guards. 'Set him to walk behind the mule. I'll not be delayed by a Saxon.'

The guards pushed the man through the undergrowth to another clearing where the rough outline of the northern road was visible. There stood a group of horses and one beleaguered mule, clearly labouring under the weight of the travel bags. By its side, a small, rotund figure huddled in a dark cloak stamped heavily on the ground, muttering indistinctly to herself.

'Emma! We are done and ready to go.' Madselin hurried over to her ageing maid. The poor woman had suffered greatly over these past few weeks on the journey north and she doubted if Emma could carry on much longer. Tough though she was, at forty years Emma was not young.

'About time, too,' came the querulous retort. 'A body could die of cold before you lit a fire.' Emma raised her pinched white face from the folds of her travel-stained cloak, pulled her hood close round her ears and lumbered towards her uncomplaining horse.

Madselin stared after Emma, her mouth twisting in a wry smile. The woman was impossible. It was Emma who had insisted on accompanying her, despite all Madselin's well-founded reasons for wanting her to remain in her brother's manor in Normandy. She had relented only when it became clear that Emma would suffer from Alice's cruelty if Madselin were not there to protect her.

Sighing heavily, she turned to find the tall peasant staring at her in a most insolent manner, almost as if he understood what had been going on. Despite the fact that he had been tied to the mule, he stood proud and erect with such self-possession that it caused Madselin a moment's doubt.

A keen howl suddenly rent the air and froze her blood. It had come from some distance hence, but only a fool would linger in a spot like this. Shouting her orders, Madselin mounted her horse gracefully with the aid of a fallen trunk and the party headed north once more.

From time to time, Madselin glanced back at the captive peasant, but he walked easily and she could discern little discomfort in his long stride. His cloak, she noticed, was lighter and shorter than theirs. Like his boots and his breeches, it was also mud-spattered and torn.

Just as the thick cloudbank rolled over the last of the daylight, a shout from the scout ahead caused Madselin to send up a prayer of thanks. At last they had arrived. Breathing a sigh of relief, she trotted on to the bend in the road where the scout awaited his orders. Not far beyond, like a bright jewel in the dark, lay the stone-built keep held by Sir Richard d'Aveyron. Torch flames lit every corner, offering welcome and warmth to the cold, weary travellers.

The scout galloped ahead to warn the guards of their arrival whilst Madselin made a vain attempt to brush some of the dust from her cloak and restore her appearance. She knew that the wind had torn her dark hair from the tight braids into an unruly bird's nest — little short of a miracle could do aught about it. Madselin would be needing more than one miracle tonight.

'Left your brother's demesne? Are you witless, girl?' Sir Richard d'Aveyron's handsome, swarthy face had turned almost red with apoplexy.

Madselin faced him calmly, deciding that it would be best to ignore his last reference to her status. They were the same age yet, whereas he was one of the King's favoured barons, she was being tongue-lashed for displaying the same mettle.

'Nay,' she returned quietly, ignoring the sea of interested faces turned in her direction. It was most rare for Sir Richard to lose his temper. 'I have not run away at all, but I have no doubt my sister-in-marriage is likely to see my journey in that light.'

Calmed somewhat by the soft, reasonable tone of her voice, Sir Richard grunted at the mention of Alice de Breuville. Alice had been a beauty, and he himself had not been averse to her frail, delicate charms, the white-gold hair and her seductive green eyes. But over the past five years of her marriage to Robert de Breuville, Alice had turned into a spiteful shrew who had made Madselin's life a misery.

He gulped down a mouthful of the sweet red wine he favoured before turning back to face his cousin. 'I received word from Robert some days back. He is convinced you are about to dishonour the family name.'

Madselin stared stonily at Richard. 'Alice wanted me to marry Goddefroi de Grantmesnil.' Her arms crept about her slender frame in protection. 'He is old, cruel and has already killed off three wives.' Madselin's chin rose a little in her defence. 'Nor has he ever produced any children.'

Richard gave a weary sigh. Domestic trivia irritated him. He was a soldier. 'He is of noble blood, Madselin. Your duty. . .'

'My duty?' she interrupted. 'Would you wish to lie with that stinking heap of flesh?' The deep flush of her cheeks betrayed her true anger. Richard d'Aveyron drank deeply from the silver goblet before eyeing his cousin thoughtfully.

'So,' he said after a moment or two, 'I take it you have a desire to marry, but not the Sire de Grantmesnil?'

Madselin looked up at him warily. When Richard was quiet, he was at his most dangerous.

'Aye.'

'He must also be young, kind and lusty?'

Madselin nodded slowly, a frown creasing her brow.

'Tell me,' asked Richard quietly, 'do you have a candidate in mind?'

She held her breath. Had Alice sent word about Hugh, too? And yet, this might be her only chance. Her only one to choose.

'I had always hoped that Hugh and I might. . .'

'Hugh?' D'Aveyron raked his memory.

'Hugh de Montchalon,' she supplied. 'His father's land marches with ours.'

There was silence as Richard digested this piece of information. 'Is he perhaps a younger landless son?'

Richard's dark eyes bored into her with cynicism born of experience.

Madselin's shoulder's drooped. 'Aye, but he is hoping to gain some property soon.'

'He is younger than you,' came the harsh reply. 'Do you not think he might prefer a more...biddable maid?'

Had not Alice said as much a million times over? Was it not that very taunt that had caused her finally to search out the head of her family and gain his permission?

'Six and twenty is not so very old and I have been patient these last eight years whilst my brother dithered over my future. His interests were paramount.'

Eight years? Had it really been that long? His mind flitted back to a moment that seemed etched forever in his memory. He remembered her as a beautiful bride of eighteen, her heart torn to pieces by what to Madselin had been the senseless act of a Saxon mercenary.

Madselin sat down on a wooden seat, weariness overcoming her. 'Please,' she whispered. 'I am begging you not to send me back to Alice.'

Staring at her face, Richard noticed for the first time the telltale lines of strain about her mouth and her eyes. She was tired and overwrought and he needed time to think on this.

He bent to kiss her on the brow. 'We'll talk further about this on the morrow. What we need is some food and drink.'

Madselin nodded slowly. What she truly wanted was a hot tub of water and a soft mattress. Her recent experience of England did not give her much hope.

Richard d'Aveyron's lands had been granted courtesy of Roger de Poictou, one of King William's most feared barons. Brother of the notoriously cruel and traitorous Robert de Belleme of Montgomery, de Poictou had been implicated in the rebellions that swept England during 1088.

Most of Rufus's barons owned lands in Normandy and England and many believed their other lord, Duke Robert of Normandy, should have received England's crown before Rufus. With the help of his loyal men and the English army, Rufus had crushed the rebellions, but had deemed it prudent to treat the majority of his barons leniently.

For this reason, de Poictou had retained his lands, although his activities were viewed with extreme suspicion. De Poictou's north-west lands stretched from the border with Scotland down to the foothills of the Pennines and played a vital role as a guard against the destructive nature of their Scottish enemies.

The responsibility of safeguarding the northern borderlands rested on d'Aveyron's broad shoulders and he chose his tenant knights with care. Treachery amongst the greedy, self-serving Normans was a problem that William the Conqueror had had to contend with and one that now kept William Rufus ever on his guard.

Life amid the never-ending, cold, wet forests, snow-covered peaks of the long hills and treacherous coastal marshlands was hard and lonely. His men were of necessity gritty, tenacious and tough, their women likewise. But his duties lay not only in England. The king was locked in endless fighting with his elder brother, Robert of Normandy. The demands on his barons' coffers and on their knights' service were consequently high.

Madselin gazed around the richly furnished feasting hall, dazzled by the unexpected display of colour and finery. Beeswax candles hissed and fluttered in the draughts caused by the servants carrying in numerous platters of meats, pies and other tasty morsels.

Richard did not stint on luxury, it seemed. Bundles of dried herbs were strewn amid the rushes on the floor and hung from the ceiling rafters to scent the air. The top table was covered in a snow-white tablecloth and boasted several wine goblets of fine silverware and an exquisite silver cellar filled with crumbly salt.

She shared a deep trencher with her cousin who plied her with several choice slices of roast pork, chicken and succulent kid. But, although polite, Richard was distant. His mind was clearly on other things. It would seem that she had been very lucky to find him at his keep.

'Tell me, de Vaillant—' Richard leaned across Madselin to address her neighbour '—have you any more information about Orvell? He's been a thorn in my side for too long.'

Ivo de Vaillant was a small, stocky man of middle years with a shock of thick black hair and very broad shoulders. Keen brown eyes stared out intently beneath shaggy black brows. He was, she decided, the surliest man she had ever met. The knight shook his head before burping loudly. Madselin's cheeks flamed red. Such uncouth manners! He was, however, apparently oblivious to her haughty stare.

'Not yet.' His voice was almost a growl, and Madselin noticed that his massive hands sported a pelt of black hair. 'I've heard rumours that the Scots are on the move. No more than that.'

He slurped noisily from the delicate goblet before wiping his mouth with a filthy sleeve. Clearly his very ruddy complexion owed much to his drinking habits. Reaching across Madselin, de Vaillant helped himself to a chicken and began to tear it into smaller joints before stuffing them into his mouth.

Oblivious to the appalling manners of his man,

Richard d'Aveyron nodded silently. 'Any plans?' he demanded curtly.

With obvious relish, Ivo de Vaillant licked his greasy fingers before rubbing them clumsily across the front of his woollen tunic. Madselin shuddered. 'I'll take some men along the coast, but Isabella won't hear of me being away after All Hallows.'

Madselin digested this piece of information with incredulity. 'Isabella is your wife?' she asked faintly. She could not imagine anyone telling him what to do.

The brown eyes bored into her before returning to his trencher. 'Aye. A good woman. Always nervous when she's near her time.' His thick features had softened a little and Madselin perceived that, beneath his coarse exterior, Ivo de Vaillant was a man who regarded his wife with some affection.

'How many children do you have, Sir Ivo?'

'This will be the tenth,' he said gruffly and without hesitation. 'The good Lord has seen fit to bless us.'

'Let's hope this one's a girl, then, Ivo.'

Madselin looked up to see the laughing blue eyes of Albert Mallet on her neighbour. 'Nine boys are enough for any one man, surely?'

Ivo de Vaillant merely grunted good-naturedly before pouring more of Richard's red wine down his throat. Madselin permitted herself a smile. It would appear that Ivo de Vaillant was not the ogre she first thought him to be.

It was not until Richard bemoaned the lack of good venison at their table that Madselin finally remembered the poacher she had caught.

'Here? You caught a poacher?' Richard stared at her as if she were mad. 'The peasants hereabouts are so scared they'd never dare. I have to see this one for myself.' Ordering the prisoner to be brought to him, Richard rose to stand closer to the fire.

From the look of the peasant, he had spent an uncomfortable few hours outside in the rain. A twinge of conscience overcame Madselin until she caught sight of the man's eyes. Mutinous was the only word for them. Banishing any weakness of spirit, Madselin held his glare for what seemed like an age. His temper, she decided, was not at all downtrodden.

Despite his wet clothing, the man walked with all the assurance and arrogance of a knight. Tall and well built, she noticed how the eyes of the women slid over his body. His profile was that of a confident man. not at all like the cowed villeins on her brother's demesne.

'Edwin?' Richard's outraged voice boomed across the dais as he stared at the peasant.

'My lord.' The words were uttered in perfect Norman French with a calm designed to aggravate and irritate. Madselin could feel the blush stealing over her cheeks. She could do no more than stare dumbly at him. This was not likely to end well for her.

'Do we starve you, Edwin? You had only to ask for more!' Madselin could tell instantly that Richard's jovial bantering was misplaced and that the man had truly had enough.

'I see you are acquainted.' Her voice was aimed at both men but her eyes were trained on the accused.

Once more she felt the full blast of his contempt.

'I take it, lady, that I am now permitted to speak?'

The blush turned into a deep, burning red. She could only managed a brief nod of her head in reply.

Sensing at last the awkwardness of the situation, Richard unsheathed his hunting knife and hurried to cut Edwin's bonds. Within seconds he had a goblet of fine wine thrust into his hands and was ushered closer to the fire.

'It was merely target practice, my lord. The lady chose to believe it was poaching.'

Madselin's eyes were riveted on the rushes at her feet. It was true she had not thought to look for evidence, but any fool could make up that excuse. 'You said naught in your defence. I took you to be a peasant. That is not so difficult to believe.'

'Only a fool would enter the forest in finery,' he countered, his grey eyes flinty in the firelight. 'And if you remember aright, my lady, you forbade me to speak.'

She was grateful at least that he did not repeat her exact words. 'Then it surprises me that the guards said naught when you were brought in.'

'The guards are not likely to question the word of a Norman lady over that of a mere peasant.'

'Enough.' Richard's stern voice cut through their anger. 'Edwin, this is my kinswoman, Madselin de Breuville. Edwin Elwardson is a crack archer from Cheshire. I would hope, Madselin, that you can repair the damage done to Edwin's pride.'

'My apologies, sir. I hope you did not suffer too badly.' The words sounded prim and insincere, but Madselin did feel a pang of conscience. She could not look him in the eye.

Edwin Elwardson's eyes flickered over her with nothing less than contempt. 'I hope, my lord, that you give me fair warning when you next expect a visit from your kinswomen?'

Richard gave a shout of laughter and clapped the man on the back. Madselin shot him a look of distaste. 'Aye, but for now you're in need of a hot tub and warm meat. Go to my chamber and I'll send in my squire to tend you.'

Edwin merely nodded; he certainly did not bear the look of a man who was grateful for such care. Madselin pursed her lips.

'Who is that dreadful man?' Madselin whispered to

Richard as she watched Edwin Elwardson's broad back disappear through the archway.

'A godsend,' came the thoughtful reply. 'An honest man who does as he's bid without question. Best archer I've ever seen.' Richard smiled ruefully. 'How we conquered the likes of him I'll never know.'

Madselin shrugged her shoulders. 'I found him most surly and arrogant.'

'Perhaps, dear Madselin, if you were less impulsive, you might have fewer regrets?'

Madselin looked up at her cousin sharply. 'If that was a veiled reference to my journey here, Richard, then the sentiments were misplaced. This was no impulse. It took me months to summon up the courage to leave.'

D'Aveyron placed his goblet carefully on the table. 'And no doubt it took every ounce of ingenuity you possess to have foiled Alice.'

As Madselin was about to speak, Richard raised his hand. 'No more. You are tired and in need of your bed. Gaston will show you to the ladies' quarters. When my wife has finished her duties, she will attend you.'

She was dismissed.

'Well, my lady. We're here now.' Emma attempted further reparations to her mistress's hair with an apparent sense of relief. 'Though the accommodation leaves a lot to be desired.'

They were sitting on roughly hewn stools before a meagre fire, Emma pulling the silver-traced comb through Madselin's hair as she had done for the past twenty-six years. Despite thick woollen sleeping robes, both women were acutely aware of the chilling draughts that swept their quarters.

Madselin smiled to herself wearily. 'What would we

be doing now if we were back in Normandy? I can't remember the last time I was sitting idly before a fire.'

Emma snorted at the very thought. 'I've no wish to criticise, my lady, but Lady Alice uses you a deal too much. Your father, God bless his soul, would have a fit if he knew what your brother lets her get away with. You're no more than an unpaid skivvy. I know you do it because you love her children, but that doesn't make it right.'

Madselin shrugged her shoulders. 'If I didn't earn my keep, Alice would have found a way to get rid of me years ago. At least this way I can stay in a home that I love, surrounded by family and friends.'

A heavy hand squeezed her shoulder. 'Aye. The servants love you for your quiet kindness and thoughtful ways, despite that sharp tongue of yours.' Emma gave a wheezy sigh. 'We all know how you've suffered since that day, my lady. And the children adore you.'

Under the rhythmic motion of the comb working through her long hair, Madselin had closed her eyes and yielded to the comfort it provided. The tension that had been building up for years seemed to ebb away. It felt good to be idle. 'I miss the children,' she murmured finally. 'Especially Mathilde.'

'Aye. She's a way with her, that one.' Emma smiled fondly at the memory of a three-year-old with blonde curls and shining blue eyes. ''Tis a pity she has a witch for a mother. That child loves you more than she does her ladyship, and that's a fact. It's you she cries for in the night, not Lady Alice.'

'Hush, Emma. Alice is a busy woman.'

'Not too busy to nag your brother about a betrothal for the poor child.'

Madselin's eyes snapped open. This was the first she'd heard of such a thing. Anything that affected the well-being of the children was important to her, and

Alice could not always be trusted to have their best interests at heart. 'Has aught been decided yet?' Emma always knew what was going on.

Any reply she was about to receive was interrupted by the sudden arrival of a small, plumply pretty woman with thick blonde braids and a knowing pout.

'Greetings Lady Madselin.' Her quick green eyes swept over Madselin's serviceable bedrobe with distaste. The sketchy bob she made was bordering on insult, but Madselin was too tired to upbraid her. 'My lord begs to know if there is aught I can do for you before you retire?'

Madselin contemplated the fire for a moment, not liking the rather cocksure tone of the woman's voice.

'Thank you. . .'

'Blanche, Lady Madselin.'

'Blanche. I require two cups of spiced wine.'

There was no more than the briefest hesitation before she managed to grind out her assent. Just as the woman reached the door, she hesitated and turned back. 'Is it true that you took Edwin Elwardson captive?'

Madselin's cheeks began to burn. 'It is,' she replied calmly, sitting up to adjust the laces on her bedrobe. 'I believed him to be poaching. It was an honest error.' She looked up to catch the servant's eyes almost gloating with satisfaction.

'About time that man got his comeuppance,' she murmured, tossing her flaxen braids over her shoulders. As she left the room, she collided with a small, dark-haired woman whose rich clothes proclaimed her high status.

'Hold your tongue, Blanche. If you have naught good to say, then stay silent.' Her repressive tone quelled the insolent look on the servant's face and Blanche scuttled down the hallway. The woman remained at the doorway, frowning at Blanche's retreating back. 'That woman will reap the rewards of her own evil tongue one day.'

She sighed before turning to Madselin and Emma. 'I must apologise for her behaviour, but her head is ruled by a very tempestuous heart.' Her rather plain face was transformed by a girlish grin. 'She is most distressed that Edwin has not singled her out as the sole object of his affections. It would seem that he prefers to bestow his favours. . .quite liberally.'

Madselin was not quite sure what to make of this particular confidence, but forebore to create any further chaos by voicing her opinions about Edwin Elwardson's loose morals.

'Forgive me for prattling so,' the stranger continued quickly. 'I am Beatrice, Richard's wife. I'm afraid I missed you earlier because my son was demanding my attention.'

'Nothing serious I hope?' Madselin enquired, her interest stirred. There was something very likeable about this plain, warm-hearted woman who did not seem to stop either talking or smiling.

'No. No more than a sore gum, but twelve months is a hard age for a babe. I believe Jordan has already learned the man's knack of gathering as many women about him for comfort as he can manage.'

'He must have been watching Edwin Elwardson,' Madselin replied tartly.

At that, Beatrice put her hand to her mouth and burst out into a fit of giggles. It was hard not to warm to the woman. 'I, too, have suspected that to have been the case.'

As she advanced towards them, Madselin could see at closer range the richness of her garments. A close-fitting undertunic of fine blue wool was contrasted with a rich, wine-coloured overgown of heavy velvet. The

edges of the gown were trimmed with bands of blue
and oversewn with intricate stitchery in gold thread.
Madselin blinked up at Beatrice d'Aveyron. This was a
woman who dressed for beauty as well as practicality.

'I hope my unexpected arrival has not caused too
much inconvenience,' Madselin began, knowing that
Beatrice was expecting some kind of explanation. 'It
was necessitated by a matter of utmost urgency.'

To her surprise, Beatrice sat on the rushes before
the fire and looked up at her expectantly. 'If you want
my help,' she began softly, 'you had best explain things
carefully to me. Richard is the best of husbands and an
excellent soldier, but he does lack...sensitivity.'
Another warming smile curved her lips.

Madselin frowned. 'Forgive my bluntness, but why
should you wish to help me? We have never met
before.' Indeed, she had not even known that Richard
was married until her arrival at his manor.

A slight sigh escaped Beatrice's lips. 'Richard has
often talked of you with affection and I believe you
were ever his favourite kinswoman. He said you were
close as children.'

Madselin nodded. That had been a long time ago.
'But I have not seen him since...' She still could not
bring herself to say the words. 'For about eight years,'
she finished rather lamely.

Beatrice stared at her with a look which betokened
pity and compassion. She knew, Madselin decided. No
doubt the whole world knew. Her next words, however,
caused Madselin to look at her more closely.

'I have also conceived a powerful dislike of Alice de
Breuville and it would give me great pleasure to cause
her inconvenience.'

A conspiracy! Madselin smiled back at Beatrice
d'Aveyron. She had found a friend. This was indeed a
miracle.

Chapter Two

The commotion in the courtyard beneath her window roused Madselin from a fitful sleep.

From the soft tone of the light filtering through the shutters, Madselin estimated that it was very early. She knew that she would not sleep further and slipped from her pallet to the window embrasure, pulling on her bedrobe as she went. A blast of ice-cold air enveloped her as she opened the shutters to look down on to the group of riders assembled in the courtyard.

Huge, muscular destriers pawed the mud impatiently, whilst their riders issued curt orders to d'Aveyron's men-at-arms. From the richness of their armour and garments, Madselin was certain that these were knights from Roger de Poictou's stable and, whatever their purpose, they had caused Richard's men to scatter urgently.

Beyond the palisade, the dark forest was shrouded in mist and low-lying clouds. It looked dangerous, even in the early morning sun. The wind that swept in from the west had a salty tang that caused Madselin a shiver of adventure.

She had seen the sea but once and that had not been a fortunate encounter. The crossing from Normandy to

Pevensey had been marred by heaving grey waves the size of castle walls with white foaming swells that made their small boat lurch from side to side. Her sickness had not abated until her feet touched solid ground.

Mindful of her need to place herself in Richard's favour, Madselin washed and dressed hastily. Just as she was about to leave, a rather pale-faced Beatrice scratched on the door.

'What is wrong, Beatrice?' she demanded quickly. 'Is it bad news?'

Beatrice shook her head with a faint smile. 'Nay. The only excuse for my whey-faced looks today is a sleepless night with my son. As for our visitors, Madselin, I think you had best come down and break your fast with Richard. I doubt he will be here much longer.'

'How so?'

Beatrice rolled her eyes towards the ceiling and sighed wearily. 'Roger de Poictou is demanding knight service from his vassals. Richard is to leave this morning and I know not whether he goes to Normandy for the King.'

Madselin nodded, torn between her sympathy for Beatrice and her concern that her plans were about to be ruined. 'Come then,' she smiled, taking Beatrice gently by the arm. 'Let us break our fast, and on the way I can tell you of my remedy for sore gums that worked well for my niece.'

The hall was in uproar. Weapons and supplies were being packed and readied for loading into carts whilst Richard's men shovelled rye bread and ale down their throats. Meals would be an uncertain business for them from now on. Servants and men-at-arms scuttled through the doors causing several calamitous but non-fatal collisions. The din was awful.

Richard was sitting at his table with the strangers

and several of his house-knights. Compared to the night before, their mood was noticeably subdued and serious. All were aware that if their destination were Normandy, they would not return to their manors before the spring. For some of the younger men, no doubt the promise of adventure would be a welcome relief. For others, the call to arms posed problems of a different nature.

Madselin noticed that Ivo de Vaillant was scowling into his cup and wondered if his thoughts were of his wife. Ale and bread lay untouched before him.

A little apart from the rest sat Edwin Elwardson; it was clear that the only thing on his mind was satisfying his immediate hunger. His appearance, however, was much changed. The blond locks had been pulled into the tight braid favoured by Saxons, revealing to inquisitive eyes a determined but clean-shaven chin.

A plain, serviceable overtunic of midnight blue lent the man an air of nobility that seemed to sit well on his broad shoulders. His eyes were fixed on the food before him, although Madselin was certain that he was aware of everything that was going on around her. Irritated that she was so conscious of the man, she made a determined effort to put him from her mind and followed Beatrice to the dais.

The murmurings immediately ceased once the men noticed their presence and Madselin could feel her colour heighten as she became the target of unwelcome speculation. Her years as an older, unmarried woman had forced her to deal with such attentions quickly and effectively.

Casting a cool and unhurried eye over the assembled group, she treated the men to a look of haughty contempt before sweeping to her place at the table. Knights leaving for war were wont to tumble maids in the stables as a final attempt to stamp themselves over their home possessions, almost as if they were hoping for immortality. Madselin was gratified to note that not one tried to catch her eye.

Richard d'Aveyron stared at her silently and his expression was not at all encouraging. No doubt there were more pressing problems claiming his attention.

Madselin, unable to postpone her fate any longer, took a deep breath and treated him to a dazzling smile. 'Well, Richard? Have you made a decision?' She could feel the smile stiffen as Richard remained mute. The bread and ale put before her were ignored as she waited for his response.

'Truly, Madselin, the problem is a vexing one,' he said finally. He rubbed at the tender spots on his chin where he had barbered himself too close in his haste. 'I do not like to interfere in a family matter which is none of my making.' He glanced speculatively at Madselin before reaching to fill his cup with more ale.

Those heavy-lidded brown eyes missed very little despite their sleepy appearance, she decided.

'It would certainly not benefit me to annoy your brother, especially in such uncertain times.'

He was going to refuse her. Madselin felt her icy heart thud to the pit of her stomach. Gritting her jaw, she stared unblinkingly at the table. 'I beg you, Richard. Alice is bent on marrying me to that old man or sending me to a convent because she hates me. She has always hated me.' Her voice was almost a whisper.

'I just want a chance to choose some sort of life of my own, with a kind husband and at least the prospect of children.' Fear and anxiety coursed through her bones at the thought of returning to Alice's crowing embrace. 'I did the only thing within my power to bring that about.' She lifted her head proudly to fix him with suspiciously bright eyes.

The stern set of his face had softened a little. 'Aye,

and it was a foolhardy thing to do.' Richard cleared his throat. 'But there is no time left for me to think clearly on the matter.' He breathed deeply and rubbed the stiffness from the back of his neck. 'Since crossing the sea in winter is impossible, you will have to remain on my lands.'

'But—' Madselin attempted to interrupt.

'Silence!' From the harsh tone of his voice, Madselin knew she could do no more than obey him. 'As you have proved your courage, then you will make yourself useful to me.'

Richard gave his wife a quick, sidelong look. 'Isabella de Vaillant will need a stout-hearted companion whilst Ivo is away. I have decided that you will deal with her and her children admirably. If your suitor is as determined as you believe, then a few months longer will make no difference.'

Madselin's gaze met Richard's in frank comprehension. He had handed her a solution that would not upset her brother and would allow him some time to think on the matter.

Madselin knew she ought to be grateful, but the thought of spending the winter in this cold place made her balk. 'It seems I have no choice,' she conceded finally.

The tense look to Richard's face relaxed and he settled back into his chair. 'I thought you would be pleased.' He tossed the remaining ale down his throat and then slammed the cup back onto the trestle.

That appeared to be the prearranged sign since all the men suddenly moved to stand as one. Beatrice turned to her husband and pulled him a little to one side away from the bright glare of the braziers. Madselin realised how selfish she had been in claiming his attention. There would be no way of knowing whether Richard would return.

Turning away she caught sight of Ivo de Vaillant's
gloomy countenance and wondered if he would welcome the chance to send a few words home to his wife.
Deciding to risk his frown, Madselin approached him.

'I am to go to your wife, sir.' Her voice did not
betray the uncertainty of her feelings. 'Would you send
word with me?'

Ivo de Vaillant glanced at her briefly as he hefted an
oak strongbox onto his shoulders. 'I said it all before I
left,' he replied gruffly. 'But it pleases me that she'll
have another woman about.'

From the way he glared at her, Madselin was not at
all sure that he approved of her, but judged it wise to
nod agreement.

'Have a care, though, woman. There's strange
goings-on out there and few you can trust. Do as
Elwardson tells you and you'll be well enough.'

Madselin's face drained of all colour. 'The Saxon?'
she whispered faintly.

'Aye,' came the impatient retort. 'An honest man for
a Saxon.' Satisfied that he had bestowed the greatest
approbation on Edwin Elwardson's character, de
Vaillant lumbered towards the courtyard without a
backward glance.

Left feeling firmly put in her place and not a little
foolish, Madselin turned her head in Edwin
Elwardson's direction and found him actually smiling.
The sour scowl he appeared to favour had been
replaced by a most engaging smile, displayed, she
discovered, for the benefit of the pouting Blanche.
Remembering Beatrice's words, the two of them
seemed to be well matched and thoroughly deserving
of each other.

Suddenly, as if aware of her eyes on him, Edwin
turned the full force of his grey eyes on her and
Madselin caught her breath. For a moment, their gazes

held fast before Blanche jealously demanded his attention.

'Come,' said Beatrice, interrupting her thoughts. 'Bid the men farewell and then we can make plans.' She slid her arm round Madselin's waist and drew her towards the courtyard.

'When must I leave?'

Beatrice, sensing constraint in Madselin's question, smiled gently up at her. 'When 'tis most convenient,' she decided firmly. 'Now come.'

Once the horses and carts had clattered out of the bailey, the manor sounded strangely quiet and deserted. Richard had left half his men but they were out of sight. Beatrice surveyed the churned mud, horse dung and puddles with a baleful eye. 'Perhaps a turn around my gardens will restore us. There is much to be done, I fear.'

Madselin shot her a brief smile. For a woman whose husband had just left for an unknown destination and an uncertain fate, Beatrice d'Aveyron was remarkably calm.

'Does aught grow in this country?' she countered with mock surprise.

A suspicion of a grin twisted Beatrice's lips. 'You are too hard on this land, my Lady de Breuville. I confess to being right pleased with my home here.' She glanced up at the bright blue sky and drew in a deep calming breath. 'A woman can grow to love the place, despite the rain.'

Their eyes caught and the two women suddenly burst into laughter.

'You are very fierce in defence of this godforsaken island. Normandy is your true home, I believe?' Madselin looked at Beatrice in complete confusion.

Beatrice simply shrugged her slender shoulders and smiled. 'There is a sort of magic here,' she said airily. 'I find I do not regret my birthplace at all. And there are certainly fewer grasping women waiting to catch my husband's eye.'

Although the comment was made in jest, Madselin was sure that it was spoken from the heart.

As they talked, Beatrice had guided Madselin around the palisade of the bailey and stopped at a small gate. Opening it, she proudly bade Madselin enter a tiny, sun-filled garden which was protected from the worst of the wind by the bailey wall. A rough wooden bench had been erected to catch the sun, and they sat down to make the most of it.

It was peaceful here, thought Madselin, as she too settled back against the wall. Birdsong floated around them and the aromatic scent of herbs calmed her agitated nerves. It reminded her of a soft summer day a long time past.

'I last saw Richard on the morning of my wedding day. Alice was there, but she was very young—just sixteen, I think. . .' but then Madselin stopped. After a moment's pause, she began again. 'I doubt if I would have noticed much that day.'

Madselin felt a gentle pressure on her arm.

'Forgive me, Madselin. I had not meant to remind you of that terrible day. We shall not speak more of it.'

Aye, it was still painful, but not as it had been. The grief had dulled over the years and she was trying to put the past behind her. Alice had never made that easy with her constant references to Guy. She shook her head. 'It does me good to talk of such things and I have no wish to forget him. Truly.'

'Well, if you are certain?' Beatrice shot her an uncertain look.

'How do you know about Alice?' Madselin began to fiddle with the folds of her tunic.

Beatrice laughed sourly.

'Richard offered for her, but she dismissed him with such arrogance that it took him many years to approach a lady again. She gave him to believe her heart was engaged elsewhere and that marriage to your brother was. . .convenient.'

For no reason at all, Madselin was certain those words should have meant something. Part of her mind was reaching out to try to piece something together. Beatrice had revealed nothing new about her sister-in-marriage, however. Alice was not known for her discretion.

'That is probably the truth,' she admitted. 'It was no love match and Robert does not care to hide his mistresses from her.' She looked across at Beatrice. 'Richard seems most content.'

'Content!' Beatrice spat out the words. 'Aye, he is content.' Suddenly she turned to Madselin. 'I don't want him to be content. I want him to desire me with such passion that he can think of nothing else.' Sighing with frustration and despair, Beatrice threw herself back against the wall with a thud. 'To him I am just. . . there. Plain, homely Beatrice. I might just as well be his mother!'

Madselin was stunned by this revelation. 'Alice has never known such contentment,' she said eventually.

Beatrice blushed and turned her head. 'I know you must think me ungrateful, for I have so much. But sometimes. . .' Her lips twisted in that wry grin that Madselin was coming to know. 'Mayhap I get myself too involved in these old local customs.'

Madselin frowned in confusion. 'What do you mean?'

'The people here are very isolated. Some of their customs must have their origins in their old pagan beliefs.' A blush covered Beatrice's pale cheeks. 'Once or twice I have watched what goes on. 'Tis most. . . revealing.'

Madselin stared at her open-mouthed. She would never have guessed.

'Isabella de Vaillant is most knowledgeable about these customs.' Beatrice flashed her a sidelong glance. 'She can be very. . .enlightening.'

The mention of Isabella de Vaillant reminded Madselin of her duty and her smile evaporated. 'No doubt we shall pass many a long evening together. I shall endeavour to learn more of this Saxon culture.' Her words were uttered with distaste.

'They are not all Saxons—' Beatrice began seriously.

'It matters not,' interrupted Madselin. 'I have no real interest in these people.' She looked at Beatrice. 'It is my turn to beg your forgiveness. I do not intend to make this my home.'

'Aye, well. Perhaps I have been boring you with my nonsense.'

Madselin laid her hand on Beatrice's arm. 'Never say so, Beatrice. You are the first friend I have talked to in many long years. I have become rude and surly, that is all.'

'Hah! Do not think it!' She looked skywards again. 'Isabella de Vaillant will test all your powers of diplomacy, rest assured.'

Madselin stared at her. 'And I thought Edwin Elwardson was going to be my problem.'

'Edwin?' Beatrice looked at her in surprise. 'Nay. You mistake the matter. It is only that you got off to a poor start. He is a good man.'

'So everyone keeps trying to assure me,' Madselin said darkly. 'But I mislike his arrogance.'

Beatrice looked at her askance. 'You think him arrogant?' She thought for a moment. 'Well, mayhap we are all just used to his ways. He has been here since before I arrived, and he was very kind to me at the beginning.' She smiled, almost to herself. 'Had I not been married to Richard, I could quite understand why the women make such fools of themselves over him.'

Giving a sigh of impatience, Madselin stared at her. 'He is a peasant. How could you even think of. . .?'

'I have not,' retorted Beatrice indignantly. 'It's just that. . .'

'Spare me,' came the acid reply. 'I truly think you have become too involved with these local customs, Beatrice d'Aveyron. They have addled your wits.'

Beatrice smiled broadly at that set down. 'I truly think, Lady de Breuville, that you are going to find the next few months interesting.'

Madselin gave her a withering look which caused Beatrice to smile even more.

Mayhap there was a certain magic in the air or mayhap it was the smell of the sea on the wind? Madselin knew naught except that she had a sudden desire to escape the confines of the keep and be on her own to think. Just for a little while.

Beatrice received the request as calmly as she faced everything else. 'I do not think it wise, for you are new to the land and. . .'

'You forbid it, then?' Madselin could not hide the disappointment in her voice.

They were standing in Beatrice's private solar before a roaring fire. Beautiful tapestries adorned the stone walls and the thick, herb-strewn rushes underfoot gave the room a pleasant fragrance.

A chubby-faced child with dark curls and an indomitable will was investigating every inch of the place, followed vigilantly by a red-faced nurse. Several young women chatted as they sewed over on the other side of the solar, and one woman with long dark braids idled over a lute.

Beatrice looked down at Madselin's soft, doe-skin boots and fine woollen gown and raised her dark brows. 'No. I do not forbid it. It would not be my place.' Her eyes came back to Madselin. 'But I believe it to be ill advised. There is much trouble in this area—not from the local people,' she added hurriedly. 'Richard suspects some of the barons to the north of treachery with the Scots.'

'Scots?' Madselin repeated. 'I do not understand. He thinks Normans would betray their own kind?'

Beatrice gave a sour laugh. 'And they do not do the same on their own lands in Normandy? Nay, some think of naught but their own profit, and the Scots are forever trying to slip through the defences.' She pushed back a stray lock of dark hair.

'With Rufus being so involved in the war against his brother, he has little time to spend here. Flambards, his chancellor, has squeezed us dry with his taxes and for many, the lures offered by the Scots are tempting indeed.'

Madselin listened to this explanation with interest. 'I heard Ivo de Vaillant mention there was some such trouble near his manor,' she remembered. 'It is serious then?'

A squeal of discontent from the child momentarily diverted Beatrice's attention. 'Aye,' she replied finally, bending down and holding out her arms to her son. Much to Jordan's delight, his mother swung him high in the air before settling him in her arms. He began to explore her face with his pudgy hands.

'Especially now that Richard is absent. Once the Scots find out that de Poictou has been called for knight service with most of his men, we will be vulnerable.'

Madselin wandered to the window embrasure and

pushed aside the oiled sheet. Away to the north, beyond the forest, lay the long hills. It was hard to imagine that such treachery could lie in so wild a place. Sighing, she let the sheet flop back and returned to the fire. 'Who is left in charge, then?' she demanded curiously.

'Albert Mallet has remained here to guard the demesne,' Beatrice began, pushing her son's exploring fingers from her nose. 'But the rest. . .'

A giggling, pink-cheeked Blanche burst through the door.

'Blanche! What is the meaning of this?' Beatrice's furious countenance caused Blanche's apparent joy to subside instantly.

'I'm sorry, my lady. Edwin Elwardson is without and wishes if he might have words with you.' The blue eyes were fixed humbly on the ground, but no one could mistake the quickness of the girl's breathing.

'Send him in, Blanche, and then fetch us some wine.'

Blanche made a hasty curtsy and retreated to the door.

'That girl is a disgrace,' began Madselin. 'How do you put up with her?'

Beatrice smiled as she handed the child to his nurse. 'She is just young and fancies herself in love.'

Madselin just raised her brows in scorn. 'Then she is a fool. He appears little more than a lecherous peasant.'

'My lady.' A deep voice behind her caused Madselin to start suddenly and then blush with embarrassment. There was no doubt that he had heard her comment and had known himself to be the subject since he had placed much feeling and emphasis on the word 'lady'. It was a moment before she realised that the Saxon was addressing Beatrice.

Was she always to be at a disadvantage with this man? If the Saxon had noticed her, he gave no appear-

ance of having done so. Pursing her lips into a tight
line, Madselin affected her haughtiest demeanour and
carefully stepped further from him. He smelled of
bracken, fresh air and horses.

'Edwin.' Beatrice greeted him warmly and bade him
move closer to the fire. 'Have the baggage wains been
readied? Do you have what you need?'

Madselin watched almost open-mouthed as the
Saxon once more summoned up his compelling smile
for Beatrice. It revealed even, white teeth and a very
attractive countenance. For a Saxon, she reminded
herself quickly. Clearly Beatrice was susceptible to a
handsome face since she, too, was smiling sweetly.

'Aye, lady.' His grey eyes were gentle now for
Beatrice. 'We'll be ready to leave on the morrow. Is
there aught I can do for you before we leave?'

Beatrice looked up at the man speculatively. 'Lady
de Breuville was asking me if she could ride out for a
short while. She has need of exercise before the journey. Would you take her?'

The grey eyes shot to Madselin instantly, but they
were neither smiling nor gentle. 'Nay.' His flat refusal
drew a gasp of outrage from Madselin.

'What do you mean by "nay"? I can assure you that
I have no desire to be accompanied by you. One of the
young squires will be more than adequate, I'm sure.'
She gave him a challenging stare that brooked no
further discussion.'

'I'll not have a boy's life wasted for the whim of one
spoiled Norman woman who has nothing better to do.'
He stared back, undeterred.

Two spots of red coloured Madselin's cheeks as she
faced the Saxon. 'You are the most arrogant, rude,
abominable peasant I have ever come across. I was
only suggesting a ride, not a pillage of the country.
There would be no harm—'

'No harm!' he interrupted loudly. 'Woman, we have lost three men in the forest this last week. There's not one squire in the manor who would willingly ride out with you, but none would gainsay you for fear of their punishment.'

The anger drained from her face. 'I. . . I did not know this,' she stuttered quietly. 'You had only to explain.'

The grey eyes speared her with a bitter glare. 'It would seem, Lady de Breuville, that you are quick to demand and somewhat slower to ask. I hope that you display far more patience and tolerance in future, or you will place other lives at risk.'

'So, Saxon, you show your true nature.' Madselin glared at him, her humiliation complete.

'I do no more than ensure the safety of all the people in this manor,' he returned quietly, his anger seemingly spent. 'And as I have command here, I respectfully request that you adhere to my judgement.' He lay meaningful emphasis on 'respectfully', although from the tone of his voice, respect was clearly lacking.

He had made his feelings on the matter plain. A brief glance at Beatrice gave Madselin no hope of support since her eyes were cast to the ground. 'I have no wish to cause hurt to anyone. It was certainly not my intention,' she added stiffly. 'Although I was given to believe that Albert Mallet was in command.'

His eyes bored into her. 'Not until I leave, Lady de Breuville. Should you wish to confirm this, I am sure Mallet will be happy to oblige.'

After a moment's silence, she deemed it prudent to yield on this matter. 'I have misjudged the situation and had no idea I was causing you such problems.'

A ghost of a smile fluttered over the Saxon's handsome face. 'If you think you have caused me a

moment's concern, Lady de Breuville, then you are
sadly in error.'

Madselin raised her brows in disbelief.

He continued to stare at her, his expression unreadable. 'As we are to spend some time in each other's
company, I think it sensible if we understand one
another. You will obey my commands or you will be
returned to your brother's demesne without your kinsman's agreement. I hope I make myself clear?' Their
eyes met.

'Perfectly.'

Apparently satisfied, Edwin turned to leave but
checked himself. 'I am sure you would wish me to point
out that you err in terms of my origins, Lady de
Breuville. It would give me the greatest of pleasure to
hear you refer to me as an Angle rather than a Saxon.
Nor,' he added with a faint smile, 'do I come from
peasant stock.' After the briefest pause, he continued.
'We leave at first light. Be ready or we go without you.'

So saying, he strode from the room, leaving Madselin
staring silently after him. 'Insufferable man,' she hissed,
before snatching at her gown and stomping towards
her room. 'I will enjoy teaching him some manners.'

Chapter Three

Blanche settled herself onto the baggage cart and smiled down at Edwin Elwardson's broad back as he bent to test one of the wheels. No one could be in any doubt as to the lewdness of her expression, thought Madselin with asperity.

'Why is she coming?' Madselin eyed the woman with irritation as she fiddled with her heavy riding gown. Beatrice stood patiently at her side.

'She has a sister who works for Lady Isabella and it seemed churlish to refuse her request.'

'There is only one reason she wishes to come with us, and he does not appear to have thwarted her desires.'

A slow smile crossed Beatrice's face. 'You do Edwin an injustice. He has never appeared to favour any one of them above the rest. It is very likely he will find others. Besides, he has much else to occupy his mind.'

'I do not think Blanche is interested in his mind.'

After a brief blessing from Beatrice's priest, the party of riders and carts lumbered slowly through the high wooden gates of the manor. Dawn had broken about an hour before and the light was uncertain. Thick clouds had rolled in from the west and there was a smell of rain in the air. The black mood that had enveloped her since she had risen hung round Madselin's shoulders like an ox's yoke and she stared ahead at the sombre forest with apprehension.

As well as the two scouts, six armed guards surrounded the two baggage carts. Edwin Elwardson and a young squire of no more than fifteen summers brought up the rear. Her fears were groundless, but none the less she had taken the Angle's warning of constant danger seriously. This land was awash with outlaws and wild animals, after all.

There were no great forests like this near her home in Normandy. The Vexin was a flat land with lush meadows and slow-moving rivers; it lent itself well to crop growing and cattle rearing. Or at least, she reminded herself, it would if it were not being constantly raided and destroyed. They were ever on the alert for roaming bands of mercenaries who cared not one whit about the land or the lives that they ruined. One of their number had certainly changed her life.

The recent downpours had turned the track into a muddy quagmire, and at times the carts stuck fast. Edwin Elwardson would then direct the men and Madselin noted with surprise how quick they were to do his bidding.

At these times, Madselin would look up and find Blanche's blue eyes fixed on her with a look of intense dislike. Clearly she saw her as some sort of rival for the Angle's affections. How wrong could she be? If she was fool enough to be interested, then the woman was welcome to him. Her affections remained firmly placed elsewhere.

Hugh de Montchalon was courteous and attentive, although several years younger than herself. His cheerful humour had helped to restore her spirits in the dark days after her betrothed was killed just hours before their wedding.

Emma was finding the jolting and shaking of the cart increasingly uncomfortable and Madselin watched her greying face with a sense of growing concern. Her health had been poor since suffering a bout of lung fever last winter, and she tired easily. Travelling had never been Emma's favourite pastime; she preferred a warm fire and a comfortable chair.

Unable to watch her suffer more, Madselin slowed her horse until she was level with Edwin Elwardson. The Angle's expression remained stiff and unresponsive but at least the boy scowled at her.

'I think it would be a good time to rest.' Her voice was even and her eyes trained on the track ahead.

The Angle was silent for a moment but even without looking at him, Madselin could feel him bristle at her words.

'It's just that Emma looks most uncomfortable. I do not ask for myself,' she added quickly.

Edwin observed the women on the cart. 'Is she not well, the old woman?' His voice was curt but not harsh.

Madselin shook her head. 'The long journey has been hard for her.' Her cheeks flushed as she felt his eyes upon her. 'I would ask that she does not suffer because of me and my foolish tongue.' Madselin glanced down at the reins in her fingers, glad that the man did not interrupt her. 'She has suffered more than enough on my account and I would be most grateful if you could show her some kindness.'

'The woman must be a devoted servant indeed.'

Uncertain as to whether it was a question or a statement, Madselin turned to stare up at his sober visage. 'She is obstinate. I had not planned to bring her with me, but she was fearful of being left with my sister-in-marriage. I could not refuse her. Emma is more like a mother to me.'

His hand rubbed thoughtfully at his shaven chin before addressing her. 'And you? Are you also fearful of your sister-in-marriage?'

Madselin prickled a little at being asked so personal a question that was perhaps closer to the mark than she wished to admit, even to herself. 'We do not deal well together,' she replied eventually. 'Her anger is usually directed at those least able to defend themselves. Emma has been with me since I was born and I would not willingly see her hurt. I do believe that Alice would hurt her deliberately just to punish me.'

Such an admission of weakness made Madselin feel very vulnerable and she could feel his eyes on her, almost commanding her to look at him.

'I am grateful that you have told me about the woman—your concern for her is welcome. We have need of healthy, loyal women hereabouts and I have no desire to lose Emma through ill use. There is a good spot ahead. We will rest there.' His tone had lost the hard edge.

'My thanks, Angle.' Had she heard the man aright? Her eyes flickered over his face and registered his expression of gentle concern.

'The horses need water,' he replied quickly, before urging his horse into a trot.

As she watched him, Madselin became aware that another pair of eyes were boring into her. Blanche was staring at her with an expression of complete hatred and it made her feel most uncomfortable. Why did Blanche want to see things between them that really were not there? Well, the woman would find out soon enough how little interest in the man she had.

* * *

Emma levered her bulk back against the trunk of a large tree and sighed with exhaustion. 'I'll not last much longer on that cart, especially if I have to listen to that trollop prating on. It still feels like I'm swaying,' she groaned, closing her eyes.

Madselin shot her a look of sympathy. 'Here. Eat some of this bread and cheese. You'll feel better.'

Blanche picked her way across the muddy clearing from the cart, where she had engaged the young sergeant in animated conversation. Their discussion had been summarily brought to an end by Edwin Elwardson's harsh command, which had the soldier scurrying towards the horses. Blanche's eyes were fixed on the Angle, but he paid her scant attention and she stalked towards Madselin and Emma in a huff.

Madselin, too, found herself watching Edwin Elwardson. He was standing by the cart, checking over the equipment with an experienced eye. He looked, she had to admit, very much in control and seemed unconcerned at the reproachful looks Blanche was now casting in his direction. He was not unattractive.

'We leave when the horses are watered.' He paused a moment, patently ignoring Blanche's pouting frown. 'If you wish a few moments' privacy in the bushes, go now—I have no desire to wait longer than necessary.'

'How long will the journey take?' enquired Madselin, pushing her dark braids behind her shoulders.

His eyes flickered to the sky and narrowed a little. 'I hope to arrive at the de Vaillant manor before nightfall. Much depends on how often we stop.'

At these words, Madselin looked over at Emma. She had a grey pallor which did not show signs of abating.

The Angle had picked up her concern. 'Would you prefer a horse to the cart?' His question was directed at Emma with a tone that betokened kindness.

After a moment or two's hesitation, Emma nodded

slowly. 'But I'll not have my lady being jolted around instead of me.' Her brown eyes did not conceal any of her wariness.

He laughed and managed a rueful smile. 'I have not the slightest intention of parting Lady de Breuville from a horse she rates so highly,' he said, his eyes sliding briefly to Madselin's startled expression. 'But young Raoul seems to think my mount unable to bear me much longer. My horse, I think, would be grateful if you took my place.'

He strode towards the group of soldiers huddled near the horses. Eventually, Madselin rose to shake the crumbs from her gown. 'I'd best go into the forest for a few minutes. I'll not be long.'

'I'll come with you and show you the way.' Blanche suddenly stood up and pushed back her blonde braids with a tight smile. 'I've been this way before and Edwin does not like the women to remain too close to the men.'

The two made their way through quite some distance of undergrowth, bracken and thick mud. Overhead, the trees towered oppressively and the silence enveloped them. There was a most eerie atmosphere which made Madselin shiver. It was odd not to hear birdsong.

'The best cover is just beyond that large stone,' said Blanche, pointing a short distance ahead to a thick grey standing stone such as they had passed not far back along the path. 'You go first and I'll keep watch.'

Madselin hurried ahead, somewhat uncertain as to why they needed to go so far, but she had no wish to be disturbed by the men. As she reached the stone, the air about her suddenly seemed to grow colder. Pulling her cloak tightly about her, she noticed that the stone was covered in strange symbols. Her eyes were drawn to the picture in the centre of the stone; it was a man with antlers on his head.

'Hurry!' hissed Blanche, drawing her attention once more.

Quickly, Madselin slipped behind the stone, but to her dismay she found that the ground dropped steeply. The wet earth gave way beneath her feet and she could not stop herself from slipping further and further down the slope. Losing her footing, she fell and rolled to the bottom of the incline in a jumbled heap. Mud, twigs and bracken covered her from top to toe and Madselin hauled herself to her feet in disgust.

Looking upwards, there was no sign of Blanche although the woman must have heard her cry as she on fell. The wretch had done this on purpose.

More angry than hurt, Madselin looked wildly around. She had fallen into what looked like a wide circle of the upright stones, all bearing the same strange markings as those she had noticed on the one at the top of the slope. Within the circle, the ground had been trampled thoroughly and nothing grew there. The silence seemed to boom in her ears and her heart began to thud uncomfortably.

Picking up her skirts, she ran to the outside of the stone circle and her breathing relaxed a little. Hiding behind a nearby tree, she relieved herself quickly and tried then to restore her appearance. Time was passing though, and she had to get back to the others. The forest was a dangerous place to be lost.

Her ablutions complete, Madselin stared around the surrounding undergrowth. Refusing to give way to panic, she gritted her teeth and began to skirt round the incline to see if she could find a way up.

After several minutes, she noticed some tree roots and strong-looking bushes a few feet up the slope and decided to try them out. Madselin took a few hesitant steps and then grabbed for a root. Slowly she managed to pull herself to her feet. It was a long, drawn-out process but, by sheer willpower and strength, Madselin finally managed to haul herself to the top of the slope.

Blood seeped from the cuts on her hands and her gown was ripped and muddied beyond repair. All she felt was relief, though, and allowed herself a moment's respite.

'Hiding, Lady de Breuville?'

Madselin almost jumped out of her skin at the sound of the Angle's cold voice. Her heart was pumping furiously and she could feel her cheeks burning.

'What do you think you're doing?' she demanded breathlessly. 'Are you trying to scare me out of my wits?'

The Angle was no more than a few feet away from her, leaning with his back against the large standing stone. His face bore little sign of concern about her ordeal. In fact, he looked rather amused. 'You have the makings of a fine peasant, lady.' The grey eyes swept over her ruined appearance.

Madselin glared at him, furious that he would make light of the situation. 'You were watching me,' she accused.

'Aye. Most instructive.' He pushed himself away from the stone and came to stand before her. The hand he offered her was large and square, and she noted the myriad of white nicks across its suntanned back— legacy of swordsmanship borne by most Norman knights.

Madselin ignored the hand and pulled herself to her feet. The Angle's large hand still wrapped itself around her wrist and pulled her hand closer to his face. 'You'll heal,' he pronounced eventually after he had examined it carefully.

Madselin snatched her hand back. 'Very gratifying. How long were you watching me?'

'Long enough.'

Madselin's lips tightened visibly. The man was a true peasant, no matter how much he protested his origins. With her nose in the air, she whipped round and stalked back towards the camp. 'I suppose you blame me for wasting precious time,' she ground out as she felt rather than saw him just behind her.

Edwin's cool voice reached her from behind. 'I warned you about the dangers here. It was foolish indeed to go so far. Death would be a very high price to pay for your modesty, lady.'

His words were true but that didn't stop Madselin from feeling unreasonably angry. 'Blanche brought me here. I would never have gone so far on my own.'

He gave a snort of disbelief. 'You strike me as a woman used to making your own decisions. I find it hard to believe you would follow a mere servant rather than trust your own instincts.'

'I did not think Blanche was just a "mere" servant, as you put it,' she retorted. 'She is most keen to impress us with her. . .experience.'

He gave a heavy sigh. 'You make absolutely no sense, woman. Blanche is no more than a servant.'

'Then why is she here?' Her eyes blazing, Madselin turned suddenly to face him. Unable to stop himself from walking straight in to her, Edwin grabbed her arms and steadied them both.

For seconds, they remained silently staring at each other. 'She asked me,' came the simply reply.

'My requests do not appear to achieve so much,' she countered.

That brought his breathtaking smile to his lips. 'Perhaps it is the manner of the request that counts?'

In this strangely humorous mood, the Angle looked very attractive. That she found him so was most vexing. Her breath caught as he reached out to pluck several curls of bracken from her hair. He could be so unnerv-

ing and irritating all at the same time. 'You chance
much, Angle.' Her voice was low and menacing, but it
only made his smile broader.

'Less than you, it would seem. Did you know you
were wandering round a sacred circle? The gods of old
are not supposed to look kindly on strangers tramping
round their place of worship.' So saying, he released
her arms and moved past her. 'The others await our
return and we must be gone. You have caused me
enough delay already.'

Madselin watched his retreating back with confusion.
He was a very exasperating man. What did he mean by
a sacred circle? Shaking her head, she followed the
Angle back to the camp.

Within an hour or so of setting off once more, the rain
began to lash down with ferocity, and Madselin did
indeed begin to wonder whether she had angered the
gods of the forest. Emma rode in silence next to
Madselin whilst Blanche huddled in the back of the
cart. She had declared herself to be far too delicate to
walk.

The Angle appeared not to notice the rain. They
were now at the front of the party, just ahead of Emma
and Madselin, and it was clear that the Angle had not
relented his guard.

Every so often he would stop to listen intently at
some unfamiliar noise or disappear into the trees for
minutes at a time. Madselin found herself holding her
breath when he did this, and only permitted herself
another when he returned.

Gradually the forest began to thin as they headed
westwards, and the landscape changed. There was no
longer a green and amber canopy to protect them from
the worst of the rain, and underfoot, the earth became
stonier and more difficult to manage.

Flat, straight paths had given way to rough tracks
meandering over low, stone-strewn hills. Trees still
dotted the way, but even they were no longer the huge
yews of the Bowland. The strange white glow from the
silver birch trees gave a haunted atmosphere to the
land. Gorse bushes and tussocks of thick reeds grew in
the marshy low places.

Towards late afternoon, the rain ceased and the
direction of the wind changed. The boiling clouds were
carried inland, leaving a blue sky cobwebbed with fine
white wisps. The wind dried their cloaks and lessened
their misery a little. Imperceptibly their spirits
lightened too. As they reached the top of the hill their
first view of the grey sea spread out before them.

It was a breathtaking sight and Madselin could not
help but feel a quickening of her heart as she looked
beyond the next thickly wooded valley. Close to the
shore on a raised earth promontory stood a small, but
weather-ravaged keep built of the grey stone that lay
hereabouts. A village of sorts huddled within the
protective palisade, its tiny church standing a little
apart from the rest of the buildings.

The shoreline beyond was a mass of grassy sand
dunes, leading to a long beach covered in pebbles and
grey sand.

They stared down at the dark wood that covered the
lower part of the hill and beyond. Despite the last
warming rays of the sun, there was a brooding atmosphere about the place that made Madselin feel
uncomfortable.

'Stay close and keep quiet,' came the command.

The Angle was standing close by their horses, his
eyes squinting over the land below them. There was a
tension about him that Madselin had not seen before.
His cloak had been pushed casually back over his
shoulders, but the muscles in his neck were taut.

'Do you expect trouble here?' Madselin demanded, her eyes also scanning the area.

He took hold of her bridle and gently rubbed the horse's nose. 'Maybe.'

She was so close to him now that she could see the lines etched on his face by the sun and the rain. It was impossible to tell how old the man was; most likely close to thirty.

Sensing her scrutiny, Edwin looked across at her. His expression was sombre. 'It's probably nothing, but I thought I saw something—a reflection in the sun. There's no point in taking chances, though. I want your word you'll do as I bid.'

Madselin gritted her jaw and impatiently pushed back the wisps of hair that had been loosened by the wind. 'Aye. You have my word.' She was not at all sure why she had agreed to it or that her word would be enough for him. Apparently it was.

'Good. Most likely it's the supplies they're after. If there's trouble, make haste to the manor. Wait for no one.' He spoke patiently, almost as if he were talking to a child. Clearly he thought he was dealing with a very simple woman.

'I understand, Angle,' she replied tartly. 'The Vexin crawls with brigands, too.'

Her words seemed to catch his interest. 'You come from the Vexin?'

'I have just said so.' She was pleased to see his cheeks flush a little. 'Do you know it?' A most unlikely event.

'I went there but once.' The words were almost incoherent but Madselin could see a change come over him. 'Come. We are losing time.'

When the attack came, the keep was in sight. They had remained in tight formation, their eyes almost on stalks trying to see through the undergrowth. Every sound

made them jump. The first sign of trouble was a startled
bird taking flight suddenly, its cry shrill in the silence.
It was quickly followed by a swarm of arrows swooping
across their path. Their attackers were but silent
wraiths flickering amongst the trees.

Madselin felt strangely detached from reality as she
watched the drivers of the heavy carts whip their horses
to a faster pace, their rough faces white with fear and
determination. The rest of the guards closed in around
them, their swords drawn. Raoul pulled the screaming
Blanche from the lead cart on to his mount and
motioned to Madselin and Emma to go with him. He
was clearly following his orders to the hilt.

Edwin Elwardson had jumped on to the back of the
last cart and was sighting an unseen victim with his
bow. The arrow sped through the trees, quickly followed by a second and a third. Suddenly a group of
horsemen crashed towards them, swords aloft, and
swept through their defence. There were six of them,
but they were dressed in thick hauberks and dull grey
helms. Their leader was a huge brute with a thick red
beard and a loud raucous voice. His sights were set on
Edwin Elwardson.

The Angle was desperately trying to aim his arrows
at the horses so that his men could cut the brigands
down with their swords, but it was an impossible task.

Swords scraped against metal and bone and the
screams that reached Madselin's ears were blood
curdling. The lead brigand had reached the cart and
was lunging heavily at Edwin. The Angle had pulled
out a sword and was counter striking with swift, well-
aimed blows. But it wasn't enough. An arrow grazed
his upper sword arm and thick red blood welled rapidly
from the cut. He was weakened now, and the brute was
pushing home his advantage with relentless strength.

Madselin looked round feverishly for a weapon, but

all she could find was a thick branch. It would have to do. Without thinking, she picked it up, remounted swiftly and plunged towards the cart. With a mighty heave, she brought the branch down on the enemy's helmeted skull. For a second, the man stilled and she was sure he had felt nothing. Then he just crumpled.

'Get on my horse, Angle,' she hissed at Edwin. 'Hurry.'

He stared at her, speechless for once, but his face was getting paler and the blood was pouring from his arm. Uncertain that he understood, Madselin grabbed at him and pulled him on the horse before her. He slumped forward.

Without waiting she spurred her horse into a gallop and headed for the de Vaillant keep.

Chapter Four

Uncertain whether the body laid across her saddle was more alive than dead, Madselin hurtled through the gates of the manor. A party of ten or so armed soldiers had galloped past her in the other direction, intent only on saving the beleaguered guards and carts left in the forest. She pulled her mount to a halt amid a crowd of strange, unfamiliar faces. Unknown hands pulled Edwin's body from her.

'I can't abide women who swoon, so don't disappoint me.' A strident voice cut across the fuss and noise, drawing Madselin's attention. No more than a yard from her stood a tall, spare woman enveloped in a thick woollen cloak trimmed in fur. Her regal bearing and swollen belly proclaimed her as Isabella de Vaillant.

Thin, mouse-brown braids framed a face which might have been hewn from the local stone. Nondescript brown eyes raked Madselin from head to toe before the woman turned to several servants and bellowed at them to carry the Angle with care into the keep.

Feeling more like she had been swallowed and then spat out whole, Madselin slipped from her horse and handed the reins to a waiting servant. Her legs felt a little wobbly but there was no way she was going to allow this rude woman the satisfaction of seeing her keel over. She deemed the de Vaillants to be well matched.

They were in the muddied courtyard of a small keep that had been built on several floors. It was certainly far grander than she had been expecting. Stables and kennels skirted the inner courtyard wall and a high wall built against the southern side of the keep perhaps hid a small herb garden. A sudden gust of wind from the north-west billowed up her cloak and she noticed that it was covered in blood.

'Stop wool-gathering and come with me.' Isabella's stern command brooked no dissent and Madselin followed her to a heavy oak door.

Isabella stopped before her. She was several inches taller than Madselin and Madselin was forced to look up. 'Have you any knowledge of healing, girl?'

Close to, Isabella de Vaillant was younger than she had at first thought. She must be near two score years, but the late pregnancy was clearly taking its toll on her. Deep lines were etched round her mouth and eyes, and there was a greyish pallor which was not quite healthy. Madselin had often helped the midwife and what Isabella de Vaillant needed most right now was rest.

Gathering her courage, Madselin unconsciously squared her shoulders.

'Aye, Lady de Vaillant. I have some skill. If you would direct me to the Angle, I will see to him. You need to lie down for a while.'

Their eyes held until the merest glimmer of a smile broke Isabella's stern expression.

'Well, you seem to know what's what. I like that in a woman. I take it you are the de Breuville wench?'

Madselin's lips tightened at such blunt words. 'My name is Madselin.'

'Good. You will call me Isabella.' She paused for a

moment, waiting for a spasm to pass. 'No. 'Tis nothing.'
Her smile was wan though, and Madselin did not like
to leave her.

'Come with me. I insist you go to your chamber and
rest.' Madselin took the woman's arm and led her into
a broad hall that smelled of beeswax candles and herbs.
A young blonde woman with a small child in her arms
was close by.

'Take Lady de Vaillant to her chamber. She is in
need of rest.' The girl nodded and beckoned for help
to another woman.

'Here a few minutes and you're already taking over
the place. I'm not an invalid, so don't treat me as if I'm
like to die. It's only a baby and I've managed nine of
them before. Joanna will take you to Edwin.'

So saying, Isabella waved her servants away imperiously and moved slowly but most regally towards a
doorway at the far end of the hall.

'Can you lead me to him?' asked Madselin of the
young blonde woman.

'I'll take you myself. No doubt my sister is with him.'
She bobbed a curtsy and dropped a kiss on the forehead
of her small charge. Madselin surmised then that this
was Blanche's sister. Smaller in stature and less brazen
by nature, Joanna proved far more cooperative.

They entered a small chamber above the hall. It was
lit by several candles and a good fire. There was little
in the way of furniture or hangings, but there was no
trace of dampness or mustiness. Joanna marched up to
the small group of women crowded round the pallet.

'Lady de Vaillant has given orders for Lady de
Breuville to tend Edwin. Take Blanche to the kitchens
and the rest of you see to the baggage wains and
wounded when they are brought in.' The girl's command was quiet but firm and Madselin was not at all
surprised that the women quickly dispersed. The dark-

haired child in Joanna's arms squirmed and she placed
him gently on the rush-strewn floor. 'Be good, Philippe.
We have to help Edwin.'

The boy turned his dark, serious eyes to the man on
the bed and pointed at him. 'Edin,' he managed.

Joanna smiled at him proudly. 'Of course it's Edwin.
Now, you play quietly whilst the lady and I help him.'

From the confident way the child was smiling at the
beleaguered Angle, it was clear that Edwin was no
stranger to the de Vaillant keep.

Madselin bent down to look at Edwin's arm and
carefully pulled at the blood-stained sleeve of his tunic.

'I'll need hot water, some cloths and a cup of strong
wine,' she murmured before sitting down at his side.

Joanna nodded and picked up the child before
leaving the chamber.

Edwin opened one eye tentatively. 'Are they all
gone?'

Madselin looked at him askance. 'Aye.'

He pushed himself up into a sitting position, his face
grim. 'Stupid women,' he muttered querulously, his
eyes checking the room.

'You were shamming!' Madselin glared at him.

He glared back at her, his lips pursed. 'Not entirely.'
As if to emphasise his pain, the wretched man grimaced
as he tried to move his arm. 'But it does give us the
chance to discuss your disregard of my command. You
gave me your word you would do as I said. It seems I
can no longer trust even that.'

Madselin gasped at his words. 'I thought you might
have been a little grateful that I stayed to save your
hide.'

'You gave me your word that you would leave
immediately at the first sign of trouble. You could have
caused far more problems by being caught.' His pale
skin was flushed an angry red.

'You said yourself that they were only interested in the baggage.' Her eyes glittered with anger.

'That was what I told you. It doesn't mean that was the truth,' Edwin exploded. 'Have you any idea what they might have done to you?'

'I certainly have a good idea about what might have happened to you had I not remained.' She paused to toss her braids back over her shoulders. 'That red-bearded brute would have hacked you to pieces if I hadn't hit him.'

'You did what?' Edwin grabbed her by the shoulders and was almost shaking her.

'I hit him over the head with a branch.' Her voice was controlled once more. Madselin gave him a look of utter disdain before pushing his hands away. 'I agree that it was a very foolish action. I should have left him to finish you off.'

The blood was beginning to ooze from his wound again, and Edwin flopped back down onto the mattress. 'Why didn't you?'

Madselin rose to her feet and walked over to the fire. After a moment or two warming her hands, she removed her stained cloak and tossed it on to the pallet. 'Richard gave me reason to think that you were important to his plans and that if aught were to happen to you, the rest of us would be in danger.' She returned to the pallet and began to examine the wound once more.

'So it was not some misguided sense of honour?' he said sullenly.

Madselin flicked her eyes briefly over his face and his disgruntled expression caused her to smile. He was behaving like a child. 'Not at all, Angle,' she replied lightly. 'It was merely a case of self-preservation.'

The door opened and Joanna entered with several women in tow. Each carried their burden to the pallet and after a quick glance in Edwin's direction, they hurried out once more.

The task of mending the Angle's arm was a simple one and took little time once she and Joanna had removed the blood-caked tunic. Madselin found it difficult to keep her eyes from staring at the expanse of chest before her. His skin was a very beautiful golden colour, enhanced by the glow of the flames, and was very soft to touch.

She was not offended by seeing so much of a man's body, since she had often attended the injured soldiers and knights at her home. Yet this seemed a little different. It was the first time she had seen so beautiful a body. Her cheeks warmed at the direction of her thoughts. Quickly she finished binding his arm.

'Well, Angle. You'll live this time.' She picked up the basin of water and cloths and handed them to Joanna.

'My thanks, Lady de Breuville,' he muttered almost mutinously as Joanna left the room.

'Think nothing of it,' she responded cheerfully, quite enjoying the man's discomfort. 'But as you have lost a lot of blood, I suggest you drink of the wine and then rest. I am certain you will wish to be putting in much target practice on the morrow and you are likely to need all your strength.'

He looked at her silently for a moment and Madselin was sure he wanted to strangle her. Suddenly his expression changed and he smiled at her almost wolfishly. The man looked impossibly handsome in the firelight. 'You have the softest touch, Lady de Breuville. I shall be hard put to dream of aught else this night.'

Her cheeks burned with the implications. He was a wretch. 'I hope you writhe in agony all night, Angle,' she spat before marching for the door.

A soft sigh followed her. 'And I thought you had suffered a change of heart, lady.'

Madselin slammed the door behind her. He would pay for such an insult. Although even as that thought came to her Madselin knew herself to be guilty. Hadn't she touched that skin gently, like a caress?

'Lady de Vaillant will see you now.' Joanna smiled at her sympathetically. 'It's best to comply immediately. The lady does not like to be kept waiting,' she added.

With a heavy sigh, Madselin followed the girl down a narrow corridor to Lady de Vaillant's solar. It was a large room, but stuffy and overheated by the fire and the torchlight. Unconsciously she wiped her brow with the back of her hand.

'You're not ailing, are you?' The accusation was flung at her from the shadows to one side of the fire grate.

'Not at all,' Madselin replied tartly. 'I find the room hot.'

Isabella rose stiffly and stepped into the firelight. Her eyes glittered, almost as if she were enjoying Madselin's bluntness. 'I feel the cold.'

Madselin surveyed the woman's homely features. The grey pallor had been replaced by a slight flush, but she was not convinced that Isabella was well. 'Did you rest?' she asked finally.

'As if I could with all that clattering going on about me,' came the irritable reply. As she spoke, Isabella gestured with her hands and Madselin noticed that the woman had the most beautiful hands she had ever seen. Each of her long, slender fingers were encased with pretty rings which caught the light as Isabella waved her hands in the air.

'I wish to hear what you have to say, Lady de

Breuville.' The brown eyes were surveying Madselin thoroughly as she spoke. 'Sit and share food and wine with me. I doubt you wish to eat in the hall tonight.'

Madselin inclined her head in agreement. 'I admit I am a little tired.'

They sat at a small table near the fire and Isabella poured a large cup of sweet mead for both of them. Warmth coursed through her body, reviving and relaxing. Isabella remained silent for some time whilst a servant filled two thick trenchers with a selection of delicate meats. A manchet of white bread was broken in two and left for the women to share.

Madselin had not realised how hungry she was and ate her food with relish. Isabella did not seem to expect her to make conversation and she supposed that as Ivo de Vaillant was a man of few words, this was how it was with them.

When Isabella had finally waved the servant to clear the table, she poured each of them another cup of the sweet wine.

'You are the daughter of William de Breuville and Adeliza de Quesnay.' This was more of a statement than a question.

Madselin just nodded in agreement.

'The eldest daughter?' The woman watched her carefully and Madselin felt quite uncomfortable.

'Aye. I have three younger brothers and two younger sisters.' This questioning was making her feel irritable. 'My father died seven years ago and Robert has the estate now.'

Isabella nodded her head slowly. 'He married that dreadful Cauvin heiress, did he not?'

Despite her irritation, Madselin could not quite prevent her lips from smiling. No one had ever called Alice that before! Still, she should not show such a lack of loyalty before a stranger. 'Alice is regarded by many as a very beautiful woman. She has provided my brother with three healthy children.'

Her words were received with a scornful snort. 'From what I hear, the parentage of the last one is very doubtful.'

The strength of the wine was causing Madselin's cheeks to flush. 'I will not stay to hear my family insulted,' she began hotly and rose. 'I find I am most tired and would welcome my bed.'

Nobody moved for a moment whilst Isabella observed her keenly. Finally she gave a faint smile and waved away the servants. 'Sit down, Madselin. I admire loyalty in people, although,' she added with a sigh, 'I think it misplaced in Alice de Cauvin.'

'De Breuville,' Madselin corrected stiffly. She sat down and looked at Isabella's face. The firelight seemed to soften her features a little. 'Do you know my family?' she asked, her interest pricked.

'I knew your father. He was a hard man. As for the rest. . .' She waved her hand dismissively. 'I know as much as many others. Gossip travels far these days.'

Unsure as to the direction of the conversation, Madselin took another sip of the mead. Its very sweet, rather sickly taste was not much to her liking, but it was soothing. 'I thought I had escaped that.'

Isabella laughed. 'We knew you were coming,' she informed her, her fingers smoothing out her gown over her swollen belly.

'How?' Madselin looked at her in surprise.

Isabella shrugged. 'We have to know what is happening, otherwise we could find ourselves very effectively taken by surprise. Danger is everywhere.'

'Why do you stay?' Madselin watched Isabella rise and stretch her back.

'My husband wishes it,' came the simple reply. 'And the truth is,' she added after a while, 'I love this land.'

'It's very cold and wet and full of barbaric peasants.'

Resuming her seat in front of the fire, Isabella laughed. 'Aye, but it grows on you. Now,' she began more brusquely, 'I want to know why you are here.'

'I'm surprised you need to ask,' replied Madselin primly.

Her implication was ignored. 'I prefer to hear the truth from you.'

Despite the woman's blunt ways, there was something quite likeable about Isabella de Vaillant that made Madselin trust her. Her story was quickly told.

Isabella stared at the fire for a few minutes, deep in thought. 'You were betrothed once before, I gather. What happened?'

Madselin stiffened. 'He died just hours before our wedding.'

'Died?'

'Killed, then.'

Isabella rubbed at her back. 'Unfortunate. Who killed him?'

Madselin rose to stand before the fire. 'A Saxon mercenary.' She almost spat out the words, such hatred did she still feel for the animal who had ruined her life.

'Do you know why?' Isabella looked at her enquiringly. This was something the woman didn't know then.

Madselin shook her head. 'At the time, I was too distraught to ask anything. Later on, Robert told me the little he knew. Guy seems to have been butchered for no reason. He was so gentle and kind,' she added. 'Why should anyone want to kill him on his wedding day?'

'Why, indeed? And this Hugh. Is he a good, honest man?' Isabella stroked her belly in a gentle rhythm.

A vision of Hugh swam before her eyes. He was handsome and cheerful. Was he good and honest? 'Of course.' For a fleeting second, an odd memory of Hugh

laughing rather intimately with Alice flashed before
her. It was gone the minute it came, but it unsettled
her. 'He is greatly concerned for the well-being of all
our family.'

'I've heard he's a vain popinjay with a sweet tongue.
Think you he wants your dowry?'

The words speared Madselin like an arrow. 'You go
too far, Lady de Vaillant.' Madselin rose quickly. 'I
have need of my bed and would bid you goodnight.'

Isabella sighed heavily and pulled herself to her feet.
'As you wish.' At her silent command, a servant
appeared from the shadows. 'Follow Anne. Sleep well,
Lady Breuville.'

Madselin slept soundly, helped no doubt by the two
cups of mead poured so generously by Isabella. She
woke early to the sound of waves crashing loudly
beyond the palisade and seagulls screeching in the
wind.

Pushing herself onto her elbows, she looked around
the room. It was small but sweet-smelling and comfortable. The stone walls were draped in tapestries and
woollen hangings and the window hole was covered by
well-fitting shutters. A good fire was roaring in the
grate and the empty pallet next to it indicated that
Emma was already about.

The wooden door was suddenly pushed aside.

'So you're awake, my lady. And high time, too.'
Emma was plainly irritated as she stomped around the
room.

'What is it, Emma?' Madselin watched her curiously.

'This place is filled with idiots who cannot speak a
proper tongue. There's a great Saxon lummox in the
courtyard who certainly does not know his place. It's
got me quite of a bother and my wits have addled. The

Lady de Vaillant is keen for you to join her downstairs as soon as you can, my lady.'

Dumbfounded that the normally even-keeled Emma had been wrongfooted by a Saxon, or Angle or whatever, Madselin could only stare at her. Emma scowled at her then, so she leapt out of bed.

Isabella de Vaillant sat near the fire with Edwin Elwardson. His long legs were stretched out before him and he looked very much at his ease.

'Come sit with us, girl.' Isabella beckoned her with a gesture that looked more like a command.

From the conciliatory inclination of Isabella's head, Madselin surmised that the words spoken last night were forgotten. Edwin managed a fleeting nod in her direction and she very much doubted if he had spent the night dreaming of her soft touch!

'Edwin tells me you think he needs more target practice,' Isabella began, a tight smile on her lips.

'I may have said that.' Madselin stiffened. 'But it was merely an observation from a novice, of course.'

Edwin leaned forward suddenly, placing his forearms on his thighs. He had decided to ignore her presence. 'I'll be taking out a patrol as soon as I can muster the men. We may find something.' All pretence of teasing had been put aside and his tone was deadly serious. 'Have you any proof that Orvell was behind the attack?'

Isabella shook her head slowly. 'Gyrth seemed to think he recalled one of the dead men near Orvell's keep, but naught beyond that. The man is very careful.'

Edwin picked up his cup from the table and took a deep draught of the ale. 'I doubt if the Scots would act before spring now. Time is on our side, but we must be careful. If Orvell is involved, he'll be keen to rid himself of any problems.'

'He knows something is amiss or he'd not have

attacked you yesterday.' Isabella's loud voice dropped. 'I'd lay my life that all the servants are loyal, but there's always the chance that one might be tempted.'

Edwin drained the cup and placed it carefully on the table behind him. He turned to Madselin. 'Stay close to the keep. You have seen what they can do.'

'I am forbidden to leave the keep?' Her voice was very still. 'I had hoped to visit the beach.'

He stood up and pulled his brown cloak about his shoulders. 'I'll take you on the morrow.' The Angle left without further words.

Madselin's lips compressed tightly. No doubt he was right to be careful, but his words were insolent.

Isabella had watched them with a gleam in her brown eyes. 'Do not gainsay him, Madselin. His pride is sore after yesterday and he thinks himself entirely responsible for the loss of the soldier's life. These things go hard with him.'

The oat cakes turned to ashes in her mouth. 'He is but an Angle. Why should he feel such duty?' This was not something she could imagine of the man. Surely he was interested only in his own gain?

'He is a man of many facets, Edwin.' Isabella fiddled with the rings on her fingers. 'He is torn between hatred for the Normans and duty. Revenge and his own gentle nature.'

'Gentle? The man is an oaf.' Madselin frowned into her ale. Were they discussing the same man? 'And if he hates us all so much, why is he here?'

Isabella gripped her stomach, her face drawn. Before Madselin could move closer to help, she had raised her hand to stop her. 'Do naught. The babe readies itself, that's all.' When the spasm had passed, Isabella sat still for a moment. 'His family were killed by a renegade band of Normans, but he was raised by a Norman family with their own children. He had a happy life, it seems.'

'Well, that accounts for his French, but hardly his manners.' Madselin teased roughly at a mark on her gown with her fingernail.

'He seeks his revenge against the murderers of his family. Where else would he learn about these men? He has spent ten years on their tracks. Do not make the mistake of believing the man simple because he chooses to appear as a peasant.' Pushing herself up slowly, Lady Isabella carefully arranged her cloak about her. Madselin lifted her eyes, aware that she was the object of the woman's attention.

'I have never suggested he was simple. Merely that the man is an oaf. There is a difference,' Madselin declared with feeling.

'Hmm. Better an honest oaf than a treacherous peacock, perhaps?'

'I know not what you mean.' Madselin was beginning to wonder if the damp weather had killed off the woman's wits. She talked in riddles.

Isabella gave her a hard stare before raising one dark eyebrow. 'It's time you saw the place for yourself, Lady de Breuville. Come.'

Madselin contemplated Isabella's stiff back. Had the woman been referring to Hugh de Montchalon? Hugh was worth ten of Edwin Elwardson; she would be proud to be his wife.

Several grimy-looking children pelted through the puddles in the bailey, splashing and laughing their way to the gate. A cheery sentry allowed them through to the outer Palisade with a few words of their guttural tongue. Madselin sighed. Did everyone speak the peasants' language?

The cold and rain of the day before had been blown away in the night, leaving a blue sky full of fresh promise. A stiff wind blew in from the sea, carrying an exotic cocktail of odours that caused Madselin's spirits to lift. Perhaps she had been hasty in her view about the weather.

Accompanied by more children, several soldiers mounted on sturdy ponies rounded the far wall of the keep. They idled towards the gates and then stopped, huddled in a tight group, the horses stomping impatiently on the muddy ground.

Edwin followed them a few minutes later' astride a magnificent black courser that bore absolutely no resemblance to his tame mount of the previous day. The man himself, however, was dressed simply, as was his way, in his old brown cloak and breeches.

Despite his apparel, Madselin had to admit that he did look every inch like a noble lord. And where had that thought come from? She studied him anew. His back was straight and strong, his head held proud. Edwin Elwardson was a natural leader who commanded the respect of his fellow men.

Isabella de Vaillant had proceeded slowly towards the gate and was joined by several others who obviously wished to see the patrol leave. Amongst them stood Joanna, who held a boy of about three years in her arms. This child was most unlike the little dark-haired Philippe, who Madselin had learned was Isabella's youngest son. This one was far more sturdily built, with a thick crop of blond hair.

As soon as the boy saw Edwin, he held his arms out to him and Madselin watched, amazed, as the surly Angle plucked the child from Joanna's arms and threw him in the air. Squeals of laughter informed the crowd of the child's complete approval of the action; indeed, he demanded a repeat performance.

Madselin found herself entranced by the sight of the Angle laughing with the child. It was very clear to her that there was a special bond between the two. After glancing at them curiously for a while, she thought she saw a resemblance between them. They definitely had a look of each other.

As Edwin handed the boy back to Joanna, she noticed a look pass between them. Were they lovers? From the way he smiled at her, it was a strong possibility. The child could be his.

She had no idea why those thoughts should concern her at all, but Madselin found that they did. He had not shown any marked interest in Joanna when they were attending to his wound, but then that would not be his way. She realised that instinctively, even though she hardly knew the man. Madselin was also aware that Edwin seemed far more at ease here than at Richard's keep.

He turned then, almost as if he knew she was watching him and held her eyes for several heartbeats. Within seconds, his attention was claimed by Lady de Vaillant who was no doubt giving him his final orders.

A movement to her right caught her eye and she found herself being scrutinised by a massive giant who was leaning idly by the palisade wall. Taller even than Edwin by at least a head, the man was as wide as he was tall, with thinning blond-grey hair that straggled over his shoulders. He had survived well beyond two score years, but time had taken its toll on his weathered face.

Dismissing her with a snort, the giant thudded across the courtyard towards the patrol. Whoever he was, Madselin had the distinct impression that she had been found wanting.

Chapter Five

When the patrol had left, Isabella had slowly taken Madselin round the tiny village in the outer bailey. For her it had been a matter of great pride that these peasants had seemed cheerful and relatively well nourished. They had certainly appeared happier than those on the de Breuville demesne in Normandy.

When Isabella complained of fatigue and returned to the keep for a rest, Madselin had decided it was time to purge her soul of her recent wrongdoings. The heavy oak door of the church had opened with a loud groan and Madselin had peered in apprehensively. There was no one about, since most of the villagers were about their business, and Madselin ventured in.

As she prayed, Madselin finally became aware of another presence in the church. Turning round, she came face to face with a small man with dark brown hair and twinkling green eyes. Not young, with thick grooves etched between his nose and mouth, the man was watching her with interested eyes. His heavy brown woollen robe proclaimed him to be the priest.

'I beg your pardon, Father,' she exclaimed. 'I did not know you were there!' Madselin hastily scrambled to her feet.

'Lady de Vaillant would never recommend such reverence from a young lady as yourself. I'd be thinking I was doing some good here!' His rather harsh features broke into a warm smile. 'I'm Father Padraig,' he announced with a strange accent she could not place. 'I've been here for the last ten years and I'm still the newcomer. If you need any advice—practical or spiritual—then I'm your man.'

Madselin frowned. 'You're not from here?'

'Ireland,' he replied with a heavy sigh. 'It's across the water.'

Madselin only had a vague idea as to where that land might be but knew naught about it. 'Do you not wish to return there?' She liked the man's warm smile and his honest face. He was very different to most priests she had come across.

He laughed then, as if she had said something funny. 'And who would guide these lost souls then? Lady Isabella would have a fit if I even suggested it, and that woman has a way of knowing exactly what a man thinks. It's a most unchristian skill she has.' The last words were uttered with a gloomy shaking of his head, but his tone was rueful rather than resentful. Madselin doubted that he meant anything dreadful by his words.

'They are not of the faith, then?' she asked, her fears about these people materialising.

There must have been something about the tone of her voice that caused the good man to pause and breath in deeply through his nose. 'I would be honoured if you would accompany me for a while. It's been a long while since I've had a pretty young girl in need of a bit of advice.'

That hadn't answered her question at all, but Madselin was shrewd enough to have realised that Father Padraig was perhaps somewhat deeper than she had at first thought.

As they wandered amongst the villagers' huts, Father Padraig gave her a short history of each family. Basically of Angle stock, the villagers had gradually converted to Christianity many years before the Norsemen came.

'So this is a Christian village, then,' Madselin stated, pushing back some strands of hair.

Father Padraig raked his small hands through his hair and smiled ruefully. 'Aye,' he replied eventually. 'But you have to remember, Lady de Breuville, that old habits die hard in an isolated village.'

'Do you mean they still worship their old gods?' Madselin widened her eyes. She had heard the stories of the pagans and their dreadful sacrifices. What Norman hadn't?

The priest laughed good-naturedly. 'No. But they like to carry on some of the old traditions. It's just their way.'

'And you allow these practices?' Madselin cast him a challenging look.

'Sometimes it is best to let things lie,' the priest explained carefully. 'These people do their duty by me and the rest of their. . .activities are harmless enough.' He smiled at her, his eyes gentle and honest.

'What sort of. . .activities do they participate in?' she asked. Perhaps she was misjudging the situation.

Father Padraig put his arm across her shoulders and turned her towards the inner courtyard. 'Nothing dreadful,' he assured her with an amused voice. 'They celebrate the changing of the seasons with a bit of dancing and music. There are other times—such as All Hallows—where they dress up in old masks and costumes. It's just a bit of fun.'

They reached the gate and stopped. 'And Lady de Vaillant allows this?'

'Lady de Vaillant is a very shrewd woman who

understands the nature of these people. She is devout and sets a shining example to the villagers, but she feels it would be unwise to prevent them from following harmless traditions.' His words were uttered in all seriousness, almost as if he were trying to warn Madselin to leave well alone. 'Come, I'll tell you about one of their legends.'

They ended up at the top of the keep. Madselin caught her breath as the strength of the wind almost bowled her over. She drew her cloak close to her body and looked out towards the bay. It swept outwards, curving round in a broad arc of sand as far as the eye could see. Heavy grey waves swirled and crashed down on the rocks near the shore. A few fishing boats bobbed up and down in the distance. The beach was deserted.

'If you look over there—' Father Padraig pointed inland, towards the forest '—you'll see a lake in the clearing.'

Madselin screwed up her eyes against the glare of the morning sun. About a mile from the keep, in the middle of a wide clearing, she could see water glinting in the sunlight. 'I see it,' she shouted into the wind.

'It's called Lhin Dhu. The black lake.'

Madselin turned to him, holding back her hair from her face. 'It doesn't look black.'

'Nay. It's the nature of the water that has earned the name.' His voice was whipped away in the wind.

'What nature? Is it evil?' Madselin shivered, not all on account of the freshness of the air.

'Only God can answer that one, my lady.' He rubbed his clean-shaven chin with his hand. 'But it's said that the lake takes its own revenge on wrongdoers.'

Madselin stared at the lake sceptically. 'And how would a lake do that?' She did not trouble to hide the doubt in her voice.

'A long time ago, a giant of a Dane led a raiding

party in the area and killed several villagers. He drowned in the lake.' The words were uttered without emotion, as if he were just relaying facts. But Madselin could swear that the priest believed every word.

'If it were true,' she said slowly, 'it could just be coincidence.' Lots of people drowned since few were able to swim.

The priest smiled good-naturedly. 'Maybe. . .' he hesitated for a moment '. . .but the villagers believe it.'

Madselin sighed. 'I doubt I'll be here long enough to consider the matter too much.'

Looking across at her, Father Padraig leaned his head to one side. 'These things aren't always as simple as you think, child.' Then, as if mentally shaking himself from a reverie, he grabbed her shoulder. 'It's about time I went to see Lady de Vaillant. She'll be accusing me of turning you away from the Church if I keep you much longer.' He chuckled deeply, clearly amused at his own words.

For no good reason that she could think of, a vision of Edwin's stern, humourless face came to her. Perhaps years of vengeful thoughts could twist a good man, too? A thread of irritation stirred her into recognising that Isabella's brief account of Edwin's early life had touched her after all. She put all thoughts of the Angle firmly from her mind.

'The child is merely young, not an idiot, and I will not have you cooing at him as if he were unable to understand simple French.' Isabella glared at an unfortunate young woman who had been attempting to entertain Philippe.

The boy was as dark and swarthy as his father but, at two years of age, was displaying the inquisitive and somewhat arrogant tendencies of his mother. Rather conspiratorially, he gave Isabella a lop-sided grin which displayed two perfectly tiny front teeth, before pulling the girl's unbraided hair. Understandably deflated, the girl retreated to her unfinished sewing near the window.

Two other boys of similar colouring and precocious nature were wrestling on the other side of the room. Madselin remembered Ivo de Vaillant telling her that they had nine children. Momentarily diverted by her appearance, the two boys stared at her before resuming their game. Isabella just smiled indulgently at them. 'Charles! Benedict! Go and play your rough games in the stable, not in my solar.' Within seconds they had gone.

'Pleased to hear you in fine voice, my lady.' Father Padraig moved closer to take her hand and kiss it with more warmth than priests usually display.

'The day I stop shouting, I'll be dead,' laughed Lady de Vaillant mirthlessly. 'Now.' She speared them both with an unwavering eye. 'I take it that the good Father has sought to give you a truthful impression of himself?'

Madselin offered a quick smile at the priest, but he seemed more concerned with warming his hands than arguing with Isabella. 'A most enlightening experience,' she said quietly. That was the truth, of course. 'I look forward to seeing the rest of your lands before long.'

'You look as if you have been dragged through most of it already.'

Suddenly realising how dishevelled she must look, Madselin tried to put her wild hair into some kind of order, but Isabella halted her futile efforts with a brisk wave of her hand. 'Leave it. I think I prefer you a little ruffled. Blanche!' Although her voice did not rise to give the command, Blanche appeared from amongst the crowd of women sewing in the corner. 'A flagon of wine and cups.'

Madselin could see that the brusque order had done little to improve Blanche's expression and the girl stomped off towards the door.

'Blanche doesn't seem to get on with Joanna. Are they not close?'

At the mention of Joanna, Isabella's face softened just a little. 'They were, but since Joanna had the child Blanche feels rather. . .ignored.' She gave a dissatisfied sigh. 'A little more guidance from the Church wouldn't have gone amiss.'

Father Padraig smiled blandly and ignored the raised eyebrow. 'The girl has a mind of her own, just like her mother. Blood will out, Lady de Vaillant, as you are always wont to say.'

'Well, I certainly wish she was here now.' This was accompanied by a heavy thump of a lovely hand on the table before her.

'Where is her mother?' Madselin ventured to ask.

'Dead,' came the uncompromising reply. Isabella's shoulders sagged. 'Ten years ago. In childbirth,' she added more quietly. 'She came with me from Normandy on my marriage. I should never have let her get married to that great oaf. She'd still be here if I'd kept my reason.'

The priest lowered his head and shook it slowly. 'It would have done no good, Isabella, and you know it. Marie and Ulf were set on it.' His eyes rested on her with affection. He reached out his hand to her shoulder and gave it a gentle squeeze. 'And Ulf has done his best with the girls.'

'Who is Ulf?' Madselin felt out of her depth and quite confused.

'The head of the village. A huge great ox of a man with more brawn than brain.'

Despite the flattering description, Madselin recognised the man as Emma's lummox.

'Will you listen to yourself, my lady? Sure, Lady de Breuville must think you and Ulf are at each other's throats.'

Isabella sniffed. 'When I need your advice, I'll ask for it. Now, go about your business whilst I talk to Madselin.'

Blanche eventually arrived with the wine and poured the two women a cup each before flouncing out once again. Madselin noticed that Isabella was holding her breath.

'When is your time, my lady?' Her eyes took in the woman's wan face and white lines around her mouth.

'All Hallows, or thereabouts.' Slowly, Isabella exhaled. She hesitated before adding, 'And I hope this time it's a girl.'

'Your husband told me you have nine boys.' She looked around for more evidence, but found none.

'There's only Charles, Benedict and Philippe here. William left for Normandy last year as a page, like the others. Alain is almost eighteen and hoping for a knighthood.' Her voice had softened considerably and Madselin surmised that Isabella was not as harsh about her sons as she chose to display. 'He might be back near Yuletide.'

They whiled away several hours in conversation of a similar vein.

A horn outside shattered the peace of the keep. One of the women ran to the window and peered down into the courtyard. 'The patrol has returned, my lady.'

'Tell Edwin to come up as soon as he is able,' Isabella commanded. 'And fetch him some ale.'

Madselin started to move. She had no desire to be near him.

'Stay. Whatever he has to say will be important. If I am ill or dead, then you have to know the plan.'

Isabella's brown eyes almost challenged her to disagree, and Madselin sat down again in confusion.

'But I don't. . .'

Isabella interrupted her swiftly. 'Richard is no fool. If anything were to happen to me whilst Ivo is away, he would need to have someone run the place. You have experience.'

Madselin could not argue with the logic but it certainly changed her perspective of the whole situation. 'I'm sure Edwin. . .'

'Edwin is a man who knows much about tracking, killing and archery, but very little about running a manor. He'd never be able to control the women. He's far too soft with them. Stop being ridiculous.'

Madselin was uncertain whether or not to breathe a sigh of relief when Edwin was announced. He strode in, bringing with him the fresh smell of the forest. He greeted them with his usual nod and gladly accepted the ale Madselin proffered.

She took the opportunity to study him a little more. His skin was flushed and locks of hair had escaped from his braid. Thick mud was splashed on his boots, breeches and cloak. Hugh would never have appeared before ladies in so dreadful a condition.

Not until he had drained the cup did he speak. How like him, she thought disparagingly. 'We found some tracks, but it was difficult. The rain last night must have washed most of the signs away.' He pushed his cloak over his shoulders and walked to stand before the fire.

He looked weary, she allowed. 'Will you sit?' Madselin offered. After all, the man had lost a fair amount of blood with his injury and he had not rested for some time.

Her concern seemed to surprise him, but he accepted her offer. 'My thanks,' he muttered, eyeing her with suspicion. His expression brought a slight smile to her lips. What on earth did he think she was going to do?

'Orvell?' Isabella's single word of interruption broke their silent communication.

Edwin rubbed his wounded shoulder with a frown. 'I think so. Gyrth is watching the manor for a while. His information could prove valuable.' She'd heard the name mentioned before but couldn't place it. 'Who is Gyrth?' she asked since no one appeared to be volunteering the information.

'Ulf's son,' snapped Isabella, more or less as if she were addressing a simpleton. 'Fortunately, he has more brains.'

A smile shattered Edwin's taciturn expression and, despite the appalling state of his clothes, Madselin realised that she could see why Blanche felt so jealous. Although he was old—near enough thirty summers— he bore few of the signs of ageing that many Normans seemed to. 'He has more charm, that's all.'

'Well? What do you plan to do?'

Pulling himself up to a sitting position, Edwin shrugged. 'Nothing for the moment. I don't wish him to know we suspect him. He might make a mistake without being forced, since he's been running unchecked for so long.'

'Suspected of what?' Madselin demanded.

Edwin turned to her, his grey eyes as cold as the sea. 'Treachery with the Scots.' His eyes slid away to stare at the flames. 'He also has a liking for manhunts.'

Madselin felt cold blood run through her veins and shivered. 'Will he attack us again?' Her customary haughtiness had been replaced by genuine interest.

'Nay. But he might try another tack.'

'If he comes sniffing round here, I'll show him what we're made of,' declared Isabella, her granite cheeks flushing with indignation.

'It might be better if you did not.' Edwin inhaled deeply. 'If he thinks we suspect naught, he'll want to plan his attack. Take us by surprise.'

Isabella shot him a look of disgust. 'He's not coming through the portals of this manor.' She shifted uncomfortably on her chair; but waved away Madselin's look of concern.

'Let him in,' contradicted Edwin firmly. 'We might recognise some of his men.'

They were both thinking of that red-bearded giant, Madselin was certain. 'And what then?'

He grinned at her. 'I thought I'd let you loose on them.'

Madselin gasped. The surly Angle was displaying a sense of humour, and it was most ill timed. 'Be serious,' she hissed.

Clearly he found the thought of allowing Madselin to run amok with thick branches most amusing since he was unable to prevent the smile from tugging at the corner of his mouth. His eyes, she noted, were almost blue. This was not a side to his character she hoped to see again. It was most disturbing.

A gentle snoring from Isabella's chair caught their attention. The woman was looking very tired and Madselin did not think she was as well as she tried to make out. Pulling a thick woollen blanket over her, Madselin then turned to Edwin.

'I am worried about her,' she confided, catching her lower lip between her teeth. 'The pregnancy is not progressing as well as it should. I have some experience in these matters, but I would like a midwife to look at her as soon as possible.'

All trace of teasing was gone. 'I'll send Agnes to you. She's the old herb woman,' he added by way of explanation.

She smiled tentatively. 'That would be kind. Thank you.'

He stared up at her intently, his grey eyes searing into her. 'It's good she's got another woman with her.'

Madselin's eyes slid across the room to the gaggle of women chattering in the corner and raised her eyebrows. It hadn't occurred to her that a man like Edwin Elwardson would consider the comforts of women.

He followed her glance and exhaled very expressively before standing. 'I meant a lady,' he murmured with feeling, before stalking towards the door.

Stunned by his words if not his expression, Madselin could only stare at the closed door. She was not sure that was a compliment of any sort, but the fact that he had said it at all interested her greatly. Sinking down onto his vacated chair, Madselin sighed and picked up some discarded sewing. It was going to be a long winter.

Agnes was a toothless crone with a weatherbeaten, wrinkled face the colour of brown berries and a body the shape and size of a gnarled stick. Wreathed in a dusty brown tunic, the old woman had surveyed Madselin with silent suspicion.

Despite her unpromising appearance, Agnes dealt with Lady de Vaillant in a manner very similar to the one adopted by Madselin, albeit of course in the local tongue. It certainly proved effective since Isabella grudgingly drank of the foul-smelling potion and promptly fell into a deep sleep. As the concoction was one she recognised from home, Madselin's estimation of Agnes's skill rose.

Judging by the guarded looks the woman was giving Madselin, however, it was obviously not a mutual feeling. She wished she could have communicated more freely with the woman, but the language barrier was just too great.

When Isabella woke up hours later, she looked much improved. Her unhealthy pallor had been replaced by a fresher, brighter countenance. The inquisitive gleam in her eyes, however, remained much the same.

'Have you got a better gown than that one?'

Madselin shrank a little under Isabella's disdainful scrutiny. Her hands smoothed out a few of the creases in defence. 'It's a perfectly serviceable gown,' she protested.

'Well, it does nothing for you. A brighter colour would look better.'

Madselin's chin rose a little. 'I see no good reason.'

'Don't you? Well, I'll tell you then.' Isabella heaved herself up to a sitting position. 'All of the villagers will be present tonight and they will be viewing you for the first time.'

'I don't quite see. . .'

'They know that if aught happens to me, you'll be the lady of the manor until Ivo comes home.'

'Then they will have to take me as I am.' Her voice sounded more defiant than she felt, but Madselin suddenly felt as if she had been transported back to stand before Alice.

However, Isabella seemed to understand. 'Very well. Have it your own way.'

When she finally graced the great hall, Madselin was feeling somewhat shaky. The thought of those peasants' eyes watching her every move was a most sobering thought. She was used to merging into the background and being obeyed for who she was, not what she was. The sight that greeted her did little for her composure.

Isabella graced the centre of the table, resplendent in turquoise silk and grey coney trimmings. Madselin

was glad that she had responded to the criticism of her
green kersey and had changed into a gown of heavy
rose damask. It was old but well made and Madselin
had always felt her best when she wore it. The pink
lightened her dark colouring and somehow managed to
light up her brown eyes. Simple but effective. She was
pleased to see Isabella's mute approval.

On Isabella's left sat the chieftain she now knew to
be Ulf, and on her right, Edwin. Much to her disappointment, Madselin found that she was to be seated
next to him. She surmised the feeling was mutual, since
he barely gave her more than scant attention on her
arrival.

The quality of the food was not the best, but it was
well spiced and tasty. Potage, chicken and rabbit were
not high table fare, but Madselin found herself eating
far more than was her custom. Something to do with
the air, she was certain.

Isabella was indulging in conversation with Ulf
although, observing him closely, Madselin realised that
Isabella was doing most of the talking. Ulf merely
nodded or grunted.

Edwin was studiously ignoring the adoring eyes of
the women which seemed to be centred on him
throughout the meal. Despite his apparent ignorance,
she was certain that Edwin was finding the whole thing
rather an ordeal.

'You look as if you would rather be at an execution,'
she began conversationally.

He turned his head slowly in her direction as if
unsure as to whether her remark was intended for him.
'And isn't it?' came the dour reply.

Madselin shrugged. 'Not for me.'

For some reason, that brought a smile to his lips.
'Are you sure?'

She blinked rapidly and listened to the conversations

going on around her. None of it made any sense. 'Quite
sure.'

Her smugness was premature.

'Ulf thinks you unsuited to our land and our men.
Too haughty and too thin for child-bearing,' he said
conversationally as he bit into a piece of honey-coated
chicken.

After a moment's intake of breath, Madselin rallied.
'And why should I be contemplating anything in this
land other than escape?' She speared him with her
most haughty glare.

His eyes roved over her slowly, lingering over her
breasts and bringing a flush to her cheeks. 'Too old?'
he asked simply before reaching for a handful of bread.

Madselin's mouth compressed into a tight line as she
regarded him with utter distaste. 'Too clever,' she
managed between gritted teeth.

He chewed her answer over with the bread before
addressing the chieftain in his own tongue. An outburst
of laughter from all sides followed. Madselin could
barely keep her head up for the shame. 'What did you
say?' Her anger was barely controlled.

Edwin tossed down a cup of ale before wiping his
mouth on his sleeve. 'Just what you said.'

'Can't you talk to him in French?' Her humiliation
was complete.

'No. He doesn't understand.'

'Well, he should learn.' She slumped back grumpily
and drank deeply of her wine.

'This is not Normandy,' he pointed out. 'And in
truth, Ulf has little need of the language since all but
you speak his own.'

Madselin's cheeks flamed. He had no need to
belabour the point. She was not as stupid as he seemed
to think.

Fortunately Emma chose to enter the hall at this

point and made her way to the table. She sat down opposite Madselin, her face and body rigid.

'Why is he still watching me?' she hissed across the table.

'Who?' asked Madselin, looking round.

'That great Saxon lummox!' Emma gave her a withering look.

'Oh! Ulf? The chieftain?' Madselin stole a glance at him; sure enough, his small puffy eyes were fixed on Emma. The intensity of his gaze was most eloquent.

Emma raised her nose and tossed back her grey braids. 'Well, chieftain or not, I'll be having nothing to do with the likes of him!'

So saying, she proceeded to partake of the food on offer, seemingly oblivious as to the state of the chieftain.

Music and laughter continued for another hour or so before people began to drift away. Madselin was very glad when the ordeal was finally over. She had been asked a few simple questions which Edwin had translated, but after a while it became boring for all concerned. Most ended up just conversing with Edwin. She did not like the covert looks he kept giving her either, and felt compelled to express her disapproval by frowning at him.

'Do not look at me so,' she muttered eventually.

'How so?' He raised his eyebrows and waited for her explanation .

She opened her mouth and then shut it again as she noticed Ulf staring straight at the pair of them. His frown said it all. 'As if I were a...a simpleton.' She fiddled with the bread of her trencher, unable to look at him.

He grinned. For a stern, surly man he was developing an irritating habit of smiling. 'You seem to have impressed Lady de Vaillant, at least.'

She ignored the 'at least' for now, but noted how adept he was at changing the subject when it suited him. 'I am considered to be efficient and capable. My sister-in-marriage leaves much of the running of the manor to me.'

'And what does your sister-in-marriage do?' He sounded genuinely interested.

Madselin found that quite difficult to answer without appearing disloyal. 'Alice is most proficient at sewing and prefers to spend her time involved in other such. . . time-consuming pursuits.' It had not come out quite as she had expected and Madselin coloured as her voice trailed off at the end.

'For someone who dislikes Alice, you seem to do much on her behalf, Lady de Breuville.'

'I don't do it for Alice,' Madselin muttered. 'I do it for her children and for my brother.' She had realised early on that Alice would not make much of an effort with running the household. At least they could now be sure of tasty food, clean clothes and comfortable rooms. 'It isn't hard for me,' she added. 'It's my home.'

Edwin shook his head. 'Running a manor success-fully requires much effort, lady. I think you are too modest.'

Madselin looked up at him, somewhat confused. Aye, there were days when she was bone-tired with running round from early in the morning until she fell into her bed late at night. The only real pleasure she had was spending time with the children. A few grubby kisses meant far more to her than Alice's condescend-ing smile.'

Fortunately, Edwin did not seem to have taken her words amiss. After a moment's rather awkward silence, he looked across at Emma and then at Ulf. 'Your maid seems to have captured Ulf's attention.'

'It is not a mutual feeling, I can assure you,' she

replied tartly, directing a repressive frown in Ulf's direction.

A heavy sigh escaped the Angle's lips. 'Then he will be hell to live with until he gets his way.'

Madselin's eyes widened as she realised the implications. 'Emma is a devout and God-fearing woman. If I remember aright, she referred to him as a Saxon lummox. That hardly seems in any way encouraging.'

'Ulf rarely takes no for an answer,' was the reply.

'Well, if he thinks Emma an easy conquest then he will find out we Norman women are clearly made of sterner stuff than the Angle women.'

Chapter Six

It was the first time she had ever set foot on a beach and the only thing spoiling her complete joy was the fact that Edwin Elwardson was there too. Madselin could tell that he was observing her from his lookout on the grassy dune behind the sand, but she chose to ignore him.

A sudden desire to break out from her own mental bonds overcame her natural modesty, and Madselin sat down on the pebble-strewn sand and furtively rolled down her thick hose and removed her shoes. With a sharp glance in the Angle's direction, she satisfied herself that he had at least had the grace to look away whilst she adjusted her gown. Somehow, Madselin had known that he would.

The sand felt at once cold, soft and scratchy between her toes. Pulling up her skirts, Madselin headed for the waves. Edwin had brought her to a small, well protected cove that was hemmed on three sides by high dunes. Rocks and pebbles covered the upper part of the cove, followed by patches of coarse dry sand and then the soft wet stuff that squelched so delightfully underfoot.

Feeling like a child, she stood perfectly still in the

patchy morning sun and allowed the wind to buffet her in all directions. For a few brief moments, Madselin felt a burst of happiness course through her.

Tentatively, she placed a toe in the grey foam. The water was freezing and Madselin quickly withdrew her whole foot before it was swamped in the next wave. After several attempts, she finally managed to stand in the water long enough to allow her calves to get wet. Looking out into the bay beyond, all she could see was miles of grey, choppy waves that disappeared on the horizon. It was hard to imagine that danger could lurk there.

Turning back suddenly, she saw the dark outline of Edwin's proud, tall body as he stood on the dune looking out to the sea. She was glad that he had let her explore this new experience on her own; he had been content to watch and wait for her, allowing her to wallow in her own thoughts. It had been a very long time since she had been allowed to do anything at all on her own. Alice had seen to that.

As she paddled along the edge of the water, Madselin found it hard to believe that she had set out on her adventure only four weeks before.

She joined Edwin sitting on his grassy dune and carefully arranged her cloak so that she could sit in comfort. She had few enough gowns that she could afford to find patches of mud and grass on them.

'Well?' he murmured. 'Is this still a terrible, barbaric land?'

His long legs were stretched out before him and he had propped himself up with his elbows. The wind blew strands of his loose hair across his face as he stared out to sea. Madselin arched an eyebrow and sighed.

'No,' she allowed, waiting for his snort of derision. None came. 'It's very beautiful here. Very. . .peaceful.'

Madselin wasn't now sure what his reaction to her views would be.

'I like it here, too. It feels like home.' His voice was soft, almost a caress.

Madselin was not sure that she had heard aright. The cold-hearted, surly Angle was admitting deep feelings. It was an admission that fascinated her.

'But this is not your home, is it?'

His serious, judgemental eyes narrowed as if he had seen something. 'No. My family came from south of this place, in Cheshire.'

'Do you miss it?' Unconsciously, Madselin leaned a little closer towards him. It was hard to hear him, the wind was so strong.

'Aye. At times. I left ten years ago.'

'Why?'

Edwin drank in the fresh sea air and exhaled slowly before turning to Madselin. They were very close and she could feel her nerves tingling up and down her spine. 'I was given my freedom.'

'But if you were happy there. . .?' Madselin frowned. Why would he wish to leave?

Edwin gave a tight smile and pulled at the blades of grass near his fingers. 'It was time for me to leave. I had fancied myself in love, but the lady was newly married and there were things I had vowed to do.'

'What things?'

He turned and flopped down on his back. She wasn't sure whether he was ignoring the question or just thinking about it. 'My family and the villagers had been butchered by a small troop of Norman soldiers a few years after the Conquest. The two men in command instigated the bloodshed and they enjoyed it all. It is a custom of my people that murdered souls be avenged by the living and I vowed I would.' His voice betrayed no emotion.

'And have you?' Her words were almost a whisper.

'Not yet,' came his stark reply. 'One of the murderers still lives.'

Madselin digested this information in silence. Edwin would certainly make a formidable enemy. Even his eyes were frightening. She nodded. 'And do you still love her, this lady?'

He moved his head so that he could look at her without the sun shining in his eyes. 'She is happy with her husband and I am content for her.' He did not answer her question, but then she had no right to pry.

For a while a companionable silence existed between them and Madselin did not wish to disturb it. Suddenly Edwin sat up and reached for a water-skin. 'Are you thirsty enough for some ale?' He handed it to her without awaiting her reply.

It was a bitter brew and her facial expression must have informed him of her opinion. 'This is awful,' she spluttered as she valiantly swallowed the mouthful

Edwin raised his eyebrows and sighed. 'Aye, but it's all there is. No wonder we peasants all look so dangerous.'

It was an attempt at humour. Madselin stared up at him in amazement, and then she smiled. 'Clearly this is Lady de Vaillant's secret recipe for keeping you all under control.'

He smiled back and Madselin suddenly found her heart beating more quickly. Whatever was the matter with her? 'On the other hand,' she added slowly, 'I could be persuaded to look into the matter. My ale was well regarded by our peasants.' Now, why on earth did she say that? She had no interest in doing anything for these people.

She wasn't sure, but her words did appear to interest him. 'And what form would this persuasion take?' His eyes had an intense look. Clearly the ale was important to him. Madselin smiled softly to herself and sighed. Men didn't differ much after all.

'Regular visits to the beach,' she announced after a moment. 'Providing it is safe, of course.'

Edwin laughed then. He took another swig of the ale and then looked at her. 'You're very easy to please, my lady. For a Norman.'

His use of her title made her cheeks grow a little warm. 'Am I? Alice—my sister-in-marriage—never seemed to think so.' She rolled on to her stomach and flicked at the sand on her cloak.

'Alice sounds a most interesting woman.' He closed his eyes and placed his hands behind his head.

'Many men seem to agree with you,' she retorted without thinking. 'She is a very beautiful woman.'

She glanced at him and could have sworn that his lips twitched at that rather bitter response.

'But she does not see to the ale?'

Madselin laughed at that. The man was driven purely by very simple needs. She shook her head. 'Fortunately not. My sister-in-marriage was not. . .well trained in the more useful tasks of running a manor.'

'And you were,' he stated quietly.

'Yes. I was betrothed to a wealthy man and expected naturally to run his manor.' Madselin could not keep the sadness from her voice.

'He is dead?' Edwin's eyes remained firmly closed.

'Aye. Murdered.'

The crashing of the waves echoed in the silence.

'Did you love him?'

Suddenly embarrassed that she was having so intimate a conversation with an Englishman, Madselin found she could not tell him. 'It was a long time ago,' she replied briskly.

'And does Alice approve of your latest betrothed?'

It was a strange question that Madselin was loathe to

answer. She did not really wish to examine why that was. 'No. She does not. Alice wanted me to marry a much older, more suitable man. A widower thrice over.'

Edwin sat up, his fair hair fanned about his shoulders. 'I cannot imagine what an elderly widower would want with you?'

'Indeed,' she responded, more than a little taken aback by his disparagement. 'You and Alice would appear to have more in common than I had at first suspected.'

His laugh echoed around the dunes and it was most attractive. Despite her ill humour at his reply, Madselin found the corner of her mouth lifting.

'You mistake me, Lady de Breuville. But I have no doubt that an old man would be more interested in a quiet widow, content to spend her days at his side. You do not, in all honesty, strike me as a woman content to sit anywhere quietly.'

'No,' she conceded. 'But it is hard to hold your tongue when you are responsible for so many people, so many things, and then regarded as. . .' Her hand went to her mouth. What was she saying? 'I mean. . .of course. . .'

Before she could finish off her sentence, Madselin found herself squashed effectively under Edwin's body.

'Stay down,' he hissed. 'And say naught. Riders approach.'

Her heart thumped loudly as the Angle slid his entire body the length of hers—and presumably more. He felt warm, hard and heavy all at the same time. Never in her life had she been so close to a man. His fresh forest smell enveloped her.

'Can you see them?' she whispered anxiously. It was a desperate attempt to divert her attention from the feel of his body, not to mention her fear.

'Aye,' he replied eventually. 'If I am not mistaken, they are Orvell's men.'

Madselin could feel his breath against her cheek.

Slowly he reached across her to feel for his bow and arrows. She closed her eyes and her fingers dug deep into the sand.

The muttering of deep voices lingered in the distance, but Madselin could not interpret what they were saying. After a while, the sound trailed away and she exhaled slowly.

Edwin did not move. Their legs were entangled and his chest and arms had completely covered her. She ignored the feeling of security he had generated and concentrated on her fear.

'Have they gone?' she demanded in a hiss.

'Aye,' came the soft reply in her ear. For a moment, Madselin shivered with the feeling he evoked. Whatever he had done, she had liked it.

Slowly she turned her head to look into his eyes. 'Much as I appreciate your protection, I think it would be best if you moved.'

His mouth was very close to hers and she could not help but stare at it. Slowly he lifted his chest and turned her to face him. Madselin was suddenly very aware of his hard body and the softening expression in his eyes.

'I was wrong,' he murmured, his eyes roving over her face.

'How so?' was all she could manage.

'There is much that an old man could see in you.' It was his turn to stare at her mouth.

Their eyes locked and Madselin found herself drowning in the real warmth of his eyes. Had she not seen it before?

Gathering her wits, she smiled at him wryly. 'Do you think of your ale, Angle?'

He pushed himself up with a reluctant grin. 'I think

you are beginning to understand us barbarians after all.'

Madselin took his hand and allowed him to pull her to her feet. They had crossed a barrier, and it felt surprisingly good.

'Did you hear what they said?' She pulled her hair from her face and attempted to right her dishevelled headrail.

Edwin shook his head. 'Only partly. It was difficult to hear. I was. . .distracted.'

Madselin frowned. 'This is not the time to allow your mind to wander,' she admonished sternly and strode off in the direction of the manor.

'He is handsome, is he not?' Isabella's bright eyes shone up at her.

Madselin appeared to consider this outrageous suggestion for a while. 'Yes, if you like that sort of thing.'

For all her weakness, Isabella managed a fairly healthy snort. 'If I was ten years younger and unwed, then I would not be wasting my time on some Norman peacock.'

Stung, Madselin stared at Isabella in reproach. 'Hugh is no peacock. He is handsome and good.' It sounded even to her own ears if she was trying to convince herself.

'Then why is he still unwed?' The button eyes refused to lower, and Madselin attributed her ravings to the fever.

'Because he is a younger son with three brothers before him.' She looked away at the fire. Isabella was being most obtuse. 'Think how it will be for Philippe with eight brothers before him.'

Isabella merely sighed and waved her lovely hand. 'That's different.'

'Well, I don't see it. Besides, my brother is allowing me a good manor for my dowry.'

'Is he indeed?' Isabella's tone was almost defiant. 'That explains it.'

'Explains what?' Madselin glared at the older woman with unforgiving eyes.

'You want that manor?' Isabella's eyes challenged hers.

Her cheeks flared. 'I couldn't care less about the manor. It's Hugh I want.'

'Why?'

Madselin thought carefully for a moment. He had a handsome face, an attractive manner and a sensitivity towards others that was not usual in a man. 'I like him,' she said simply. 'We deal well together.' For some reason, the grip of strong hands and a warm body came into her mind. She rejected them completely. 'Anyway, if Edwin Elwardson is so worthy, then why is he not wed?'

Isabella raised her hands and then allowed them to drop. Really, she had the most dramatic ways for so sensible a woman! 'He fancies himself in love with Ghislaine de Courcy still. I doubt it's true, of course. Men are easily persuaded to change their minds.'

Exasperated, Madselin raised her voice. 'I have no interest in the Angle and I intend to return to Normandy and hope to marry Hugh de Montchalon.' Her lips compressed. 'Or do you find me wanting?'

'No,' said Isabella wearily. 'It's not that.' Her lips broke their granite expression. 'I like you both and I think you suit one another. It would, of course, be very convenient for me if you decided you were suited. That's all.'

'He's an Angle peasant,' Madselin argued. 'We have nothing at all in common.'

'He is no peasant. He is of noble Angle stock and I

doubt that he will remain impoverished for long. Your
kinsman is tardy, that is all. Mark my words, Edwin
will be rewarded in the spring.'

'You're impossible,' replied Madselin with a shake
of the head.

Whilst Isabella de Vaillant found her body required
increasing amounts of rest, Madselin took on more and
more of the running of the manor. True to her word,
she instigated her recipe for ale and all the men seemed
to be awaiting the new batch with baited breath. All,
that is, except Ulf.

The chieftain appeared to have taken Madselin in
dislike and, whenever in his vicinity, she tried to ignore
him. It wasn't always easy. However, wherever
Madselin was, Emma was sure to follow, and Ulf
seemed to take this occurrence as God-given. Emma
had other ideas.

'Stupid Saxon lummox,' she would mutter beneath
her breath as he watched her with lust-filled, reproachful eyes. He would draw his thick set body to its
impressive height and then leer in what he presumably
considered a winning smile. Emma would merely glare
at him before returning to the tasks in hand. Madselin
was rewarded with the usual scowl as he lumbered on
his way.

From the vehemence of the oaths he was uttering,
Madselin was not at all sure that Ulf was going to put
up with this situation for long.

She noticed that seemingly acquiescent women muttered quietly in that strange language, clearly so that
she could not understand if she did hear them.
Madselin felt irritation towards them and towards
herself. Isabella would have understood them so they
would never have done it whilst she was around.

Madselin compressed her lips. Hadn't she always

maintained that it was a dreadful tongue and not worthy of her attention? She flushed at her own arrogance. It was no good, she decided. If she was to get anywhere, she would have to learn to speak a few words.

Joanna was happy to oblige. Her eyes twinkled with a rather knowing glance when Madselin made her request. 'Exactly who is it you wish to speak to?' she enquired casually.

'Anyone,' she snapped. 'Did it take you long to learn?'

Joanna shrugged. 'Blanche and I were only young when we came to live here. When my mother married Ulf, we lived in the village with the others. It seems like I've always spoken it.'

'*Your* mother married Ulf?' Madselin repeated in surprise.

Joanna laughed at her expression, clearly expecting such a response. 'He is much gentler than he appears,' she teased. The smile quickly gave way to a frown. 'I think he is lonely though, and it makes him bad-tempered. Blanche's behaviour does not please him, but he is not sure how to deal with her.'

She fleetingly met Madselin's eye and flushed. 'She doesn't mean to be bad, lady, but she's had a passion for Edwin for some time.'

'Aye, well, perhaps it is about time I discussed the matter with Lady de Vaillant. Blanche is causing too much disruption.'

Joanna nodded and turned to go. Just as she reached the door, she turned. 'There was. . .' she began hesitantly. 'She gets on well with one of the Norman guards who came here with you.'

Madselin inclined her head to think. 'Aye, I've seen her talking to one of them quite often. The handsome one with the dark hair?'

Joanna nodded. 'Antoine.' She smiled timidly, unsure of Madselin's reaction. 'He would marry her, I think.'

Edwin seemed to absent himself more than ever, clearly aware that he was the focus of the problem. Whenever Blanche was near him, her blue eyes were fixed soulfully on his stern face. If he noticed, Edwin gave no indication but would attempt to escape at the earliest opportunity. Had Madselin not found the situation awkward, she would have found it all very amusing.

One evening, after the meal was finished, Edwin requested a private conversation with Madselin. The solar was quiet and relatively cool after the noise and heat of the great hall, and it was a relief to escape. Madselin waited for him in silence, sensing that he was trying to find the words.

He gave her a tight smile. 'There has been a problem. . .with one of the women,' he began hesitantly. 'It seems to be getting worse, and I wondered. . . I wondered. . .if you might have some advice.' Edwin's cheeks were pink with embarrassment and his large frame moved nervously on the hard seat. His strong fingers fiddled with a loose thread on his tunic and a thick swathe of his hair had escaped from its braid to hide half of his lowered face.

Madselin knew that her patient expression was hardly encouraging, but then the problem, of course, was of his own making.

'It's Blanche.' His tone betrayed a certain amount of irritation.

'May I ask the nature of the problem?' Madselin smiled benignly in what she hoped was a fair imitation of Alice's most condescending expression.

Edwin lifted his head and pushed his hair back from

his face. She could see that he was frowning and his lips were drawn in a tight line. 'She will not leave me alone,' he said finally.

Their eyes held for a moment, and Madselin was surprised to see in Edwin's normally cold expression something much more human. This was a genuine request for help, and she was not hard enough to refuse him.

She nodded. 'What have you said to her?'

His broad shoulders shrugged lightly. 'That I cannot marry her and will not take her as my woman. She chooses not to understand me and seems to think I will change my mind.'

'Blanche is an attractive woman,' Madselin said slowly. 'Many men would be flattered by her attention.'

He nodded in resignation. 'Aye, that's true enough, but I am not free.' Edwin's grey eyes stared at her, almost willing her to understand his position.

'Did you ever encourage her to think this was not the case?' she asked. The man had a reputation for womanising and it was clearly well deserved.

'Nay. She always knew that I wished to remain free.'

However he put it, his words sounded callous to Madselin. 'That's very convenient for you, of course,' she retorted tartly. 'But it does seem as though you were the main beneficiary of your arrangement.' With little thought for Joanna and her child either. Madselin frowned deeper.

'What arrangement?' he asked in a bewildered whisper.

Madselin's cheeks burned. The wretch surely did not think she was going to discuss his seduction of Blanche as if this were the sort of proper conversation ladies had all the time? She glared at him.

'I do not propose to talk about your relationship— proper or otherwise—with Blanche. Her behaviour as a result of your deplorable treatment, understandable though it is, does concern me, however. I suggest that we restrict our discussion to this in future.'

Edwin looked at her, his eyes narrowing. 'I did not lie with her, if that's what you mean.' There was no warmth to his voice now.

'That is not what Blanche says.' She stared at him defiantly.

Her words sank in. 'So you knew?' He looked at her with flinty eyes, his anger growing.

She lifted her chin, but did not comment. He would draw his own conclusions.

Edwin raked his hand through his hair and shook his head. 'Well, Lady de Breuville? Since you have such vast experience at running a manor, have you any advice?'

'Yes.' Her tone was crisp. 'I have a husband in mind for her, but I require your cooperation.'

The anger died in his eyes, to be replaced by curiosity and not a little surprise. 'Who?'

'One of the Norman guards. Antoine.' Madselin paused as he went through a mental roll-call of the men. 'I have spoken with him and with Lady de Vaillant. He is keen to wed Blanche and Lady de Vaillant will allow the match. Joanna assures me that Ulf will present no problem when the time comes.' She offered him a tight, superior smile.

If she had expected amazed delight, then Madselin was to be disappointed. A deep frown marred his tanned brow. 'And what exactly is my part in this?'

Ignoring his menacing tone, Madselin smoothed out some of the creases in her gown. 'In my vast experience,' she began, echoing Edwin's sarcastic words, 'it is usually best to be quite harsh.' She shot him an assessing glance. 'Blanche is under the impression that you find my wealth and nobility a real attraction. It might,' she hurried on to say as his face darkened, 'be a good idea to convince her she is right.'

'Nay. I'll have naught to do with Normans.' His words were uncompromisingly final.

'I thought you needed assistance?' Madselin's tone was steely. 'You need not worry that I shall take any of your overtures seriously, if that is what concerns you.'

Edwin stood up and pushed around some of the floor rushes with his toe. As Madselin watched him she was reminded of one of the young pages who was constantly torn between his duty and his desire for adventure.

'You would, of course, need to explain to Joanna.'

'Joanna?' His frown deepened.

'Aye. She should know.' Madselin was confused by his lack of concern for these women. He truly was a heartless brute.

He rubbed the back of his neck before turning to her and watching her with a strangely intent look. 'I'll do it, but I care not for the plan.'

For someone whose actions had got him into this mess, Edwin seemed very graceless. Madselin rose and was just on the point of telling him so when she found herself roughly pulled against his chest and kissed with a thoroughness she had never before experienced.

Breathless, Madselin pushed herself away from him. His solemn grey eyes were not on her but fixed on a point beyond her shoulder.

Madselin whirled round to find Blanche's white face staring up at her. Just as she was about to utter calming words, she felt a large hand on her shoulder and Edwin came to stand close behind. It was a very eloquent gesture that was not lost on Blanche.

Blanche's jaw gritted tightly as her eyes fixed on the tanned fingers gently stroking Madselin's shoulder. With as much dignity as she could muster, Blanche picked up her gown and marched from the room.

Edwin turned Madselin gently around. Wordlessly he adjusted her headrail that had come awry during their kiss. 'Perhaps you were right,' he said quietly, his grey eyes roving over her blushing face. 'It could prove a most effective plan.'

Dropping a final soft kiss on her lips, Edwin sauntered casually from the room. Madselin dropped back onto her seat. What had she done?

Chapter Seven

Isabella lay motionless on her bed. Madselin could tell from her laboured breathing that something was amiss although it was obvious she had been dosed heavily with syrup of poppies. Agnes sat quietly at her side in vigil, gently dabbing her colourless face with a damp rag. As soon as Madselin stepped forward. Agnes rose and hobbled towards her. Her narrow, flinty eyes gleamed with a suspicious brightness.

Alarmed to find the usually diffident Agnes so distressed, Madselin tried to form her questions in the Angle tongue. It was very hard, but with help from Isabella's woman and an impressive number of gestures, the two women managed to communicate. Isabella was weak and in pain, and it seemed that the child was not in the right position but wanted to make an early appearance.

Madselin approached Isabella silently and took over wiping her face. The grey streaks under her eyes had become dark smudges and her lips were almost as bloodless as the rest of her face.

Sighing, Madselin looked across the bed at Agnes. There was nothing more she could do for Isabella either and her fate rested in God's hands. Few women came through such an ordeal to nurse their babe. Had not the miller's wife, a strapping mother of six, succumbed to just the same fate last Yuletide? Madselin's eyes roved over her bloated body in pity before turning once more to Agnes.

'Is there no one who can help at all?' she asked quietly. The other woman translated. Agnes sucked on her toothless gums and then slowly nodded her head. Her dry, cracked voice mumbled several words whilst her eyes remained on Isabella's sleeping face.

'She says that there is a woman, although she is not from here. Lady de Vaillant does not approve of her, but Agnes thinks that only her skills can save the lady and her child.'

'Where is this woman?' Madselin asked quickly. 'Can you take me to her?'

After a few words, the woman turned to Madselin, her expression gloomy. 'The woman's name is Bronwen. She lives to the north of here, near Orvell's keep.'

Agnes and Madselin stared at each other for a moment and then back at Isabella. 'I will see what I can do.'

'But my lady. . .' Isabella's woman grabbed Madselin by the arm '. . .you cannot go there. . .'

Madselin shook her arm free. 'I will do what has to be done to save two lives.' With one last glance at Isabella, Madselin strode from the room.

Edwin was out with the patrol and was not expected back until at least two days hence. He had received a report about strange activities to the north and had gone to investigate. Madselin had noted that there was a look of grim relief etched over his face as he had lead the men through the gates. There was not time enough to send a messenger to him since the matter was urgent.

Two men had been left in charge of affairs at the keep in his absence. Antoine commanded the Norman men-at-arms whilst Ulf concerned himself with the Angle contingent, such as it was. Madselin knew that the only one who could really help her was Ulf.

The church was bitterly cold but the strong smell of burning candles and the lingering smell of rushes and incense were comforting. Father Padraig was kneeling before the tiny altar, his head bent in supplication. Sensing that he was not alone, the priest turned.

'Good morning, Lady Madselin. A willing soul is a rare sight!'

'I am sorry to disappoint you, Father, but I have come to ask your advice. Lady de Vaillant is very ill and Agnes is not hopeful of her survival. Her only hope is a woman called Bronwen who lives to the north of here.'

'Aye, I know of her, to be sure,' he said uncertainly. 'Her skills are well known.'

There was a deep frown on his kind face that caused Madselin a moment's hesitation. 'But you do not approve of her?'

Father Padraig inhaled deeply, his hands clasped behind his back. He considered Madselin steadily before turning his eyes towards the wooden cross. 'She is not of the faith,' he said abruptly. There was a pause. 'But I daresay her love of gold would ensure her full attention.'

Madselin's eyes widened at such assessment. 'Not of the faith?' she repeated dumbly. 'Is that why Isabella's woman was so against her?' Isabella's piety was of the strictest nature.

The priest nodded. 'Aye, to be sure it is. But the good Lord has put her on the earth for a reason and I'm not about to stand in your way if you think she's able to save Lady de Vaillant.'

Madselin nodded. She would have to take the risk. 'Edwin is out on patrol and I will need an escort to get the woman. Ulf does not appear to approve of me and I wondered if you might. . .help me to persuade him.'

He smiled bleakly. 'You'll not need to persuade the man if it's to help Lady Isabella. But come. I'll explain for you.'

A soft wind gusted around the village huts and brought with it the smell of rain. Madselin stepped carefully around the puddles in the bailey as she and the priest headed for Ulf's abode. Larger than the rest, his hut stood proudly in the centre of the village. A thin trail of smoke threaded its way from the hole in the thatch. After no more than a brief tap at the door, Father Padraig entered the gloom within. Madselin followed warily.

Ulf was sitting before a well-banked fire, his craggy face creased in concentration as he whittled a piece of wood. A pile of roughly hewn arrows lay scattered at his feet, awaiting tips and feathers. Isabella's two young sons, Charles and Benedict, sat close by, watching him with rapt attention. Ulf was clearly their hero.

Ulf's eyes flicked over his visitors for a second before returning to scrutinise the stick in his hand. They were in a lofty room with beautifully carved rafters and a large table. Leather-bound shields and evil-looking spears adorned the walls. Madselin shivered despite the warmth from the fire.

The two men engaged in a desultory-sounding conversation which Madselin found hard to understand. Irritatingly, Ulf tended to mumble his words into his beard. Some parts of their discussion were perhaps best left unintelligible anyway. Every so often, Ulf's blue eyes would settle on her and then move back to his knife. At one point he shook his head slowly and spat viciously into the floor rushes. Bronwen's reputation was well known, it seemed.

Eventually, after several harsh-sounding utterances, Ulf wiped his knife against his thick breeches and placed it carefully in a sheath at his waist. Standing slowly, he turned to Madselin and nodded, muttering a few words which sounded like an agreement.

Madselin managed a brief smile and looked towards the priest. 'He'll do it?' she asked hopefully.

'To be sure he will,' came the reply. 'His bark is far worse than his bite and we'll be safe enough with him.'

'We?' Madselin frowned. At this rate there'd be more people traipsing about the land than in the keep.

'Aye. You're not thinking I'd be letting a young innocent girl like yourself go gallivanting around the country without some spiritual support?' Father Padraig looked most put out. 'Besides, you might need to persuade Bronwen with more than a bit of gold.'

'Oh. I see.' She wasn't at all sure that she did see, but the thought of the Father being close by was some relief. 'Very well. How long will it take before we can set off?'

After a moment or two of hurried discussion, it appeared that Ulf could gather an escort of his men within a candle notch. Madselin nodded and hurried to the keep. She had much to organise.

Gripping her hood tight round her face, Madselin tried to protect herself from the driving rain strong sea-wind snatched at her cloak and froze her blood as they raced along the coastal path.

After a time, Ulf slowed the pace and turned the party inland towards the forest. The horses' hooves sank deep into the mud as they tramped stoically further north. Beyond the forest, far in the distance, Madselin occasionally caught a glimpse of the towering

wild hills whose peaks already boasted a covering of
snow.

Father Padraig nodded towards a steep hill about an
hour's ride hence. 'Bronwen's village lies on the other
side of that hill. Let's hope God is with us and she still
lives there.'

That thought hadn't even crossed her mind. 'Is she
old?' Madselin realised she knew nothing about this
woman either.

The priest shook his head. 'Bronwen has a liking for
gold, men and usquebaugh. She's left the village many
times on account of all of the three.'

A delicate flush on her cheeks was the only sign that
Madselin had heard the words. No wonder Isabella did
not approve! However, it seemed the woman was the
only hope. Stiffening her back, Madselin resolved to
bring Bronwen back, no matter what.

Straight ahead, at the top of a steep, rocky incline
stood a large, grey keep. It menaced the skyline and
robbed the valley of its peace. This must be Orvell's
keep.

The village was no more than a ragged collection of
tumbledown huts huddled around a makeshift-looking
church. When they reached the church, Madselin and
the priest dismounted, leaving the escort to glower at
the three impoverished inhabitants who had gathered
about. Feeling very conspicuous, Madselin followed
Father Padraig to the very last hut, where, he had been
informed by a suspicious old man, Bronwen still
resided.

Despite its dark interior, Bronwen's hut boasted
several lavish touches. There were beeswax candles
instead of the tallow most peasants used, several woollen wall hangings and a handsome, carved stool close
to the fire. On the table stood a jug of wine and several
cups.

Although grubby, the hut appeared cleaner and sweeter smelling than other such places and Madselin was intrigued. Bronwen was clearly a woman of some standing. At the far end of the hut lay a simple wooden pallet bearing a mattress and soft coverings that Madselin herself would be proud to own. Next to the pallet was a beautiful wooden chest.

'What do you want?' The words were spoken in heavily accented Norman French.

Madselin whirled round to find herself confronted by a tall, slender woman with long dark hair outlined in the doorway. Suspicious brown eyes raked over her and Father Padraig before the woman sauntered inside to the table and poured herself a cup of the wine. Ignoring the deliberate insult, Madselin forced herself to smile.

'We are here to request your assistance.' Her gaze did not flinch from the woman's bold stare. 'Lady de Vaillant is in need of your skills and Agnes has sent me to see you. You are the only one who can save her and her baby.'

The woman had an almost feral look about her, which was enhanced by the soft brown colour of her skin. She walked with the lightness of a cat, moving with fluid grace towards the fire. Still holding the cup of wine, Bronwen sat down on the stool and stared into the fire.

'Why should I help? Isabella de Vaillant has been no friend of mine.'

Madselin unlaced a pouch of coins from her kirtle. 'I have this for you.'

Bronwen glanced across at the offering and flicked her long, unbraided hair back over her shoulders. 'I have no need of your gold,' came the bored reply. 'What is there to spend it on here?' Her gaze returned to the flames whilst she stretched out and pushed open her cloak. It revealed a red woollen gown tied at the waist with a golden kirtle. Riches indeed for a peasant.

Madselin frowned. She had not expected a blatant refusal of the gold. 'Is there something else that would bring you to the de Vaillant keep?' she asked finally. Anger would not help, despite her true feelings.

Bronwen's soft laughter filled the hut. It was a beautiful sound, like a young girl's—although Bronwen herself must be of a similar age to herself. 'Have you a handsome, rich man for me? A keep of my own?' A soft sigh escaped her full lips and Madselin was certain she glimpsed the longings of a very lonely woman.

Madselin shook her head. 'Helping the lady would bring you friendship,' she ventured.

Her words were greeted with a look of intense scorn. 'What need have I of friendship? Does not every woman around turn to me in their hour of need?'

Father Padraig raked his hand through his dark hair. 'Will you not come to help her, woman?' His eyes held hers for a moment. In that brief space of time, Madselin caught the change in the atmosphere between them. Something had gripped the both of them and they were pulled along in its wake.

'What goes on here?' A loud voice addressed them from the door. All three turned at the same time.

'My lord?' Bronwen's question held a certain edge to it, making it clear that their relationship was more than peasant and master.

The man was tall and very slender. Thick brown hair swept back from a broad brow and hung in waves around his shoulders. The grey locks at his temples softened the effect of his dark clothing and Madselin estimated his age at about two score years. His body, however, could have belonged to a much younger man. There was no evidence of the over-indulgence in ale, wine and meat so many of her brother's friends enjoyed. Soft grey eyes glared at them.

'My lord,' managed the priest after a moment's hesitation. He turned to Madselin. 'I beg to introduce you to a guest of Lady de Vaillant. This is Lady de Breuville, recently arrived from Normandy and kins-woman to Richard d'Aveyron.'

White teeth gleamed when he smiled and Madselin found herself responding in kind. 'Henry Orvell, my lady de Breuville. It is a great pleasure to meet such a charming visitor in so. . .unexpected a place.' Stepping forward, he gently lifted her hand to his lips and place a gentle kiss on her fingertips.

Confusion flooded Madselin. So this handsome, charming man was the ruthless Henry Orvell? Surely someone so obviously cultured and gentle could not be guilty of the crimes Edwin believed him to be?' 'It is an honour, my lord.' She smiled up at his frankly admiring eyes. 'I hope you do not take offence at our presence here, but my Lady de Vaillant is in urgent need of Bronwen's help.'

Reluctantly he let her hand go and stepped back. Casting no more than a brief glance in Bronwen's direction, Henry Orvell nodded. 'She will go with you. Take whatever you need and keep her as long as is necessary. My thoughts will remain with Lady de Vaillant this night.'

Ignoring Bronwen's gasp of outrage, he indicated to Madselin that he wished to step outside. Father Padraig remained inside to help Bronwen. Madselin noticed the old man still watching them. His eyes followed Orvell like a hawk. For a moment, she was certain she could see hatred burning there with the fear.

'That is most generous of you, my lord,' she said, breathing deeply of the fresh air.

'No. The pleasure is all mine, I assure you. It is not

often I get the chance to be of assistance to a beautiful young maiden in distress.' His eyes regarded her with amusement. 'We are somewhat isolated in this place. Few ladies venture this far.'

'Nevertheless, we remain in your debt. Lady de Vaillant is a good woman. There would be much sorrow if aught were to happen to her.'

'Just so.' Henry Orvell smiled, revealing his perfect teeth. 'Father Padraig tells me you are kin to Richard d'Aveyron. What brings you here?' He turned to her and folded his arms across his chest, surveying her carefully.

Madselin hesitated for no more than a few seconds. 'I had come to visit Lady de Vaillant since she is needful of another woman at such a time.'

Henry said nothing, merely smiling and rubbing his beard with his hand. 'It must have been most vexing to find your kinsman leave so suddenly.'

'Aye, but I was glad to be of help. I am used to running my brother's manor in Normandy.' Madselin brushed a few spots of dust from her cloak. Whatever was the matter with her? Her tongue was running away with her.

'De Breuville? De Breuville?' he murmured the name almost to himself. 'The name is most familiar, but I am sure I would remember having met you before.'

'Oh, no. I do not recall having met you. You are mistaken,' she replied quickly.

He stilled suddenly and looked at her. 'Were you once betrothed to Guy de Chambertin? Forgive me for such a question, but he and I were once very close. . .'

Madselin could feel her blood change to ice when Orvell mentioned Guy's name. 'Yes,' she responded in almost a whisper. 'He was killed on our wedding day.'

'Then you are Madselin?' He moved closer to her

and placed a hand gently on her arm. 'Guy used to tell me so much about you.'

'When did you know him?' Madselin was grateful that her voice sounded close to normal.

'We were together on campaign in the north of England. Many is the night we spent talking of the future.'

Madselin found herself warming to this gentle man who seemed to know much about Guy. He had rarely spoken about his early days on campaign in England. She sighed softly. 'I know so few of his friends,' she confided. 'It is nice to be able to talk to someone who knew him well.'

'I am sorry.' he said, his eyes concerned. 'This must be a most distressing conversation for you.'

'Not at all, my lord.' Madselin smiled. She was certain that Edwin was wrong about him. 'It does me good to talk of him. Guy is not forgotten.'

Orvell inclined his head. 'Then you must be my guest at the keep. When Lady de Vaillant recovers, of course.'

Touched by his sensitivity, Madselin would have liked to have accepted his invitation. 'I'm sorry. Lady de Vaillant insists we stay close to the keep for fear of attack from the Scots. I should not be here now, were it not for the emergency.'

The grey eyes flickered over her once again. 'Aye, well, you can't be too careful.' He hesitated. 'However, I am not sure Lady de Vaillant is quite correct in her assumptions. The Scots are not our enemy at the moment. I fear the danger lies closer to home.'

'Oh?' Madselin looked at him askance. 'Who is our enemy if not the Scots?'

Orvell turned to stare up at his keep. 'I am informed that a band of renegade Angles and Saxons plan an insurrection in this area. So far my. . .investigations have proved fruitless, but I believe they are led by a man who may be known to you.' He paused to let his words sink in. 'I can prove nothing as yet, but I have eyes and ears in many places.'

'Who is this man?' Madselin could feel her heart in her throat.

'Edwin Elwardson.'

'Are you sure?' She could barely get the words out.

He shrugged his broad shoulders. 'Positive. But he is a clever man and will twist events to suit himself. He is most credible and very dangerous.'

Madselin remained silent, trying to make something of this new information. Her mind had gone completely numb.

'I speak to you for your own protection, Lady de Breuville. You must inform no one else or he may escape.'

Bemused by all that he had said, Madselin managed only a nod. Perhaps her first instincts had been right all along?

'When you have no further need of Bronwen, escort her back with the men and visit me.' His grey eyes were soft and pleading.

'I will try.' Madselin could only form a weak smile. Her throat was tight and raw, and nausea threatened.

Chapter Eight

It was a measure of his regard for Isabella de Vaillant that Ulf harried them back to the keep before the night clouds had rolled in from the sea. His harsh tongue chided men, women and priest alike if they failed to keep up or do his bidding.

Madselin had been surprised at the man's loyalty since she had not expected it of so uncouth a Saxon. Whatever his reasons, she was grateful to him.

The party audibly sighed with relief as they thundered through the gates of the keep. A babble of voices surged towards them once Ulf had drawn to a halt. Bronwen, who had doubled up behind him, sprang from her imprisonment like a wild cat with a fire on her tail. Ulf had clearly made a strong impression on her.

Madselin watched Bronwen as she stared around her, drinking in the sight of the keep and the strength of the people.

It struck her then that Bronwen was a most dangerous weapon in Henry Orvell's hands, if he was indeed the monster that Edwin believed him to be. He had offered Bronwen's services without a second thought,

either because he wanted to help or because he
intended to make use of whatever she could find out.

Madselin had spent the hours in the saddle between
Orvell's keep and the de Vaillant keep deliberating the
problem. How could Guy have befriended a traitor?
Henry Orvell had seemed so good and honest that it
was truly hard to think him evil. And yet he had named
Edwin a traitor in turn.

Madselin rubbed her throbbing head. Despite her
hatred of the English race, too many people she did
trust held Edwin Elwardson in high esteem. She would
have to tread carefully.

Bronwen halted before Isabella's door, almost as if she
were afraid to enter. 'What will happen to me if she
dies?' she demanded, flicking her hair over her
shoulder.

Madselin stared at her. 'Nothing,' she replied indignantly and pushed the door open.

Agnes looked up as they entered the chamber and
put her fingers to her lips. At least Isabella was asleep.

The heat from the fire was overwhelming and
Bronwen carelessly tossed her fine cloak onto the
rushes before moving closer to the bed.

Bronwen murmured a few questions in the local
tongue as she gently examined Isabella. Agnes shook
her head mostly and sucked on her toothless gums.
Madselin surmised that Isabella had not improved.

Pulling back the covers on the bed, the woman
placed deft brown fingers on Isabella's swollen belly.
Lowering her head to her fingers, she listened to the
sounds of the baby for several minutes. Madselin could
hear only the fire crackling and the neighing of horses
in the bailey.

Slowly, Bronwen righted herself and moved her
hands gently over Isabella. Her face was unreadable as

she replaced the covers. Without a word, she sauntered to the table and poured herself a goblet of wine. Madselin and Agnes watched her, half-fascinated, half-angry that she could keep them waiting so.

Wiping her mouth with her sleeve, Bronwen turned to face them. 'I warn you now that I can do nothing for your lady. She will not live beyond this night and no earthly power can save her.' The harsh words echoed round the hot room. Madselin could do no more than stare at her and then at Isabella.

'You lie,' she hissed finally. 'There must be something you can do.'

Eyes darker than her own bored into her. 'I can do something for the child, but that depends on you.' Bronwen turned to look at the sleeping woman. 'Your lady is all but dead. Only her willpower keeps her alive. If I act now, the child may survive.'

'What can you do?' Her words came out in a whisper as Madselin felt a surge of frozen blood rush through her.

Isabella murmured something unintelligible, drawing all eyes to her. It was impossible to believe that she was dying.

'The child would never survive the birthing,' Bronwen stated simply. She sat down on the edge of the pallet and softly began to wipe Isabella's gaunt face. 'To cut the child free now would be the only way it could live.'

'That would kill Isabella!' The horror of the situation washed over Madselin. It had to be a lie!

Bronwen picked up Isabella's hand and drew tiny circles on her palm. 'There is no other way,' she reiterated softly. 'It is her fate. You must decide within the hour. Beyond that, they will both be dead.'

Isabella's eyelids flickered open. Dull brown eyes turned up to Bronwen and made their assessment before rounding on Madselin. 'Save the child,' she muttered faintly. 'You must save the child.'

Drawing closer to Isabella, Madselin took a cold hand in hers. 'You will not die, Isabella. You are too strong.'

Isabella de Vaillant summoned all her remaining strength to form her granite smile. 'The woman is right, Madselin. I order you to save the child.' Then, turning to look at Bronwen, she gripped her arm. 'I give you my life for hers. You must keep her safe. Stay with her.'

For moments their eyes locked and Madselin felt they were in another world. This was something between the two women that excluded all other beings. Yet it did not make any sense to Madselin.

Bronwen, however, seemed to understand perfectly. 'Do not make me responsible,' she cried out. 'I did not want to come.' She would have stood, but Isabella still had hold of her arm and gripped it even tighter.

'You cannot refuse,' came the implacable reply. 'Now send me the priest.'

Whilst Father Padraig was closeted with Isabella and Agnes, Madselin took Bronwen to the still room to make the necessary preparations. For all her wild and sluttish appearance, Bronwen was neat and efficient in her dealings with the herbs and potions. Finally, she took a small knife from the leather pouch at her waist and unsheathed it. The blade glimmered in the soft torchlight and Madselin shivered.

'It must be sharp.' Bronwen thrust it into the flames of one of the wall torches.

'Can you save her the pain?' Madselin asked quietly, watching the blade in fascination.

The woman's eyes remained on the knife. 'Aye. The potion will put her into a deep sleep before her heart stops. It will be quick.'

Closing her eyes, Madselin sought to quell the nausea

that threatened. When she opened them again, she found Bronwen looking at her. 'Where did you learn the skills you have?' she asked eventually. Everyone seemed to have much faith in her, but yet she could not put from her mind those strange reactions that Bronwen provoked in both the priest and Isabella.

With a slight shrug, Bronwen smiled and considered the heated blade before her eyes. 'I watched my mother birth ten babes that I can recall. There were others,' she added lightly. 'When she died, I went to live with an old herbal woman who had learned her skills from her travels. She took me with her and I watched what she did. Eventually, Dunne became too old and people called for me instead.'

'What exactly did Isabella mean when she said you must keep the child safe?' Madselin's question seemed suddenly loud in the quiet of the small room.

A small sigh of frustration escaped from Bronwen's pursed lips as she replaced the knife in the sheath. 'It is the way of things in these parts. In taking your lady's life to save the child, I am bound to the child by the deed.' Their gazes held over the table. 'It is time.'

Isabella de Vaillant faced death as she had faced all other challenges in her life. When Father Padraig performed the last rites, her eyes glittered with courage and determination, and she insisted on administering the fateful potion herself.

'Courage, Madselin,' she whispered softly as she lay suspended between life and sleep, 'Trust in Edwin. I want your word on it.'

Numb with shock at the speed of events, Madselin could do no more than nod as she gripped Isabella's hand. Isabella, apparently satisfied, closed her eyes for the last time.

* * *

Maude de Vaillant entered the world silently as the lifeblood of her mother seeped away. Bronwen plucked the tiny, blood-streaked girl child from Isabella and gently placed her on her mother's still breast. Instinctively, the child seemed to know that Isabella could offer her nothing and she mewled like a new-born kitten for the hands that would give her the warmth she craved.

Almost hesitantly, Bronwen picked her up and looked down into the hazy eyes of Isabella's daughter. It was a moment when the whole world seemed to hold its breath, a moment that few women ever forgot. Maude's innocence and vulnerability wrapped themselves around Bronwen's lonely heart and pulled tight.

'I will keep you safe, child,' she murmured as she gently kissed her soft black hair.

Madselin and Agnes watched in open-mouthed disbelief as the untamed Bronwen sat quietly in the firelight, crooning softly to Maude. She relinquished the baby only when a wet-nurse was found to provide the nourishment for her that Bronwen could not.

Madselin could not prevent the tears from coursing down her cheeks. Isabella had given her life for her child, yet she would never know that she had given Ivo his much-wanted daughter. Nor would she ever know how beautiful her baby was.

Madselin's heart had melted the moment she saw Maude de Vaillant's vulnerable eyes and crop of black hair. When she held her for the first time, she ached with longing to hold her close for the rest of the night. She had felt the same for Alice's children too. Regretfully, Madselin had relinquished Maude once more to Bronwen's open arms.

Giving Isabella one last sorrowing look, she thought of the three young boys who were now without a mother. They would have to be told in the morning.

Satisfied that they could do nothing more for Maude, they set about preparing Isabella's body for burial. Despite the pain that she had suffered, Isabella's face was calm and at peace and, in a strange way, Madselin found comfort in that.

When they had finished, Agnes refused to leave. It was her right, she declared in her strange tongue, to watch over her mistress through the dark hours of the night. The brown eyes of the old woman glistened with unshed tears, and Madselin nodded her assent.

She left the room quietly to go in search of Ulf. He would be the best one to tell the boys of their mother's death. They would be able to cry with him far more easily than with a stranger.

Edwin and his patrol returned to the silent keep not long after first light. Ulf's messenger had reached him quickly, but none the less he must have ridden at breakneck speed to have arrived back at such an hour.

He found Madselin sitting before the fire in the hall, her gown still bloodspattered and her face white. As he approached her, Madselin began to stand but he placed a large, strong hand on her shoulder and forced her to remain where she was.

'Ulf told me,' he murmured, his grey eyes taking in her grief and her calm. Unpinning his cloak, Edwin turned to pull another stool close to Madselin's and slumped down at her side.

Madselin noticed there were raindrops sparkling in his hair and resisted the temptation to flick them away. Instead, she busied her fingers with the end of her dishevelled braid. 'I know I disobeyed your orders.' Her eyes glanced at him quickly, not at all sure of his mood. 'But there was no time to delay and I had to...'

Edwin raised his hand to halt her flow of increasingly gabbled words. 'You did what I would have expected.

There is no need to explain,' he said quietly. With deliberate slowness, he placed his hand over hers, almost as if he were afraid to startle her. 'Are you all right?'

His question surprised her as much as the comfort she found in his hand. 'Aye.' Raising her eyes to his, Madselin managed a curt nod. Fanciful though it suddenly seemed, Edwin's strong hands and the way he had placed his long body between her and the rest of the hall made Madselin feel fragile and protected. Imperceptibly, she leaned a little closer towards him and he did not move away.

'There is much to be done. I have no idea why I am just sitting here.' Dragging her eyes from his, Madselin attempted to look over his shoulder, but, tall as she was, it proved impossible.

A gentle tug at her braid brought her eyes back to his. 'You are tired and upset. Just admit it for once. Go rest for now.' He pulled again on her braid as if to emphasise his words. 'It's an order, my lady.'

His face was so close that Madselin could see every bristle of the thick brown stubble on his face. Suddenly, without warning, he placed a gentle kiss on her lips and then stood up before she could say or do anything. Looking down at her from his great height, Edwin gave her shoulder a squeeze.

Madselin watched him leave, her mind reeling from his gentle treatment of her. This was surely not the same brute who was forever frowning at her or criticising her? It was, however, the same man who had kissed her so thoroughly two days before. Alerted, Madselin scoured the hall. There was no sign of Blanche. The man's behaviour was a complete mystery.

Putting his odd reaction to her to the back of her mind, Madselin rose and hurried to her chamber. She was tired and she was certainly upset. Besides, an order was an order!

Isabella was buried on sacred ground close to the edge of the coastline. It was a sombre, soul-wrenching time which drained Madselin and every member of the village. For all her bluntness and brusque words, Isabella had been respected and loved.

Beatrice had journeyed from her keep, bringing Jordan and a small army of soldiers as escort. Her kind, smiling face had been a welcome relief to Madselin as she struggled to come to terms with Isabella's fate.

'Come, now, Madselin,' she soothed, as they sat before the warm fire in the solar. 'You did everything humanly possible to save her. Isabella would not want you to blame yourself.'

Madselin could only smile grimly. 'It all seems so unfair. Isabella was strong and had borne nine sons without any problems. Why should one small daughter have caused her death?' Flicking her damp skirts above her ankles, she stretched her feet towards the hot flames and tried to bring a little warmth into her frozen blood.

Beatrice did the same. 'You know,' she confided very quietly, 'Isabella had sensed that all was not quite right. That was one of the reasons for you being here.'

Madselin turned to look at her friend. 'She knew? Why did you not say anything?'

When Beatrice finally spoke, her voice was less certain. 'She did not wish it and I had no desire to countermand her will. Would you?'

Visions of the strong-minded lady of this wild land floated before Madselin's eyes. Shaking her head, Madselin pushed back some loose strands of hair that had escaped from her braid. 'What now, Beatrice? Have you heard from Richard?'

'Nay, but Sir Albert despatched a messenger to him and he will inform Ivo.' The heavy sigh escaping her was most eloquent. 'It will go hard with him.'

The thought of facing Ivo de Vaillant plunged Madselin into deeper distress. He had never seemed a man of gentle manners and she greatly feared his reaction to the news of Bronwen's part in his wife's demise. 'It is well that Maude is strong and healthy. At least he will have her to console himself with.'

'Aye,' conceded Beatrice. 'Isabella did say that Ivo would be more than glad to have a daughter, if only because they were running out of relatives and friends who would take on the boys.'

Madselin could just imagine Isabella making so wry a comment and smiled in response. They had already farmed out six boys as pages and squires with three more still awaiting their seventh birthdays. She had a vague recollection of Isabella telling her that her eldest son was perhaps coming home over the Yuletide festivities. She would face that event when the time came.

'Have you heard any more news of trouble in the area?' Madselin leaned forward to poke the fire with the iron pole at her feet and then sat back to watch the flames splutter and shoot up.

'Aye. Our scouts have reported much raidıng and looting near the border areas, but Sir Albert fears these attacks may just be a cover By diverting our soldiers, they have more chance of success.' Beatrice's eyes met Madselin's in a steady gaze. 'What of Edwin?'

Madselin shrugged her shoulders as she sat back. 'The patrols have reported odd things but nothing certain as yet.' Hesitating, she turned her head towards her friend. 'You do trust him, don't you?'

Beatrice thought for a moment, giving no sign of surprise at such a question. 'Aye. I would leave my son in his care gladly. Richard is always wont to say that

Edwin is the most trustworthy of all his vassals, and he does not say that lightly.'

There was a silence whilst Beatrice waited for Madselin's reasoning behind such a question.

'Henry Orvell thinks he is stirring up trouble.'

'Orvell? You have met him?'

'Aye. Bronwen comes from his lands. He ordered her to help Isabella.' She frowned down at her fingers, which had twisted round a loose thread on her mantle. 'He spoke of Guy. They fought together in England.'

Studying Madselin's tangled fingers, Beatrice was aware of Madselin's confusion. Their friendship was not yet so deep that she could demand to know what had happened, but she guessed that whatever had taken place had affected Madselin greatly. 'He can be very charming when he wishes,' Beatrice responded carefully. 'Did he give any good reason for such accusations?'

Madselin shook her head. 'He has no proof yet, but believes Edwin to be the leader of some Anglo-Saxon rebels.'

'I see.' The reply was guarded intentionally to see if it would draw Madselin out further. 'And what do you think?'

Madselin's jaw tightened and she snapped the twisted thread from the material. 'I no longer know what to think. Henry Orvell was a friend of Guy's and I cannot believe he would involve himself with someone less than honest.'

'That was a long time ago and people do change, Madselin.' Beatrice only voiced Madselin's own concerns, but because she echoed her misgivings she responded with more than a streak of irritation.

'Do you not think I know that?' The sharpness of the retort echoed in the silence of the room. Beatrice remained still. 'Yet the last thing Isabella told me to do was to trust Edwin. It was as if she knew what had gone on.'

Recognising the emotions that had prompted Madselin's outburst, Beatrice reached out her hand and placed it on Madselin's arm. 'Well, then. Just place trust in Isabella's judgement and do not rush into a hasty decision about Orvell. He may be innocent, after all. The rebels could indeed be far cleverer than we imagine.'

Madselin looked at the small hand on her arm and smiled. 'Aye. It's as well for me that you are sensible, Beatrice.'

Beatrice laughed softly. 'I thought you were supposed to be the sensible one.'

'So did I, but I rather think that Edwin is not of the same opinion.' Madselin's humour had been replaced by a rueful sigh. 'I have no idea why I even thought to question his motives, but I suppose my feelings towards the English go deep.'

Beatrice picked up her cup of spiced wine and sipped at it thoughtfully. 'Are you at least talking to Edwin?'

'Talking? Aye.' She smiled to herself. 'In fact, our relationship has developed apace.' In very broad terms, Madselin explained to Beatrice her plan to rid Edwin of Blanche.

'Do you wish me to take her back?'

Madselin shook her head. 'She would never get over it then. No, we agreed to do this and hopefully Blanche will be so involved with her new husband before too long to pay much attention to him.'

'Well, if you're sure?'

'Very sure,' voiced Madselin, not quite certain why she felt more light-hearted than she had for days.

Beatrice and her men stayed on for several days and she gladly accepted Madselin's invitation to remain for the All Hallow's Eve celebrations. Despite the mourning period, Madselin and Beatrice had felt that the event was too important to cancel. Besides, as Beatrice and Father Padraig pointed out, Isabella had always enjoyed the festivities and would not have wanted them to be missed.

The whole village and manor house busied themselves in preparation. For a day, at least, the grimness and solemnity had lost its cruel grip on them and Madselin could feel the lifting of their spirits.

Catching sight of Bronwen hurrying towards Agnes's hut, Madselin decided she could wait no longer to find out more about Henry Orvell. It was some time before Bronwen returned, Maude gripped tightly in her arms.

Madselin had not seen much of either of them since Isabella's death and the change in Bronwen surprised her. Her hair was still long and wild, but there was a softness to her eyes that had not existed before. Instead of the tight-fitting red robe. Bronwen wore a plain mantle of soft green. It suited her far better. Maude slept contentedly in her arms. Clearly Bronwen suited her, too.

'My lady.' She greeted Madselin with her customary wariness, however, and gripped the baby tighter. It was almost as if she expected her to snatch Maude away, although that made no sense.

'Bronwen, I wonder if we might talk somewhere in private?'

'What about?' Her tone was suspicious, but Madselin supposed she had a right to be wary. Few of the villagers even acknowledged her presence. Only Agnes had shown any interest in her.

'Come to the orchard. No one is about there.' Firmly Madselin led her to the orchard on the south side of the keep. It was small but enclosed and they would not be disturbed. They found a wooden bench by one of the old apple trees.

'I wish to ask you some questions.'

A strong gust of wind caught Bronwen's long hair and it whipped across her face. Pushing it back, she turned to face Madselin. 'About Henry Orvell.' It was not a question.

'Aye.'

'I have been expecting it.' Bronwen stared amongst the trees and along the keep wall. 'I'm not sure I have the answers you seek.'

'I'll be the judge of that,' replied Madselin tightly. Conscious that those words had sounded harsher than she had meant, Madselin reached out to put her finger in Maude's tiny hand. Instinctively, the delicate fingers gripped hers in an iron-strong hold. 'What can you tell me of him?'

Bronwen's dark eyes held Madselin's in a cold, intense stare before dropping to watch the baby sleep in her arms. 'Henry Orvell is a harsh man if you cross him.'

Irritated by her reticence, Madselin frowned. 'Most men are.'

Bronwen shook her head and looked away into the distance. 'He is not like most men. The man is evil.'

Alerted by the vehemence of her words, Madselin stared at the woman and child at her side. 'How is he evil?' Her words were almost a whisper.

'Orvell cares not how he achieves his own ends. If other people die, he thinks nothing of it. His men follow his example since they are too afraid to do anything else.'

It was hard to believe this of the charming man she had met no more than three days before. There was more than a chance Bronwen was lying for some petty revenge. 'What did he do to you?' she probed, hoping to catch her out.

'To me? He did not lay a finger on me. He had no need.' Bronwen's tone was scathing. 'But he had my man torn to pieces by that hound from hell he loves. He was the quarry in a manhunt.'

Bronwen's sunkissed face had paled and every muscle in it was taut. Hatred poured from every inch of her.

'Manhunt? What do you mean by manhunt?' Madselin could feel the bile rising in her throat, but she had to know the truth.

'Owain was his scout and afraid of no one. Not even me,' she added with a bitter smile. 'Orvell and his men had been drinking and had taken it into their heads to go hunting. But this time, they decided it would be more interesting if there was a human quarry.' Her cold eyes dropped to Maude, whose face was twitching as she dreamed.

'They hauled one of the village boys in from the bailey, half-dead already from fear. Only Owain stood up to them.' Her eyes were shining as she gently stroked Maude's forehead.

'But there were too many of them and none of the villagers would dare lift a finger against their lord. Not even Owain's own father, coward that he is. Orvell released the boy and gave Owain a hundred paces headstart. Orvell laughed as he told me later that Owain nearly made it to Lhin Dhu before the dog ripped him to pieces. Had he made it, the water gods would have saved him.'

The silence between them lengthened as Madselin absorbed her words. There was no doubt in her mind that Bronwen was telling the truth and it would explain Orvell's hold over her.

'He even killed the boy later,' she added between

gritted teeth. 'Just so that everyone knew what would happen if they tried to argue with him.'

'I am sorry,' murmured Madselin, knowing full well how inadequate the words were. 'I could not have known.' She felt numb. Surely Guy had no idea what sort of a man Henry Orvell was? Perhaps it was as well he had never known. 'If you wish to stay here, Bronwen, you are welcome.'

A smile twisted her lips. 'I have no choice, Lady de Breuville.' Gently brushing Maude's soft black down with a finger, Bronwen's eyes roved over the sleeping baby. 'Lady de Vaillant demanded my services for the child. I will not leave, but I am sure that Henry Orvell will have something to say about that. He does not give up his possessions easily. You had best tread warily about him, for things are not always as they seem.'

They sat in silence for a while, listening to the screeching of the hungry seabirds. 'You must hate the Normans,' Madselin said eventually.

Bronwen stood up and looked back down at her. 'As much as you hate us, my lady.' Without a backward glance, Bronwen walked back through the orchard towards the gate.

Madselin was left alone to contemplate those strange words, for she had said nothing to Bronwen about her hatred of the English. Perhaps it just showed in all she said and did.

Chapter Nine

Madselin could not fail to recognise Edwin amid the mêlée of All Hallow's revellers. He was the only one not wearing some sort of mask or costume. Idly making inroads into the ale, Edwin sat in the corner of the feasting hall whilst all around him people chattered loudly. Every so often he would smile to himself as a few of the villagers broke out into song to accompany a rather drunken harpist.

Edwin's very stillness amid the hubbub attracted Madselin's gaze and she found herself wondering more about this enigmatic man. Despite her desire to hate all Englishmen, her instinct was to trust him as Isabella had commanded. Blunt and surly he was, but ever honest.

It was very evident, however, that his lack of charm did not deter some of the women from trying to attract his attention.

All, Madselin noted wryly, were treated to the same tight-lipped indifference, although this did not marry with his reputation for being a womaniser. The sudden and very unexpected memory of his kiss caused her blood to warm inexplicably and Madselin could feel her face turning pink.

To make matters worse, Edwin appeared to have chosen that very minute to glance over in her direction. In order to cover her confusion, she summoned a servant to refill her cup and hastily threw herself into her duties as lady of the keep.

Once the feasting was over, the revellers cleared back the benches so that the dancing could begin.

Amid raucous shouts of encouragement, the musicians burst into action but, despite much clapping and tapping of the feet, no one moved to dance. Madselin was quite at a loss until she suddenly felt a heavy hand on her shoulder.

'I think we are expected to take the first steps.' Edwin stood before her, his eyebrows raised in question. 'It's a tradition for the lord and lady of the manor to start the dancing. We appear to be. . .ah. . .the next best thing.'

Glancing around, she realised that most people were watching them. This was not the time to decline. Nodding curtly, Madselin rose gracefully and placed her fingers on his arm. He led her to the centre of the hall and they waited for the music to begin.

As the first note struck, Edwin dispensed with any nicety of manners by grabbing her waist and whirling her round and round in an exhausting jig. Breathless and with her blood pounding in her ears, Madselin could only clutch helplessly at his sleeves.

'For the love of God, Edwin,' she hissed into his shoulder. 'We're only trying to dance, not run for our lives. Slow down.'

She sensed rather than saw his smile. 'My dancing is not to your taste, lady?'

'This is not dancing. I would describe it as torture,' she gritted through her teeth. 'And if you do not slow down, I will be sick.'

That earned her another grin, but Madselin was

gratified that he did at least take heed of her words. Once they had charged around the hall in a full circle, the more enthusiastic of the revellers joined them and Madselin sighed with relief.

Confident that Edwin would revert to his normal, surly state and return her to her place shortly, she allowed herself to relax a little in his arms. For a large man, he was certainly light on his feet and it had been a very long time since she had taken part in such festivities.

'You adjust well to our customs, Lady de Breuville.' His words were murmured so that only she could hear him and Madselin shivered a little at such unsought intimacy. 'Perhaps we'll make an Englishwoman of you yet?'

Pushing herself away from him suddenly, Madselin speared him with a haughty glare. 'A most unlikely occurrence. I was merely following tradition. Besides,' she added with a sniff, 'I haven't danced for years.'

Edwin's grey eyes roved over her flushed face and grinned. 'Too old?' he divined with disheartening accuracy.

Madselin's colour heightened if that was possible. 'Alice felt it was undignified for a woman of my years. She preferred me to watch.' Madselin caught her breath as Edwin pulled her closer to him and whirled her round again.

'A mistake,' he said softly, squeezing her waist in a most familiar manner.

'You've had too much to drink,' she accused his ear. 'Take me back.'

'So you prefer to watch from the side after all. I was sure you had more spirit than that.' Edwin's rather endearing grin had subsided into regretful sigh.

'I did not say that.' Madselin shot him a vexed look. The man was very trying. 'I was merely pointing out. . .'

'Do you not dance with your betrothed?' he interrupted, his eyes gazing down at her solemnly.

'No' she admitted. It was a sore point, for she would dearly have liked to on many occasions but Hugh did not care for dancing. This was something she would not admit to Edwin. 'He is of the same opinion as Alice.'

'They seem well suited, your sister-in-marriage and your betrothed.'

Ignoring his rather unhelpful comment, Madselin tried vainly to place some distance between her body and his, but Edwin held her fast. 'He is not my betrothed yet,' she grumbled. 'We still await Richard's decision.

With a heartfelt sigh she gave up trying to distance herself from Edwin and looked up at him. His hair was neatly braided and his chin barbered more skilfully than was his habit. Gone, too, were the muddy tunic and breeches he favoured, replaced by a finer, softer tunic of blue edged in red and gold. With so gentle a smile, Edwin did, indeed, look most attractive.

Unconsciously, her fingers slid over the bulging muscles in his arms and she swallowed hard as one of his hands responded in kind by roving over the curve of her hips.

Even though the fire had been damped down a little, the heat in the hall was almost unbearable. The shutters were open to let in some cooling air but all that seemed to do was cause acrid smoke to billow through the hall whenever the wind gusted. Madselin was glad of the excuse to cover her flaming cheeks. 'I shall have to sit down or I am afraid you will be left carrying me back,' she muttered into his tunic.

'I had not realised you were so wan, lady,' he countered quickly with concern. 'If you wish me to carry you to your room, I shall be happy to oblige.'

Madselin's cheeks flooded with embarrassment as she stared up at him. Had she misinterpreted his meaning or was he genuinely concerned? The wretch gave no indication as to whether he was teasing her or not but she was certain he was aware of the double meaning. 'No,' she gabbled hastily. 'I merely meant that the heat is oppressive. Please do not be concerned since I am noted for my good health.'

He removed the offending hand with a wry smile before grinning at her. 'Your body has always appeared to be most healthy to me, Lady de Breuville.' His grey eyes twinkled down at her as he watched her confusion.

'This is not the time for you to display your tasteless wit, Edwin Elwardson,' she hissed at him. Clearly he had drunk far more than she had thought. 'I shall forget your strange humour and we shall sit down.' So saying, she stalked from the centre of the floor to be followed by Edwin.

Almost hurling herself onto her chair next to Beatrice, Madselin was able to observe the festivities from a position of relative safety. Edwin stood casually at her side as if naught was wrong and that irritated her immensely. Glaring at the dancers, she gradually realised that Edwin's very simple but enthusiastic steps had been but a far cry from those of the others.

'I see Emma has finally succumbed to Ulf's charms,' Beatrice observed with raised eyebrows.

Disbelieving her, Madselin's eyes followed the direction of Beatrice's accusing finger. 'It looks like he has managed to pour a casket of ale down her throat to achieve it,' she responded in concern. 'I do believe Emma is drunk.'

They watched as Emma careered about the floor, her cheeks red and her eyes merry, before Ulf gently guided her to a seat at the far end of the hall. She confounded all of them by promptly plopping herself onto his lap. Ulf beamed in obvious pleasure at so unexpected a conquest.

Open-mouthed at such unlikely behaviour, Madselin was about to go to Emma when a familiar hand at her shoulder prevented her.

'Emma does not look as if she wishes to be rescued,' Edwin pointed out.

Pushing his hand from her shoulder, Madselin jumped up and turned to Edwin.

'It is my responsibility to protect her from such things,' she argued, staring at him with a frown. 'Besides, I have no idea how she is managing any sort of conversation since he speaks no word of French.'

That raised a smile from Edwin, who watched her thoughtfully. 'Emma is more resourceful than you give her credit for. Her fluency in our barbaric tongue improves daily.'

Madselin's eyes narrowed at that barb, but she admitted to herself that she had been neglecting Emma of late.

'If you are that concerned about her, I will watch over her should she go with Ulf to Lhin Dhu, although I cannot promise preserving her virtue if she does not wish it.'

Her glittering brown eyes met his grey ones and she saw the humour there. 'You do not appear to be in any fit state to help anyone. I shall have to go myself—and besides,' she added with a sniff, 'it is fitting that I should see these traditions first-hand.'

Beatrice stared at her for a moment or two, her eyebrows raised in faint surprise. 'You cannot mean that, Madselin?'

'Why not?' Madselin looked at her friend curiously.

'Well. . .you are not married,' she replied quietly. 'It is not at all proper for someone like you. . .'

'I am older than you,' Madselin pointed out. 'And I

am quite aware of what goes on in the forests on feast days. I doubt very much that England is so different to the Vexin.'

'Then I suppose I shall have to extend my protection to you as well, Lady de Breuville.' Despite Edwin's solemn tone, there was a flush to his cheeks that Madselin could not quite trust and she vowed to keep away from him as far as was possible.

Festivities were interrupted by the loud blare of a hunting horn. A very tall, well-built man dressed in a long green cloak and a hawk's mask leapt onto the high table and slammed a long stick three times into the table. A gruesome horse's skull stared out from the top of the stick.

'Come,' he shouted to the cheering crowd. 'Let the souling commence.'

In the wake of the horse's skull, everyone surged through the doors taking with them burning torches and the yew tree branches that had adorned the hall. Their strange masks gave the procession a very eerie appearance that Madselin had never before seen. Fascinated, she allowed herself to be pulled along with the crowd.

Lhin Dhu was fully deserving of its reputation as a sacred lake. All around the banks grew thick reeds where the sad, dark water lapped mournfully. Cold gusts of wind from the sea sent tiny ripples shivering across its murky surface.

'It's fascinating, don't you think?' Father Padraig had come to stand silently at her side.

She turned to look at him, his green eyes shining in the torchlight, and wondered what he had been like as a young man. 'You aren't at all what I am used to, Father. Most of the priests I know would frown darkly

on such heathen practices and beseech the wrath of
God to smite the perpetrators on the spot.'

'Aye, well, I wasn't always a priest,' he confessed as
his eyes followed the progress of a particularly buxom
villager.

'Rest easy, Father. I have no intention of changing
their ways.'

Father Padraig did not look at her but nodded
quietly, his eyes fixed on the village woman. Madselin
did notice, however, that his grip on the cross had
tightened and she deemed the moment ripe to move
on.

On the other side of the lake stood three large
stones, similar to the ones she had seen in the forest
before. The stick with the horse's skull rested against
the largest of these and Madselin found herself drawn
to look at it more closely. Unconsciously, she reached
out to touch the stone. Etched deep into the stone was
the same carving of the horned man she had seen before.

'Do you feel the magic, lady?' Edwin's soft voice
behind her made Madselin jump and she pulled back
her hand quickly.

'I feel vexed that you keep creeping up behind me,'
she retorted, unable to keep the waspishness from her
voice. 'Why do you not dance with Joanna?'

The words had come with no forethought, but all the
same, Madselin wondered at their origin.

'Joanna has already found a partner for the night.'
Edwin turned to the dancers and nodded to a couple
who were closely entwined.

'Does that not upset you?' Madselin asked quietly,
wondering at his lack of emotion. He truly did not
seem concerned.

'Why should it?' A frown betokened his confusion.
'She dances with Gyrth.'

As they watched the couple dancing, Madselin recognised Joanna's partner as the tall man who had led the revellers to the lake. The name sounded vaguely familiar. 'Gyrth?' she asked eventually.

'Ulf's son and. . .' he paused significantly '. . .Joanna's husband.'

'Her husband? But I thought. . .' Well? What had she thought? That Edwin was Joanna's lover and father of her son. 'I have not seen him before,' she pressed on hastily. 'Where has he been?'

Edwin sat down at the base of a stone and leaned back. Staring out at the lake, he picked up several tiny stones and threw them into the water. 'Watching the coastline. Searching for information.'

Aye, she remembered that she had heard Isabella and Edwin talk about this Gyrth. 'Did he find anything out?' Keen to hear, Madselin moved to Edwin's side and sat down.

He turned to look at her, his eyes searching her face. Madselin was most glad that she was shrouded in darkness since he would not see the blush on her cheeks. Why on earth he had this effect on her she had no idea.

'Enough to concern me greatly.' There was no humour in his voice now.

'What? Can you tell me?' Inadvertently, Madselin had placed her hand on his arm. She pulled it away quickly.

'Orvell plans to make a treaty with a clan who live just beyond the border. They have been harrying our land for years without much success.'

'Why would he make a treaty with them?'

'For their men. Whilst the king and his earls are busy in Normandy, the path is clear for Orvell to take what he wants. In return, he would offer the Scots land, gold or even some rich heiress.'

On hearing his last words, Madselin drew her cloak

closer to her body. It was very hard to believe that Henry Orvell could commit such treason.

'He suspects you of leading a revolt,' Madselin said. 'Did you know?'

'Aye.' His voice was grim. 'But it gladdens my Angle heart to know that you did not believe it.'

In the silence that followed, Madselin could almost hear his mind working.

'You did believe him,' he said eventually.

'I wanted to,' she allowed. 'But I could not.'

'Well, I suppose I shall have to be content with your honesty at least.'

'I am sorry.' Madselin placed her hand back on his arm. 'I am a naturally suspicious person. Trust does not come easily to me.'

Edwin rubbed his face in his hands as if he were tired. 'And yet you risked your life once to save mine.'

'I was not thinking aright and had clearly forgotten you were an Englishman.'

That drew a smile from him. He stood up and offered Madselin his hand. After a moment's hesitation she took it and allowed him to haul her to her feet.

'Have you seen enough?' His chin lifted in the direction of the dancers.

'Aye, although I have been wondering about the horse's skull?'

Edwin turned to pick up the stick, testing its weight in his hands. 'It is a symbol of fertility, to ensure a good crop growth next year.' He replaced it carefully before turning back to Madselin. 'Well, my lady, I had best take you back to the keep unless you are keen to taste my dancing skills again?'

'I think not,' she replied with a laugh. 'Although I was perhaps somewhat hasty in my criticism earlier this evening. I did. . .enjoy dancing with you. It has been a long time since I last danced and I think I was just embarrassed.' The words were hard to say but she felt she owed it to him.

Her words seemed to have a much greater impact on Edwin than she had thought possible. She could feel his eyes turn on her and could not help her cheeks beginning to burn under his scrutiny. Beyond them, the drums pounded in an age-old rhythm that strangely matched the beating of her heart. Madselin wondered if Edwin could hear it too.

'Perhaps I was too rough?' he began very quietly. 'I am used to the village girls and. . .'

'No. It was not that at all.' She could not quite find the courage to look up at him. 'I think perhaps I was enjoying myself and I did not want to.'

A finger lifted her chin so that she was forced to look up. They were standing so close that Madselin could feel the heat from his body. Strange longings suddenly welled up deep within, and Madselin found it hard not to reach out and touch him. Could it be the magic of the night?

'A Norman enjoying herself in the arms of an Angle?' he teased gently. 'Mayhap we ought to test it once again to see if you were right?'

Madselin could feel the heat flood through her body as Edwin slipped his hands around her waist once more. Without waiting for her protest, he pulled her hard against his body and lowered his lips to hers.

Unlike their last kiss, this one was gentle and teasing. His lips were soft and sweet, and tasted of ale, but were irresistible. Gently they coaxed a response from her and Madselin found her hands slipping again over his arms and around his neck. Her body moulded against his, swelling and rejoicing in this forbidden taste of passion. And when had his soft gentle kisses turned so passionate?

Madselin found herself caught up in an embrace so

wild that all feelings of control deserted her. Without knowing how, Edwin had pushed her back against the sacred stone for support whilst his hands had begun to slide over her aching body. She in turned had begun to push herself harder against him, wringing a groan from Edwin's hot mouth as his lips brushed gently over the tingling skin below her ear.

'Come into the forest, Madselin,' he urged, his hand beginning to stroke the soft curves of her thighs.

His words penetrated her confusion. 'Nay,' she whispered, pushing him back. 'We cannot.' How had she allowed this to happen?

'Cannot?' he groaned, his hand stilled on her tingling skin. 'Is an Angle lover not good enough?' The bitterness in his voice cut through the air.

'Nay,' she replied breathlessly. ''Tis not that.'

'Then what is it?' Edwin straightened up and stepped back from her.

'I. . .I. . . It is not right,' she managed finally, watching his expression in the flickering torchlight.

For a moment his face mirrored his confusion and then suddenly both of his hands covered her cheeks. 'Are you innocent?' he asked incredulously.

Stung at such lack of belief in her virtue, Madselin shook herself free of his hands and pushed him away. 'Is that so hard to believe?' Pushing her hair from her face, she tried vainly to bring some order to her appearance. She ignored the pointed silence.

'How old are you?' he asked eventually, his voice no longer passionate nor angry.

'Six and twenty. Why?' Her words sounded harsh in her embarrassment.

Gently he took her hands in his and ignored her attempts to push him away. 'You kiss like a woman.' Turning each of her hands in his he kissed the centre of her palms and a tingle shot through her disappointed body like a bolt of lightening. 'I find it hard to believe that your betrothed has not. . .' He did not finish the sentence.

'Hugh is a true knight and would not even think of it,' she countered with hauteur. He had never kissed her like Edwin either, but she chose not to dwell on that. 'I am sure that there are women aplenty who would do as he wished. He would not think of tumbling his wife in the forest.'

'Ah,' came the maddening reply as he stooped to pick up her discarded mask. 'So you would prefer your husband to tumble wenches in the forest rather than yourself?'

Well? Would she? Somehow, Madselin could not imagine herself doing any such thing with Hugh, whether in the forest or a bedchamber for that matter. It just didn't seem quite right. 'This is a most improper conversation. Will you take me back to the keep?' It was more of a command than a question, but Edwin forbore to say anything. He passed her the mask in silence and stalked on ahead to the keep.

Madselin stared at his back for a moment before following. His question—or more particularly her reaction to it—disturbed her greatly. Whenever Edwin seemed to talk about Hugh, she began to feel uncomfortable and it annoyed her.

Pulling her cloak close about her, she hurried after Edwin.

Chapter Ten

Madselin stared at the bowl of grey lumpy porridge before her and groaned. Glancing over at the silent, whey-faced Emma, she firmly replaced her spoon in the bowl and went to stand before her. They were attempting to break their fast in Madselin's chamber since the hall was still awash with the remains of the feast. Madselin took her chance and enquired wryly after her maid's health.

'Like I've been kicked in the head by a mule,' Emma managed grimly as she significantly placed her chubby fingers over her mouth.

'Do you remember what happened?' Madselin asked speculatively. There was no telling what Emma may or may not remember but she had best tread lightly to begin with.

'Of course I do,' came the petulant reply. 'I was only drunk, not deprived of my wits.'

'What about Ulf?' It was now or never, thought Madselin. She would have to tell her sooner or later so best to get it over with.

'Ulf?' A deep frown stole across Emma's face. 'What do you mean?'

'Well,' began Madselin doubtfully. 'You appeared

to. . .er. . .see him in a more positive light than before.'
There really was no easy way to broach this.

'Ye-e-es,' allowed Emma somewhat warily. 'That is
so.'

Alerted by her maid's rather hesitant reply, Madselin
pressed on. 'So you do remember dancing with him? I
thought he was a great Saxon lummox?'

'Aye, well, that was before,' Emma conceded rather
grumpily.

'Before what?' This was most certainly news to
Madselin. She stared down at Emma, waiting for a
reply.

Emma shrugged her plump, rounded shoulders, but
Madselin noticed that there was still a bit of a gleam in
her eye. 'It was the night Lady Isabella died. You were
with her and I was downstairs helping with the young
boys as you had asked. The poor things knew that
something was up but couldn't find out what it was.'

A shadow passed over Emma's face as she thought
back to that night. 'It was young Charles who did it.'
Emma's fingers twisted the corner of her tunic. 'As
soon as Ulf came in the hall, he ran to him and began
to cry. Ulf said something to Joanna and nodded.' She
sniffed as if the memory was still painful.

'Well, he sat down in her chair and called Charles
and Benedict to sit on his knees, just like a father
would. He told them then, the poor little mites, and the
three of them just cried their eyes out together. I'll not
forget that sight in a hurry. A huge man like him, not
worrying about crying in front of women like us. In the
end, we were all crying too.'

A lump caught in Madselin's throat at the thought of
it. She was glad she had asked Ulf to tell the boys
about their mother.

'He is a lonely man, Joanna says.' Madselin watched
Emma's reaction.

The woman just smiled, a rather soft, secret smile. 'Aye, but I reckon I put a bit of a smile on his face last night.'

Madselin laughed. 'Aye, that's true enough. Although he wasn't smiling when he came back to the hall after taking you out.'

Emma sighed and tugged harder at the edge of her tunic. 'No. He was probably thinking of her.' Her brown eyes glistened with unshed tears.

'Her?' Madselin had not seen him with any other woman.

'His second wife. Marie. She's been dead these past ten years. Every All Hallow's Eve he goes down to that lake with the others and talks to her.'

This was definitely a side to Ulf Madselin could never have imagined. 'I didn't see him down there.'

'You went down there?' Emma whispered in shock. 'Why, there's no telling what could happen there.'

'Edwin Elwardson was there too. He had offered me his protection.'

A most unladylike snort came from Emma's tight lips. 'The way that man watches you, I'm surprised you managed to get home at all.'

Madselin was prevented from thinking up a suitable reply by a loud scratching at the door. It was Joanna.

'Ulf bade me bring you this,' she said quietly to Emma. 'He said it would aid recovery.' Carefully she placed a pitcher of foul-smelling liquid before Emma and nodded at her in encouragement to drink it. 'It does work, once you have been sick,' she added with quiet conviction.

Madselin looked at her glowing cheeks and cheery smile. Clearly Gyrth had a good effect on Joanna. On reflection, it was certainly odd that she could have attributed any such signs of well-being to Edwin. In truth, they rarely passed more than a few words together. It was most odd the tricks a mind could play.

Emma drank the concoction without hesitation. It was several hours before they were able to resume their conversation.

There was no sign of Edwin anywhere in the keep and Madselin heaved a sigh of relief.

The more she had thought about what had happened, the more confused she had become. He had always been overbearing and abrupt with her until that time on the beach. Since then, she noticed, his behaviour had changed. He had smiled at her, even teased her on occasion, and was gentler in his treatment of her.

And what of herself? Had her attitude towards Edwin changed? Aye, she admitted eventually. He was no longer the ruffian peasant in her eyes.

He was a well-respected, trusted steward of her kinsman who commanded a keep with authority and intelligence. The men grumbled at their duties as they would for anyone who demanded vigilance and discipline. No one seemed to resent the fact that Edwin was an Englishman rather than a Norman. No doubt they might think it, but the men wisely kept such thoughts to themselves.

November had dawned cold and grey with the first cock crow. Her feet crunched over the iron-hard earth as she crossed the bailey, the noise echoing loudly in Madselin's head. All Saints' Day was traditionally the day they began preparing for the winter months. Judging by the noise coming from the barns, the slaughter of the herds was well underway and she decided that for now she could not face the stench of fear and fresh blood.

Killing most of the animals at the start of winter was the only way most keeps could survive the long, cold months ahead since they were unable to provide enough food for the animals to last through the winter. All the same, Madselin could not help but feel it was a terrible waste. The beef would be salted carefully in barrels whilst the hides would be made into leather. Nothing went to waste.

The bailey was seemingly awash with women carrying pails of milk or laundry, screeching hens and hounds scavenging amongst the piles of rubbish that had accumulated. Madselin made a mental note to have it cleared away since the stink would be putrid and she loathed the rats that it always drew. A shout from the sentry caused her to stop and turn.

'Riders approach!'

After a moment or two desperately trying to think who the visitors could be, Madselin gave up the struggle and hurried inside the keep. Whoever it was, she had best make sure the hall was in some sort of order and that all the drunkards sleeping off the after-effects were surfed out.

'Henry Orvell requests entrance, my lady.' The guard stood to attention as Madselin digested the information. A cold, gnawing pain plucked at her innards.

'How many men are with him?'

The soldier blinked as he mentally added the number. 'Six others. All soldiers, my lady.'

Nodding her assent, Madselin cast her eye around the hall and found it in a tolerable state. Its very dinginess was oddly comforting. Ordering ale and wine, she went to the hearth and held out her hands before the flames. Her fingers were ice cold and she was afraid. Much would depend on her handling of the situation.

If the men were to be believed, Orvell was as dangerous as he was charming and if he suspected that she had an inkling of his activities, then he could wreak terrible devastation on the de Vaillant lands. He believed her to be innocent of such knowledge and therefore useful to him, as was Bronwen. Breathing deeply to calm her nerves, Madselin lifted her chin and thought of Isabella.

The heavy door was wrenched open and Henry Orvell strode in, bringing the freshness of the morning air with him.

'Lady de Breuville.' He smiled as he reached for her hand and touched her fingers lightly with his lips. His grey eyes watched her carefully as he performed the greeting with effortless grace. Resisting the desire to pull her hand back, Madselin nodded with the haughty acceptance that Alice always used and schooled her lips into a dainty simper.

'This is indeed a surprise and a pleasure, my lord.'

His somewhat hawklike expression relaxed at those words, and Orvell offered her a brilliant smile. 'The pleasure is all mine, Lady de Breuville.' He accepted a cup of wine before removing his cloak and throwing it over the table.

Madselin glanced nervously in the direction of his two men who had planted themselves conspicuously on either side of the door. Her own guards were stationed somewhat laggardly around the hall but appeared more concerned with their throbbing heads than any possible danger from Orvell. She hoped it was just the impression they created. 'Perhaps your men would care for some ale?'

Orvell shook his head. 'They can wait. It does them no harm.' He sipped the rich wine and savoured it slowly before sitting down before the fire. 'I was most sad to learn of Lady de Vaillant's death.'

Despite his disarming smile, Madselin was aware that those grey eyes missed nothing. 'It was very unexpected,' she replied simply, dropping her gaze to the floor rushes. 'But at least Bronwen was able to save the child.'

Her reference to Bronwen caused Orvell's eyes to flicker but he said nothing. Taking another sip from his wine cup, he nodded silently. There was nothing in his behaviour or expression to cause her concern, but Madselin could feel the tension in him mounting once again.

'Bronwen has indeed been a godsend,' she remarked carefully. 'Lady de Vaillant expressly requested before her death that she take sole charge of Maude. I had hoped to persuade you to allow Bronwen to remain here.' Madselin held her breath, unable to discern from the expression on his face exactly what he was thinking.

'Ah.' That one word was uttered without the slightest inflection. Pushing his dark hair back from his brow, Orvell regarded her intently, his fingertips carefully placed against each other below his chin. Madselin was reminded of one of the stable cats playing with a mouse.

'The baby is much taken with her,' she felt obliged to offer.

'Then of course she must stay,' came the bland reply. Inhaling deeply, Orvell flicked carelessly at the soft, rich wool of his tunic. 'However, as Bronwen has skills which can be. . .shall we say. . .most valuable, I would require some compensation.'

'Compensation?' Madselin echoed the word in a whisper. 'What sort of compensation?'

A rather curious smile broke out on his face. 'Rest easy, my lady. I meant no more than bid you dine at my keep after a day's hunting. My land is well stocked with game and my cooks provide passable fare. Shall we say a week hence?'

'I'm not sure. . .' she managed quickly.

'I have some things of Guy's,' he continued, almost

as if he hadn't heard her, although she was certain he had. 'You might wish to have them. I know he would have wanted that.'

At the mention of Guy's name, Madselin felt her blood go cold. How could Guy have been involved with such a man? 'What sort of things?' Despite her hesitation, Madselin could not help feeling curious. Anything of Guy's would be precious to her.

'Ah, my lady! That is where I have the upper hand.' His face was alight with humour and it was almost irresistible. 'If I do not tell you, then you will have to come to see for yourself. Guy often mentioned your quick wits and your inquisitive nature.'

Smiling her capitulation, Madselin nodded. 'Very well. A week hence.' After all, he was most unlikely to attempt harm to a Norman lady.

'Good.' Henry Orvell rose to his feet in one graceful movement. 'I shall not detain you further.' He turned to leave the room. 'Perhaps you would bring Bronwen so that she can take her things. I'm sure she needs them.'

'I shall ask her.'

Their eyes held for a moment, before Orvell nodded curtly. As he quit the room, Madselin felt a wave of relief flood through her body. At least he had gone and had made no real fuss about losing Bronwen. Perhaps they had underestimated him? Somehow, she did not think it would be so easy.

Beatrice had left the de Vaillant keep not long after Orvell's departure since she wished to be within her own keep walls before nightfall.

Once her friend had left, Madselin could no longer put off her talk with Blanche and resumed her search in earnest. The girl, however, remained inexplicably elusive. No one had seen her since the early hours of the morning. Madselin eventually gave up with a sigh. There was much to do. Blanche could wait.

Edwin found Madselin in the cellar overseeing the salting of the meat. Trying to take her mind off the meeting with Orvell, Madselin had thrown herself into the most arduous of household tasks. Dust from the salt floated in the stale air and it was hard to breathe. The light from the wall torches barely penetrated the gloom at times.

Just as she had thumped a large leg of beef into the grimy salt box, Madselin felt a hand on her shoulder.

'A word, lady.'

Edwin stood behind her, his face grim. There was no gleam in his eye this morning and Madselin half-wondered whether he had also partaken of Ulf's cure. Nodding, she shook the salt from her hands and rubbed them on her gown covering. Several of the women were watching them with intense interest.

'We'll go above.' Without waiting for Edwin's reply, she turned and made her way to the solar. Madselin could hear his light steps behind her and knew a certain pleasure in being able to command so easily a man as truculent as Edwin. She doubted, however, that his cooperation had anything to do with her. More like he wished to deliver his own words in private anyway.

Eventually they reached the privacy of Isabella's room. Her unfinished tapestry lay on her chair, cast carelessly aside as was Isabella's impatient habit. She looked away from it and turned to face Edwin.

'Well?' To cover her embarrassment, Madselin had adopted a tone that did not encourage intimacy.

Edwin's grey eyes betrayed nothing. 'Gyrth tells me Orvell came earlier.'

'Aye. You were not around so I felt it best to see him on my own.'

'What did he want exactly?' There was a steeliness about him that made Madselin wary.

'To offer his condolences and to ask about Bronwen.'

Edwin's lips formed a tight, bloodless line. 'Did you believe him?'

'I'm not sure,' she admitted. That particular question had dogged her for several hours already and she had not arrived at any conclusion. 'I suspect he was here to see how the land lies.'

Without taking his eyes from her, Edwin considered the reply. His jaw tightened. 'And how does the land lie?' he asked softly. There was no mistaking his meaning.

'Quiet,' she retorted indignantly. 'And he invited me to hunt and dine with him.'

'Which you refused,' he finished confidently.

'No. I accepted.'

The silence between them was charged with tension and Edwin's narrowed eyes made her nervous. Madselin had to remind herself that she had done nothing wrong. 'Did he threaten you?' Edwin's tone had an icy quality that chilled her to the bone.

She shook her head. 'He said he had some of Guy's possessions.' Madselin glared at him, discomfited that he had made her admit such a thing.

'Who is Guy?' His frown deepened even more.

Straightening her back, Madselin lifted her chin. She refused to be cowed by Edwin Elwardson. He was, after all, only an Englishman. 'Guy de Chambertin was my betrothed before he was cut down like a dog on our wedding day.'

Unexpectedly, Edwin's face drained of colour. He stared hard at her as if viewing her for the first time, his fingers rubbing at his stubbly chin. 'Why would Henry Orvell have some of his things?' he asked eventually, his voice quiet and very controlled. There was an intensity in his eyes that Madselin found uncomfortable.

'I believe they were on campaign together in England. Orvell was Guy's commander.' His reaction to her words was not at all understandable.

Edwin looked as though he was about to say something, but bit the words back and reached for a cup of wine. That in itself was strange since the man usually drank ale from preference. All the same, he was not acting himself, so Madselin held her tongue and waited.

'Did your betrothed ever mention Orvell?' The wine cup was held before his lips as he awaited her reply.

'Nay. But then I had not seen Guy for years before our wedding. I do not recall him being a guest, although it has been eight years since. . .'

Edwin gulped the wine down in one and she noticed a little of the red liquid dribble down his chin. The man was not at all himself.

'He is a dangerous man,' Edwin said finally, wiping his chin with his sleeve. 'It seems very likely that he is the man responsible for killing my family and I would not trust him with a dog. You will not go to his keep, lady. The man is as treacherous as a trapped wolf.'

Madselin watched him, sensing his controlled anger and something not unlike anticipation. She doubted that Orvell was the man who killed Edwin's family. Orvell was far too much a Norman knight—although she had reason to believe his treachery with the Scots.

Her mind whirred on despite herself and she traced the trail of a strange thought. If Orvell had been responsible, then that could mean that Guy. . .no. It was too absurd. 'If you believe that to be the case, then why did you not act earlier?'

Refilling his cup, Edwin swirled the liquid round thoughtfully. 'I have no proof beyond recognising him and d'Aveyron will not act on that alone. He has stayed my hand these many months as he doubts the King would view my killing of Orvell on such grounds as anything other than murder. I am willing to pay the price but your kinsman plays a deeper game.'

'I don't understand,' she said, her tone somewhat softer. It was not often that Edwin spoke of his inner thoughts and she savoured the confidence a little.

With a heavy sigh, Edwin frowned once again at the flames in the hearth. 'I am to take him committing an act of treason. That way, Richard can justify Orvell's death by courting Rufus's fear of treason. He has reason to believe the King will be well pleased.'

'So,' she finished wryly, 'your revenge takes second place to my kinsman's desire for favour with the King. I had not thought Richard so blatantly avaricious.'

'Your kinsman treads a fine tightrope, Lady de Breuville. His liege-lord is suspected of treason and Rufus will be keeping a careful eye on de Poictou's vassals. D'Aveyron acts not only in his own best interests, but in those of his family and his tenant knights too. I, also, have reason to be grateful for his shrewdness on more than one occasion.'

Fascinated, Madselin raised her brow in question but Edwin shook his head. 'I gave him my word I would do as he says.'

Madselin remembered Richard telling her that Edwin was one of the few men he could trust to do his bidding to the letter. At the time she had thought that strange, since it did not accord with her own view, and it still did not ring true. He was loyal, she was certain, but capable of independent action none the less.

Edwin carried on, unaware of the nature of her thoughts. 'Gyrth has heard a whisper that a small retinue of Scots are due tomorrow eve. They come by boat whilst the moon is low over the channel. I'll arrange a patrol to await their arrival. If we can capture

one alive, then we could point more than a finger of
suspicion at Orvell.' He glanced up at Madselin's white
face. 'Give me your word that you will not visit Orvell,
Lady de Breuville.'

Glancing across at the unfinished tapestry, Madselin
remembered Isabella's last words to her. Aye, she
would trust this strange man. 'You have it, Angle,' she
replied so meekly that his brows lifted almost in
question.

He inclined his head in acceptance before allowing
his gaze to rake over her. 'Do you know your face is
covered in salt dust, Madselin?' Without awaiting her
reply, Edwin turned to leave the room.

Quickly wiping her cheeks with her grimy hands,
Madselin glared at the truth of his words. Why did the
man always have the last word? And yet he had allowed
her to stand there the whole time with a dusty white
face and said nothing at all. Irritated beyond measure,
she stalked back to the cellar.

Madselin paused at her sewing and listened to Maude
de Vaillant's fierce cries vie with the strains of the harp.
For a tiny baby, she was certainly more than capable of
expressing her displeasure loudly.

Madselin stilled for a moment, more concerned for
the baby than she cared to admit. Bronwen shushed
and caressed Maude gently in the shadowy embrasure
of the solar whilst Madselin and Emma sat busy with
their mending before the fire.

'The babe is restless tonight, Bronwen. Is she ailing?'
The early days were often the most dangerous for the
newborn and any discomfort could be the first sign of
impending death.

Bronwen looked up and shook her head firmly. 'Nay,
'tis either the weather or Morwenna. The woman drank
more than her fair share of ale yestereve and I'll wager

her milk curdled with all that dancing.' Gracefully she stood up and placed Maude across her shoulder, rubbing her back to the rhythm of the harp. 'What with her and that Blanche, you've got your hands full.'

Madselin ignored the harsh snort that came from Emma's direction. 'What about Morwenna? I had thought she was working well as the wetnurse.'

Unable to hold her tongue any longer, Emma interrupted. 'Aye, until she gets herself with child again. If I'm not mistaken, that won't be very long.'

Casting a quelling look at her maid, Madselin turned back to Bronwen. The baby was clutching at her thick braid and snuffled loudly into her tunic. 'Are you not pleased with her?'' she questioned. There had been little time to oversee Morwenna since Isabella's death and she had thought that since Bronwen had not mentioned it, she was happy with the woman.

Bronwen shrugged her slender shoulders with indifference. 'She does what she must, but Emma is right. There is a good chance she will get herself with child soon.'

A frown creased Madselin's brow. Aye, she had noticed the priest's interest in her, but other than Emma's caustic words there had been no other indication that he had been dallying with Morwenna. 'When did her husband drown?'

'It's been five moons she said,' Bronwen replied absently, her lips brushing gently over Maude's soft brow. 'She's just lonely,' she offered in excuse. 'But lying with the priest is no way to find herself another man. Her best chance would be to wait until the spring celebrations. There's many good men around who'd be more than happy to have her tie their hands. She's got two healthy sons and is still young and strong.'

Fascinated at such a barbaric method of finding a husband, Madselin mused that perhaps it had its merits.

Were it the same for Norman ladies, she would never choose an old man like Goddefroi de Grantmesnil.

Had she the choice, like Morwenna, who indeed would she pick? In a place as wild and treacherous as this, only the strong and the bold survived. It was hard to imagine Hugh pitting his strength against the elements that shaped their lives here. At least, she amended quickly, not for long.

'And that Blanche has been missing since this morning.' Emma's censorious tone interrupted her thoughts. 'The woman has no morals. That young man of hers has been searching for her everywhere. No doubt she'll turn up when she's good and ready with her nose in the air as if naught was wrong. Leading him a merry dance, she is.'

Madselin sighed and rubbed her aching head. 'Aye. I'll speak to Father Padraig about marrying her soon. Is he missing, too?' she enquired distractedly, stifling a yawn.

'He was at Lhin Dhu with the others,' murmured Bronwen, rocking the now-quiet Maude. She made her way to the wooden crib and bent down to settle the babe amongst the fleeces and blankets that lined it.

Madselin raised her eyes to the woman. 'Why were people at Lhin Dhu?' She dry-washed her face with her hands in an effort to wake up.

Bronwen offered her a wry smile as she straightened and walked back towards the fire. 'Just adding your Church's approval to our traditional ways. They'd lose us otherwise.'

Madselin did no more than raise her brows at this cynical view of the old ways of the villagers versus the religious zeal of the Church. She was coming to realise that perhaps it was better to accommodate than to sweep clean. Besides, she had quite enjoyed herself at the celebrations.

'Did you know that Henry Orvell came?' At last she had broached the subject that had been bothering her most. Bronwen's gaze did not even flicker.

'Aye. What did he want?'

Madselin ignored Emma's hiss of disapproval at such bold questions. She approved of Bronwen's straight-forward approach. 'To invite me to hunt and dine and to find out if you were coming back.'

The silence between them was tense.

'What was your answer?' The woman's tone was cool but Madselin was certain she detected a slight quiver in her voice.

'Yes to the first and no to the second. He did not appear overly concerned,' she added as the frown on Bronwen's face deepened.

Bronwen shook her head. 'The man goes deep and he has his eye on you. There's something there between you. A link.' She shrugged carelessly before placing her hands before the fire. 'It was just a feeling I had, that day you came.'

Debating whether or not to divulge this link, she decided to bite her tongue for the time being. There was no need to mention Guy at all and his connection with Henry Orvell was making her uncomfortable. Madselin stood up in a fluid movement. The candles had reduced only a notch or so since they had first retired to the solar.

'I feel in need of a bath,' she announced to Emma. 'Have the tub and hot water sent to my room. There's no need for you to come too,' she added hastily, seeing the startled look on her maid's face. Madselin sus-pected that Emma had made some sort of secret tryst with Ulf for later on and she had no desire to interrupt their plans. For once she had a yen to be on her own.

* * *

Madselin closed her eyes as she lay back against the oiled cloth in the tub. The fragrant scent of herbs and the last of her precious oils enveloped her in a steamy mist that she found most relaxing. The deep ache that had gripped her head for most of the day had lessened as the water lapped over her. Well, it was in fact just a tiny tub with barely much room for sitting in, but it served its purpose.

The latch on the door rattled but Madselin ignored it. A strong gust of wind, no more than that. She carefully removed the damp lock of hair that obscured her view, just to be on the safe side.

'Had I realised how unconcerned you are of your reputation, I would have breached your haven earlier. You are a most difficult woman to pin down.'

With a strangled squeak, Madselin sank into safety but re-emerged, spluttering with indignation. 'Get out of here, you. . .you. . .'

'Angle?' Edwin offered helpfully, the broad grin on his handsome face indicating clearly how much he was enjoying her discomfiture.

'Barbarian!' Madselin hissed vehemently. 'Have you been drinking again?' she accused, eyeing his large, solid body doubtfully.

That question caused a slight flush to his tanned cheeks but she was gratified that he did not come any closer, none the less. Edwin was leaning against the door as nonchalantly as any well-built warrior could, but then he had the upper hand, she reasoned. He was effectively blocking her exit and preventing anyone else from coming in.

As he didn't immediately leap at her, his purpose for sneaking into her room was not apparently as straightforward as she had at first assumed. Her embarrassment subsiding a little, Madselin managed to glare at him in the haughtiest manner she could summon.

'Pray explain why you should wish to pin me down at all, Angle.' In echoing his words, Madselin had not at first realised the *double entendre*, but his somewhat amused expression told her that he had.

'Why indeed, lady? A question which has been plaguing me much of the day.' He finished the statement with a rather despairing sigh, and Madselin could have sworn there was a certain look of regret in his eyes.

Dismissing any such notion, Madselin glared at him. 'What do you want?' she demanded slowly. She felt very alone, exposed and. . .well. . .intimate with this great lummox. No! Not lummox! Emma had shown how lummoxes lured a good woman down the wrong path. Barbarian was far more apt. Barbarian. The word echoed round her mind for a moment as Edwin appeared to be mentally preparing what he was about to say.

Now it was her turn to be confused. 'For God's sake, Edwin. What is it?' She was not in any frame of mind nor in any kind of position to be trifled with.

His eyes watched her for less than a few seconds but Madselin could see he was not feeling at all perturbed at confronting a fully naked woman in her bath. And then she saw the blood-red colour steal upwards from his neck and he looked away.

Despite her anger and humiliation, Madselin could not help feeling as though she may have been having more of an effect on him than she had at first thought. Fascinated, the germ of an idea gnawed at her.

Sighing loudly, Madselin raised her brows and delicately soaped her arms. 'Well,' she said in her most matter-of-fact tone, 'as you are clearly going to take some time over this, I would be more comfortable before the fire.' Gratified at his deepening colour, she continued mercilessly, 'You may as well bring me the drying sheet.' Her hand waved carelessly in the direction of the vital cloth.

The silence between them grew until she heard his soft footsteps on the rushes.

'Here!' The word was snapped out gruffly and Madselin was relieved to see that he was standing awkwardly with his back to her, the cloth dangling from his outstretched arm.

Slowly, and very daringly, she rose and allowed the water to cascade down over her body before stepping out of the tub and wrapping the cloth carefully around her. Her tangle of still-damp hair was tossed back over her shoulders as Madselin slipped a bedrobe on—she felt a little less naked with two layers on.

Finding herself quite enjoying this somewhat bizarre charade, Madselin turned then to Edwin. He was nearer than she had expected and had to step back a little. A faint flush crept over her own cheeks.

'Well, Angle?' Her voice was a little squeaky. 'Have you remembered what was so urgent that you could not wait?'

Those grey eyes missed nothing of her, from the top of her wet, dark brown hair down to her blue-tinged, bare toes. Slowly they took their fill of her, roving upwards once more to her mouth, lingered a while and then returned to her eyes. Madselin was certain that as far as Edwin was concerned she was stark naked.

'No.' The word was uttered in a half-groan, bordering on a very intimate whisper. Cold trickles of sweat trailed over her skin as he slowly raised his hand to her face. She was rooted to the spot as his fingers curled around her neck and pulled her across the inches that separated them. 'But something else comes to mind.'

'Indeed?' Madselin managed, crushed as she was against his chest. The strong, musky scent of him lingered on his tunic as she pressed her fingers vainly against it.

'Can you use a knife or a bow?' He stared down at her from his great height, his expression fathomless.

His question was like a douse of cold water. Strength flooded into her bones and she pushed him away with considerable force. 'Of course not,' came the confused retort. 'I am not a peasant!'

'Hmm.' Whether that noise was uttered by way of dissent or distraction, she did not know for sure. 'It's time I gave you some lessons then, lady.'

'Rest assured, Angle, I have no desire to add those particular skills to my repertoire. My betrothed. . .'

'Betrothed-to-be,' he interrupted with surprising alacrity.

She grimaced her thanks before she continued. 'My betrothed-to-be is most appreciative of what I have to offer as a lady.'

'Apparently not.' The wretch grinned lewdly, his eyes resting on her curves. 'He's neither bedded nor wedded you, girl. The man doesn't seem in much of a hurry to me.'

Despite her anger, the gibe stung. 'It just goes to show how much you know about the meaning of knighthood.' Her waspish reply was cut short by his hands pulling her hard against him once more and her mouth covered by those gentle, coaxing lips. Within a heartbeat she was drowning in his passion again.

'You're right, lady,' he said somewhat breathlessly. 'I know little about Norman knights but I do know some of the ways between men and women.' His soft mouth hovered just above hers and Madselin had to school herself not to draw up on tiptoe to respond. 'When I first laid eyes on you, I wanted to lie with you there and then on the forest floor and take that haughty smile right off your face.'

Outraged at such an idea, Madselin's hand swept towards his face. His hand wrapped around her wrist. 'You barbarian!' she spat, her cheeks burning. 'You wouldn't have dared.'

He laughed and pulled the offending hand down behind her back. 'Had you been alone, I would most certainly have tried.' The smile faded as the pressure on the base of her spine increased. She could feel every contour of his hard body. 'As you can tell,' he added wryly, 'nothing has changed.'

There was indeed clear evidence to support this theory, and although innocent of what went on between men and women, she was not unknowing. Even as she struggled to free herself, Madselin realised she was fighting a losing battle.

'That's what you get for tempting the devil, lady.'

Gulping loudly, Madselin belatedly realised that he was right, but it in no way excused his brutish behaviour. 'Let me go,' she hissed.

Brows raised, he shook her gently. He was clearly awaiting her apology. Grudgingly she gave it, adding sullenly, 'But I did not invite you up here.'

Grinning down at her almost impudently, Edwin released his grip on her wrist. 'That's true enough, but I reckon we're even now. You achieved what you set out to do,' and he glanced ruefully at the area about his waist causing Madselin to blush to her very toes. 'And I'll be content to leave with your word you'll practise some. . .ah. . .native skills.' He uttered those words with the confidence of a victorious man.

'I said no such thing!' Madselin lifted her chin in retort.

'Aye, but you will.' His large hand gripped her chin firmly. 'Or I shall kiss you again and may not find I can control my. . .barbaric. . .nature.'

Her lips tightened in anger. 'Richard was right,' she muttered eventually. 'Very well. You have my word.'

Satisfied with that, Edwin nodded his head. 'Tomorrow, then. Before I leave.'

'There really was no need for all this,' she grumbled. 'You could have simply asked me in the morning.'

'Ah, but then I would not have been able to kiss you,' he pointed out with a frown.

'That was not your purpose in coming here, surely.' The man made no sense.

He sighed in response. 'No, but it reminded me of our plan.'

'Blanche isn't here.'

'Nay, but you're in sore need of practice, lady.'

Ignoring so pointed a comment, Madselin shook her head. 'If you cannot remember what you sneaked up here for, then I think it best you leave. It would hardly do much for your reputation, being found alone with a Norman.'

Edwin's face suddenly became sober, as if she had reminded him at last of his true mission. 'Aye, well. As to that, it can wait a while.'

He left as suddenly as he appeared, leaving Madselin to stare at the closed door. In truth, no matter how much he irritated her, it was hard to dislike the man when he was in his strange, humorous mood. Sighing, Madselin turned to the bed.

Chapter Eleven

The beach lay windswept and deserted, save for a lone gull pecking with determination at a morsel stranded there by the thrust of the waves. A cold gust of rain blew through every one of the six layers Madselin had put on that morning and she turned, blue-lipped, to face her pitiless torturer.

'I see no good reason for doing this, Angle. You might feel at home here in the wild, freezing cold, but Norman ladies are used to gentler living and warmth. I can assure you that ladies have no such aptitude for fighting. We leave that to men and peasants.'

Edwin had planted himself solidly before her, his face seaward and his braids floating a little with the strength of the wind. 'Believe me, woman. I've seen a Norman lady do this afore now with my own eyes.' Those same grey eyes skimmed over her once again, earning him another glare. 'As far as I can tell, your body is not ailing and your eyes. . .'

She raised her hand impatiently to draw a halt to any further speculation on his part. Edwin appeared to have surveyed her person with a thoroughness that was most unexpected. 'I did not say there was anything wrong with me, just the activity.' Her teeth began to chatter and she pulled her heavy cloak about her.

'Orvell is a clever man,' he explained slowly as if to a rather backward child. 'It will do you no harm to learn to protect yourself.'

'I thought that was your job?' she pointed out with a superior sniff.

'Aye, but there's always a chance I'll not be there. You are a most difficult woman to. . .'

'Pin down,' she finished tersely. 'Aye, you mentioned that, but I have not noticed you having that much difficulty creeping up on me or lurking close by in dark places.' Her disgruntled expression caused Edwin to grin.

'I had no idea my presence unsettled you so much.'

'Oh?' she uttered in disbelief. 'As to that, I would say that your presence is more of an irritation, in fact.'

The grin deepened. 'Very gratifying,' he added.

'Look,' Madselin gritted out between clenched teeth. 'As you have dragged me outside in this. . .this. . . howling gale, could you just get on with it?'

He inclined his head before giving their surroundings a narrow-eyed inspection. They were standing at the edge of the beach since it provided, he pointed out gravely, the softest landing for her. The forest beyond seemed quiet compared to the noisy waves that crashed heavily onto the beach. Edwin then turned back to Madselin and eyed her speculatively.

'You're well built for a woman and probably far stronger than you imagine. Perhaps we should try a few basic moves without a knife first? To get you used to a man's strength.' His grin had been replaced by a solemn expression that led Madselin to believe the man was truly serious.

'Whatever you think,' she grumbled with a distinct lack of enthusiasm.

'Madselin,' came the stern rebuke. 'I am trying to be of help to you.'

She sighed. 'Very well. What will you have me do?'

For at least a candle notch, Edwin proceeded to show Madselin some of the more effective methods of warding off a strong man. Although at first clumsy and unsure, she eventually began to feel more confident. A wave of something akin to pure glee surged through her when she finally managed to floor him with a heavy thud.

'Hah!' she crowed at Edwin's inert body. 'It would appear you men have been fooling everyone for years. This is not so difficult.' When she received no answer, Madselin looked at him more closely. There was no movement and his eyes remained closed. Panic assailed her and she looked around wildly but could see no form of help.

Kneeling at his side, Madselin gently patted a stubbly cheek. 'Edwin? Edwin?' Her voice became louder and she placed her faced directly above his to see if she could detect any signs of breathing. There were none. 'Dear God,' she whispered. 'I've killed him.' She just sat there, staring at him in stunned silence, her heart thudding loudly and her fingers gently stroking his cheek.

Suddenly, two strong hands squeezed her arms tight and pulled her full length on top of him. Quickly he rolled over so that she was effectively trapped beneath him. A pair of shining grey eyes blinked down at her.

'I thought you were dead.' Her fear had been replaced by a slow-burning anger. 'I was just about to send up a prayer of thanks,' she hissed.

His nose and mouth were no more than a fingertip above her own and his weight was considerable. There was absolutely no possibility of escape. 'Aye, I felt you battering my face with your fingers,' he smiled.

Until that point, Madselin had felt relatively safe, but the minute he smiled at her in that certain way he had, her innards turned to water and her limbs refused to cooperate with any command she gave. It was, however, becoming increasingly difficult to breathe. All she could manage was a breathless 'Wretch!'

'We men are wily creatures.' He pulled her arms above her head and imprisoned them between his fingers. 'You should always be prepared for the unexpected, lady. Never assume a man is no threat just because his eyes are closed.'

Madselin gaped at him, somewhat chastened by his speed. Well, then. He wasn't the only one who could be wily. 'Perhaps this is exactly where I want to be, Angle,' she managed a little breathlessly and studied his expression. A tide of red rose gratifyingly up from his neck and he heaved himself a little further away from her nose to look down at her more comfortably.

This small distraction was not quite enough, however. 'If you moved a little to the side, I could show you what I had in mind?' Her eyes shone at him with what she hoped was barely concealed excitement and it certainly earned an instant response from her tutor. Edwin shifted on to the sand and let her hands go. As he was reaching for her, Madselin managed to jam her fist in his throat and her foot in his shin before scrabbling to safety.

This time Edwin writhed in agony on the sand. She deduced that this was a more successful ploy than his. 'You win,' he groaned, before rolling on to his haunches and heaving himself to his feet. 'I'll not tumble another Norman lady in a hurry.'

Madselin folded her arms and smiled up at him smugly. She was beginning to enjoy herself. 'It was very simple, Angle. I relied on your baser instincts coming to the fore. It would seem you are a most predictable man.'

Edwin rubbed vigorously at his throat and shook his head ruefully. 'Aye. Ghislaine used to say that.'

'Ghislaine?' she enquired, as if she didn't really know.

'Ghislaine de Courcy. My former mistress.'

There were two—or possibly three—ways of looking at that statement, but Madselin decided it would perhaps be prudent to concentrate on the 'former'. 'A most astute woman,' she murmured. After a brief hesitation, Madselin decided she wanted to know more about this Ghislaine. 'Is she pretty?' she asked curiously.

Edwin sat back down on the sand to attend to his leg. 'Pretty? Aye, I thought so. Long, wild red hair and dangerous eyes. Skinny.' He flickered her a glance. 'Younger than you, of course.'

Stung, Madselin turned on him furiously. 'I asked you if she was pretty, not young,' she snapped. 'Perhaps our lesson is concluded? If not, I have many pressing concerns back at the keep and would be most grateful if we could finish.'

'If you say so, lady.' He hauled himself to his feet and produced a small dagger from under his tunic. Its cold blade glimmered menacingly under the stormy grey skies. 'Hold it,' he commanded.

Taking the weapon into her hand, Madselin knew a shiver of forbidden strength. It felt cold, hard and very dangerous. When she had gripped it comfortably, she looked up at Edwin. 'What now?'

Without taking his eyes from hers, Edwin threw off his cloak and pulled up his tunic. Acres of goose-bumped brown flesh stood before her and Madselin felt her own chest constrict as she remembered how soft his skin had felt. He reached for her dagger hand

and pulled the point into a spot just above mid-centre. 'Aim here. It will kill quickly if you push up hard enough.'

He watched her agonised expression with an amused grin on his lips. 'You'd best try. It's harder than you think.'

Madselin pressed her lips together tightly. What on earth was she doing with a half-naked English man on the beach in the middle of a gale? 'I hope,' she said repressively, 'that I would have attempted something long before my attacker was in a semi-naked state. Even you have a tendency to wear a hauberk when you go out on patrol.'

Edwin stiffened. 'Aye, but I was just showing you where to aim for. You said you were innocent and I took you at your word. I assumed you have little knowledge of a man's body. Other than a sick one, that is.'

'I've learned more than enough for a lifetime since I came across you,' she retorted quickly. 'Now put your tunic back on before you die of a chill and force me to observe far more of your body than you had intended.'

Surprisingly, he obeyed without dissent and Madselin put his speed down to the freshness of the wind.

Lunging, jabbing and ripping were the most important features of using a dagger and although her efforts were competent eventually, Edwin was not happy at her lack of killing instinct.

'For all our differences, Angle, I have surprisingly no real wish to injure you,' she observed sardonically.

A look of disbelief wiped the grin from his face. Edwin laughed out loud. 'You can't hurt me, woman.'

'Then what is the point of this charade?' she ground out. 'Obviously there are few men with as magnificent a physique as you, but I assume there must be similarities.'

'Magnificent?' Disconcerted by Madselin's description of his body, Edwin blushed.

Watching him, she realised he really had no idea of the effect his body could have on a woman. 'Fortunately,' she continued unabashed, 'your brains are clearly lacking and your body has to compensate where it can.'

Recovering quickly, Edwin frowned. 'Then if that is the case, you should have no fears about being outwitted by me. I suggest,' he finished menacingly, 'you put it to the test.'

'Fine!'

The contest was over in less time than it took to blow out a candle. Edwin emerged unscathed and Madselin glared at the dagger lying in the sand.

'I've had enough, Angle,' she muttered disconsolately. 'Take me back.'

He stooped to pick up the weapon. 'Aye.' His lips smiled at her tone. 'You've done well.'

'For a woman, you mean?' Madselin raised her brows in question.

'For a Norman lady,' he corrected, blatantly ignoring her reluctant smile. 'I was right about one thing, though.'

'Oh?'

'That body of yours is very healthy.'

Madselin's cheeks remained red all the way back to the keep.

It had become her recent habit to don her coney-lined cloak before the late meal was served and spend a little time up on the battlements. Standing with her face pointing seawards and her hair blown back by the wind, Madselin had grown to love those solitary moments of pure peace.

Such fragments of time were unknown to her at her

own home. At those moments when the world hovered between light and dark, she would feel something close to a deep contentment. No matter how much she at first wished to deny such a ridiculous idea, Madselin gradually came to accept that she no longer hated living there.

Madselin sighed. It would be harder to go home now and she was glad that she had until at least after Yuletide before returning to the Vexin.

The sound of the gong calling the keep dwellers to the meal interrupted her thoughts. Slowly Madselin descended the stone steps, the icy cold almost burning its way through the soft leather soles of her shoes.

Her mind dwelt on the coming ambush and of Edwin and his men who might not return. Her stomach lurched a little. She did not doubt for a minute that the Angle would not give in without a terrible struggle, but in her mind's eye Madselin remembered the face of the red-headed butcher who had led the previous ambush in the forest. Edwin was indeed a marked man and Orvell had made it clear how much he wanted to kill him.

The subject of her thoughts crashed into her as he raced up the steps.

'Oof. You stupid. . .'

'Angle?' he offered once more, along with his hand.

Madselin straightened up, furiously brushing the dust and dirt from her cloak. 'If this is meant to be a further lesson in combat. . .

He held his hand to stay her tongue. 'Nay. Emma told me where you were and I was afraid you might miss the meal. After all,' he added with raised eyebrows, 'a healthy woman needs her strength.'

Madselin gave him a withering stare. As he was stood two steps below her, they were almost eye to eye. 'Are you not afraid I would put your lesson into practice, Angle? I now have the experience to do much damage even to a large man as yourself.'

'Hmm,' he muttered thoughtfully. 'I think I preferred magnificent.' He bent his head for a moment as he fumbled at his belt. 'Here. Now you can use it, you'd best strap it to your leg. It will be safe enough there,' he added wryly.

Under the flickering torchlight, a silver dagger lay on Edwin's outstretched palm. It was not the same one she had used with him that morning. This one was smaller and more intricately patterned. His expression was most solemn.

Speechless, Madselin began to shake her head. 'No,' she began quietly. 'I couldn't take that. It's yours.'

His eyes watched her gravely, drinking in her flustered expression. 'It was my mother's.' His eyes flicked down to the sharp blade. 'It has tasted Orvell's blood. She would wish it so,' he added.

Touched beyond all measure, Madselin gulped silently and then held out her hand to take the weapon. This one was warm to her touch and very pretty. 'Would you not wish to give this to your wife?' Her voice was almost a whisper as she examined the dagger closer to.

'Aye, but I think it an unlikely prospect. I aim to kill Orvell or die in the attempt. My chances of survival are not good either way. The King is not in the habit of allowing natives to murder his barons.'

Tears pricked unexpectedly at her eyes and Madselin willed herself to stay in control of her emotions. For all their ruffling of each others feathers, she realised that there was a certain intimacy in it. His death was impossible to contemplate.

She smiled shyly. 'Then I accept your kind gift.' Their eyes held. 'But I cannot take it without you having something of mine.' Seeing that he was about to object, Madselin quickly placed a finger gently on his lips.

'It is a custom of my people. Say nothing.' Slipping a tiny ring of intertwined gold threads from her finger, her lips twitched in amusement. 'It's not very manly, but I would be honoured if you accepted it. My mother gave it to me.'

His cheeks burned in pleasure as he placed the ring reverently in his belt pouch. 'I shall keep it close.'

He looked up at her. 'Amongst my people, we have a custom too. When a man bids farewell to a woman, they offer no words. Just a kiss.'

'Oh.'

It was a chaste, almost brotherly kiss that left Madselin with a raging desire to put her arms around his neck and pull him close. Instead, he did it for her. 'That was the custom,' he whispered in her ear. 'This is for me.'

This time, Madselin had absolutely no cause for complaint. His kissed her hard and with a thoroughness that left her completely breathless. If it hadn't been for the noise of the sentry clattering down the stone steps, Madselin could not have been certain that either of them would have been able to stop. As it was, Edwin broke away first. 'Perhaps you would accompany me to dinner, Lady de Breuville?'

Madselin could only manage a contrite nod before the interested eyes of the sentry.

The feasting hall looked very festive that evening and Madselin supposed that it was Joanna who had ordered the additional greenery adorning the walls. A wonderful smell of pine and forest invaded the whole room and seemed to have affected everyone. The noise of excited chatter was dreadful.

Food and drink had not been spared and everyone participated with gusto. Well, she noted, at least amongst those who would remain at the keep. The men leaving later appeared to be drinking sparingly of ale. Madselin herself had no stomach for the wine. High up, the shutters rattled with the force of the wind and despite the heat of the room, she felt herself shiver.

Edwin, sitting to her right, had been engaged deep in conversation with Gyrth for much of the time. When there was an apparent lull in their dialogue, Madselin took her chance.

'Have you a plan?' she asked quietly.

Edwin stopped chewing on the mutton bone and looked up at her, slightly askance. 'A plan?'

Perhaps he had drunk more than she had thought? 'Of attack,' she clarified. Madselin noticed that Gyrth had also stopped eating, clearly awaiting Edwin's reply.

'Aye. I have a plan.' He continued gnawing the bone. 'But I think it best if you know nothing of it.'

'So you still don't trust me,' she replied huffily and not a little hurt. Madselin pushed her trencher back.

'Aye, I trust you. It's Orvell I don't trust. He has no scruples about hurting women. You're safer not knowing.'

Eyeing her somewhat impatiently, he rubbed his chin.

'But someone here has to know what's going on. Isabella would have insisted.'

Edwin and Gyrth exchanged looks before staring back down at their ale cups. Seizing her moment, Madselin pressed on. 'If Orvell is as clever as you say, then the keep could very well be in danger anyway. The visit yesterday was most likely so that he could find out more about our defences.'

He shifted on his seat before answering that one. She decided Edwin was looking a little perplexed and she could almost hear him thinking to himself. 'Most likely.

That's why I've sent two messengers to Mallet at the d'Aveyron keep. He'll send more men.'

'Oh.'

Putting his bone down somewhat regretfully on his trencher, Edwin turned to look at her. 'You'll be well protected, lady. Ulf remains here with enough men to last out until Mallet sends his reinforcements.'

She raised her eyes slowly to his. 'And what happens if they don't arrive? Orvell will have the keep under observation, no doubt. A couple of messengers are not likely to prove difficult to kill.'

'Whatever happens, stay here.' His eyes flickered to her leg. 'If. . .if his men find you, use the knife on yourself first. They won't spare you, since you know too much.' He looked at her steadily. 'Orvell enjoys subjecting people to degradation and pain. God would understand.'

Despite the din all around them, Madselin was sure that the two of them inhabited at that moment a very private world. She suddenly realised just how much she had come to respect his solid, reassuring presence and how much faster her blood ran whenever he was there. Her head moved imperceptibly closer to his. 'You'll take care, Edwin.'

Despite their audience, a large hand crept gently over her much smaller one. It felt warm and strong as his fingers squeezed hers gently. 'I wish you well in your marriage, Madselin. I hope he's a strong man.'

That little piece of humour dispelled the strong emotional pull that Madselin felt for her erstwhile foe and she smiled grudgingly. It was sometimes hard to remember Hugh's face. 'My thanks.'

A chance remark by one of their neighbours broke the spell and the meal continued with very little further communication between them.

* * *

The patrol left not long after when the night clouds had
blanketed the land in a blackness that was almost evil.
Madselin could see nothing as she watched Edwin and
his men melt into the night as they slipped silently from
the keep. If Orvell was watching, he made no move.
Unsure of what she could do, Madselin made her way
to the church. A prayer might help.

An urgent tapping on her shoulder made Madselin
jump in surprise. She was kneeling before the altar,
concentrating so hard that she had heard no sound
behind her. Father Padraig stood there, dripping wet,
his face creased with worry. 'The guard sent me to you.
An old tinker is outside the gate, demanding entry.'

Before Madselin could say a word, the priest held his
hand up to forestall her. 'He says he has news of a
young woman that sounds much like Blanche.'

Rising quickly, Madselin turned to Father Padraig.
'Take me to him.'

Despite the raw, wet night the old man was barely
covered. Rain dripped from thin, matted strands of
grey hair and the rags he wore were thoroughly soaked.
His bones were the size and shape of twigs, ready to
snap at the first gust of wind.

Clearly exhausted, the old man could barely stand
and supported himself against the gate.

'Let him in,' she commanded against her better
judgement. Trap or not, she could not allow an old
man to die out there. The soldiers had been shooting
wolves as target practice for the past few days. If any
remaining wolf caught his scent, he'd be dead before
they could find anything out.

Once the old man had stumbled through the gate,
Father Padraig wrapped his own cloak about his
shoulders and Madselin sent a soldier for a bowl of
pottage and a loaf of bread. As the man could barely

walk, the priest hauled him to his feet and led him to the sentries' hut.

The hut offered little more than protection from the elements and only a little warmth from the brazier, but the man accepted it all with gratitude. At least, Madselin thought he did, but even though her command of the local tongue was improving, it was hard to understand him. His teeth were long gone and as a result, his diction was very sadly lacking. Father Padraig understood.

The priest pinned his fierce eyes on the old man and fired a multitude of questions at him. Thanks to his occasional explanations Madselin was able to follow more or less what the man had to say.

His name was Saer and he came from Orvell's village. The villagers had heard of Edwin's endeavours to take Orvell and they wanted to help. Their lord's cruelty and viciousness were killing them all and it was agreed between them that this would be their chance.

Orvell and his men had left that morning and not returned, having planned a secret meeting with the Scots not far from the de Vaillant keep. Saer had volunteered to run the risk and warn Edwin. It would seem that he was making his way through the forest when he heard someone crying out.

At first he was frightened, thinking it was a boggart or one of the spirits that haunted the place, but as he hurried on, he realised the voice belonged to a woman. A terrified, pitiful wailing that speared him to the heart.

Father Padraig's expressive brows were raised in disbelief at this juncture, but Madselin could see the man was in a world of his own. He was picturing the scenes and reporting it carefully.

The woman had long, blonde hair which was filthy and matted. He could tell from her well-nourished body that she was no simple peasant, but her clothes were in muddy tatters and she was bleeding.

Confused, Madselin demanded to know why he hadn't brought her back with him. Father Padraig hesitated a moment and then asked him. The old man's face drained of colour and he pursed his thin, cracked lips around his toothless gums. He spat out an answer that left the priest staring at him in silence.

'What?' She shook Father Padraig's arm. 'What did he say?'

The silence stretched on.

'She's been chained by her neck, beaten to a pulp and left for wolf bait,' he replied tonelessly.

'Dear God,' she whispered, feeling her blood turn to ice. 'Why?'

He ignored the question and spat a barrage of words at the tinker. His response was to shake his head and point a shaky finger in a northerly direction.

'Orvell. He's made use of her and now he's left her to die.'

He said a few words to the old man, who nodded and stood shakily on his feet. 'I'll get her and the old man will take me to her.'

Madselin nodded. 'Take Ulf. If it is a trap, he'll be some protection.'

'No doubt Orvell did not expect Blanche to be found so quickly. It can be the only reason the old man survived this far.'

Madselin nodded wearily. 'Go quickly.'

As the three men left the keep, Madselin watched them, wondering exactly what sort of man Henry Orvell could truly be. The man's soul was evil. Heartsore, she rested her forehead on the cold wood of the gate and sent up a prayer for their safety.

Chapter Twelve

The candle had burned down two notches before the sentry called out that strangers approached. Until then, they had all sat in the hall on tenterhooks, not sure of anything save that they could all be in danger. Especially Edwin.

Joanna was sat with her son sleeping in her arms, her face pale and drawn. It was hard to know who she was more concerned for, since Gyrth had gone with Edwin and Blanche, despite their differences, was still her sister. She had said little, answering distractedly in monosyllables, bending occasionally to kiss her son's blond hair.

Bronwen had been strangely quiet as she helped Madselin to prepare salves and ointments that they might need for Blanche if she had survived. A small bed had been made up in Isabella's solar and a pail of hot water steamed by the fire.

Practical as ever, Bronwen had insisted on some usquebaugh being on hand, since that was the only thing that would bring her through the shock. Once everything was readied, there was nothing else left to do save wait.

When the call was heard, they sprang to their feet,

speechless, before rushing to the gate. The sentry had identified four strangers, but only three appeared to be moving. The fourth hung limply in Ulf's arms. When they finally staggered through the gate, Madselin put her hand to her mouth and hoped to God she would not be sick.

Blanche was unrecognisable. Her pretty, pouting face was broken and bloody. From the gaping wounds in her scalp it was clear that thick clumps of her hair had been pulled out. Father Padraig had covered her body with his cloak but he had been unable to hide what was left of her mangled feet. They looked as if they had been clubbed until they were no more than a bloody pulp.

Ulf gently carried the girl into the solar. All the while he muttered words in his strange tongue which seemed to have a calming effect on Blanche. Bronwen whispered that he was offering a prayer to the old gods and Madselin decided that it couldn't do any harm.

It might have been better had she died straight away. There wasn't a part of her body that hadn't been beaten or whipped. Her teeth, nose and several ribs were broken and Madselin was not at all sure that one of her eyes would recover. The girl had been subjected to an appalling assault and cruelly left to die slowly and in fear.

Madselin reached for the poppy juice so that Blanche could at least be spared the pain for a while. 'No!' shouted Joanna suddenly. Kneeling at her side and gently lifting her head up, Joanna tried to rouse her. 'What did you do, Blanche?' she demanded urgently. 'Tell me what you did.'

Blanche rolled her head from side to side and moaned, trying to push her sister away. Joanna would not go. 'What did you do for him to have done this, Blanche?'

One eye blinked rapidly beneath its blue, swollen lid and her cracked lips moved a little. Joanna moved close to her mouth.

'Louder, Blanche. Speak louder.'

The others shifted uncomfortably, compelled to watch all the same.

'I told him.' The voice was barely more than a broken, hoarse whisper but they all heard it.

'Told him what?'

'About Edwin.' Blanche's head drooped to one side, but Joanna pulled it back again and gently patted her cheeks. The pain quickly brought the girl round.

'What did you tell him about Edwin?' Joanna demanded.

'About tonight.'

Joanna looked up at Madselin. 'Dear God. He knows they'll be there. They don't stand a chance.'

'Edwin sent a messenger to Albert Mallet for re-inforcements. They may come in time.' Madselin picked up the pail of water and laid it by Joanna.

'Messenger dead.' There was no misunderstanding Blanche's meaning.

Joanna shook Blanche lightly. 'Why? In God's name, Blanche, why did you do it?'

The eye flickered in Madselin's direction and the lips cracked into the ghost of a smile.

Madselin stared down at her. The girl had done it out of jealousy. She had gone after Orvell and told him what she knew of the ambush. All because of her.

'There's no way of telling them now. No one knows where they are.' Madselin's voice was flat and toneless. It was her fault the men were going to die. She had thought up that stupid plan and made Blanche think that she and Edwin were lovers. He had not wanted to, but she had insisted.

Whilst Joanna administered the usquebaugh and

Emma ushered the men from the room, Bronwen drew Madselin to one side. 'I know where they will be.' Her voice was low and her eyes solemn.

'How?' Madselin looked at Bronwen in amazement. Edwin had refused to tell her but she found it hard to accept he would have told Bronwen.

Bronwen stared at her with bold eyes. 'I overheard him talking to Gyrth. Besides, I know this area well enough to work out the most probable landing sites for the Scots. It isn't that hard. Edwin will be close.'

A little disconcerted by Bronwen's willing admission, Madselin realised that it was in fact a good job she did tread quietly. 'Can you tell me?'

Assessing her for a moment, Bronwen finally shook her head. 'You'd never find it in broad daylight, let alone a cloudy night. Besides, you'd be dead before you got there. If the wolves don't get you first, Orvell's men will.'

'Well, there has to be a way or we're all in danger. Can you think of anything better?'

The dark eyes glanced at the other occupants of the room. 'I might,' she said. 'But it's still very dangerous.'

A deep groan from the bed made Madselin shiver. Why indeed was she wanting to risk her life for these people? They should mean less to her than her own people in the Vexin and they were also English. But her conscience would not let her go. She had created this problem and she would have to do something at least.

Almost as if she knew what Madselin was thinking, Bronwen sighed heavily. 'She'll die within the hour. There's no saving her. It's just as well, perhaps.'

Anger and helplessness fired through her blood as Madselin gazed at Blanche's broken body. 'Tell me.' Her voice was firm and decisive.

'Well,' she began, 'old Saer could take you. He

knows every blade of grass hereabouts.' Her eyes glittered down at her and Madselin was certain it stemmed from excitement. Could she trust Bronwen? Was she Orvell's creature after all?

'You know Saer, then?' Madselin asked, her suspicions aroused.

'Aye, although I'm surprised he had the courage to come here. The man's never been keen to cross Orvell.'

Frowning, Madselin considered her options. Saer, too, could just be another in Orvell's pay. Just because he brought Blanche back proved absolutely nothing. Orvell could have planned it that way. Inhaling deeply, she looked over at Blanche. Or it could just work. With little more than a brief regret at breaking her word to Edwin, she gave a curt nod. 'I'll do it.'

It wasn't until Bronwen exhaled loudly in relief that Madselin realised the woman had been holding her breath at all. 'What are my chances, do you think?'

Bronwen raised her hand to touch her face. 'You have a strong face to match a strong will, lady. I hope your God smiles down on you.' With no more than a brief nod, she put her arm in Madselin's and led her to the door. 'Come. There's no time left.'

If Saer was Orvell's creature, then he was indeed a very wily one. For an old man who had appeared on the point of death not long before, he had achieved a most remarkable recovery.

It could, Madselin supposed, have had something to do with Ulf and the rather threatening words he heaped about the old man just before he lead her through an ancient, unused side door. His black eyes gleamed somewhat wickedly in the flickering torchlight before the thin shoulders shrugged their reply.

Ulf grabbed Madselin's shoulder and squeezed it in a gesture she now recognised as that shared by the fighting Englishmen. It signified respect as well as farewell. Clearly she had risen somewhat in his estimation and despite the smile that curved her lips upwards she could also feel the tears pricking her eyes. There was nothing they could say to each other. Ulf stood back to let them pass.

Her companion showed a surprising amount of speed and agility. He was clearly possessed of cat's blood too, since he was the only one who appeared to be able to see the path ahead. There was no moon to light the way.

Scrambling quickly down the steep, rocky path, Saer did not look back to ensure that Madselin was managing to keep up. Obviously, she told herself wryly, he was not used to walking with Norman ladies. Muttering some choice oaths that she had picked up in the keep, Madselin pulled up her skirts and scrabbled after him.

As they reached the lower part of the hill, the sharp stones gave way to muddier earth and malicious gorse bushes that ripped her clothes and her skin to shreds. Saer then began to zigzag his way down with increasing speed until he reached a small clump of alder trees.

Madselin arrived moments later on her backside, her dignity, as well as her cloak, in tatters. Her colourful language caused Saer to offer her a toothless smile. 'Not bad for a Norman,' he muttered in heavily accented French.

'You speak French?' she accused through gritted teeth.

'Of course,' he replied impatiently. 'Get down, lady, or I'll not be answerable to that great ox for your death.' For an old man he had a surprisingly youthful tone to his threat, but Madselin decided this was not the time to discuss it. 'This way.'

Surprised that they had managed to reach the forest without being attacked, Madselin now realised that the danger here was far greater. The silence about them was as deep and impenetrable as the dark, but she could feel the hairs on her body stand on end. It had naught to do with the cold or the rain.

'The wolves aren't far now,' came a rasping whisper close to her ear. 'They can smell the girl's blood and they're hungry.'

As if to illustrate the point, one wolf howled loudly and plaintively, causing Madselin's blood to freeze. Saer lifted his head, like a horse smelling the wind, before pulling her swiftly to the left. Whether she trusted him or not, Saer was her only hope of survival and she followed where he led.

Every so often, Saer would pause to listen and, God help her, she could hear it too. Light rustling to their right alerted her to the fact that they were, indeed, being followed.

'Have you a knife, lady?' Saer's voice was little more than a whisper.

'Aye.'

'Then have it at the ready. The beast is close by.'

With her heart in her throat, Madselin pulled the dagger from the strap round her thigh and ruefully acknowledged that Edwin might have been right. She was not at all confident that his advice could be used against a four-legged attacker, but she would be willing to try. Gripping the dagger until it bit into her fingers, she edged forward with Saer.

'Just one on its own for now. If we can kill it first, we might have a chance.'

She was so close to Saer that she could smell his rancid breath and unwashed body, but nevertheless she would have moved closer even still if it were possible. There wasn't a fibre of doubt that this was a trustworthy man. Suddenly his hand grabbed at her arm. It was surprisingly warm and despite the rain felt like parched leather.

'Here it comes. Hold still. If I miss it, aim your knife for its belly.'

A pair of yellow eyes now blinked at them a short distance away, waiting patiently. Madselin was feeling sick and faint but determined not to die.

The only sign of the wolf moving was no more than a faint rustle, but Saer was ready. There was no sound bar a growling and then a suppressed yelp. Then silence.

'Saer!' She was terrified to move.

'Aye. I'm still here, lady.' The old man crawled back to her, breathless but alive. 'A rabid old beast he was,' was the only comment he made before urging her on.

Madselin estimated that they had covered another two miles or so before Saer pulled her down again.

'There's someone ahead. Wait there.'

She had an uncontrollable urge to drag on his arm and demand he take her with him, but did not actually think it would have any effect on the man. Dutifully she crept behind the trunk of a massive old tree and crouched down to wait. Edwin would have been impressed, she thought, and then wondered if she would ever see him again.

Her eyes were out on stalks and she flinched at every sound until Saer returned a few minutes later. 'Hurry, woman,' he hissed. 'I can see the lights of the boat. They're close by.'

Madselin had not even been aware that they were near the beach, but did not need telling twice. Rising quickly to her feet, she walked headlong into a hawthorn bush. She felt its spikes rip the skin over her cheeks but pushed it aside. This was no time for female hysterics.

Heart hammering, she gripped the dagger even more tightly, although she was certain that she would be frozen to the spot if the worst came to the worst. It did, however, give her a feeling of security. They crept through the undergrowth until ahead of them she could sense rather than see a clearing. The darkness about them had also been changing in quality and somehow seemed lighter.

Madselin had been aware that the forest was thinning out and the tangy smell of the sea was stronger. The wind that edged along the coast caused the trees to sway and creak in an alarming fashion. Madselin clutched at what was left of her cloak.

'Wait here.' Without discussing the matter further, Saer disappeared, only to reappear a few seconds later with Edwin.

Although she couldn't tell who it was exactly, the tone of his voice was enough.

'You broke your word.' His voice was harsh and uncompromising.

'You're in danger,' she hissed at him, half-overjoyed to still find him alive, half-wanting to throttle him for his ungrateful attitude. 'Orvell knows you're here.'

There was a gratifying silence whilst Edwin absorbed her words.

'Why did you have to come? Saer could have come on his own.'

'Saer could easily have been killed. We were attacked by a wolf as it was.' The half of her that had been pleased to find him alive was very quickly subsiding into the remaining half.

Muttering several oaths that Madselin had never heard before, Edwin grabbed her arm and pulled her further away from Saer's interested ears.

'When I give you an order, I expect you to obey it, you foolish Norman.' He sighed heavily and by the sound of it, he was rubbing his hand over the stubble on his chin.

To her horror, Madselin could feel the tears pricking

at her eyes. Angrily she dashed them away with her hand and was just about to tell him exactly what she thought of him when a shadowy figure approached them.

There was a hurried, confused whispering and then the man left quickly.

'The boat's about to land. Now,' he tugged at her arm, 'wait here and don't make a sound.'

'But Orvell will be waiting.'

'Aye, but I've a plan. If you hear fighting, wait. No one knows you're here. You'll be able to escape when the light comes. Do you understand me, woman?' He gave her a shake that would cause several bruises to her arm.

'Very well.' All tender feelings had vanished, to be replaced by a definite hardening of the heart. 'The next time you need rescuing, I shall leave it to God to save your miserable soul.'

Her note of absolute sincerity must have roused some finer feelings in the brute since he gave an exasperated sigh before pulling her hard to his chest and squeezing the breath from her. Without another word, he pushed her from him and disappeared into the shadows.

The world was black and silent for several heartbeats before a familiar smell assailed her nostrils.

'Saer?' she whispered.

'Aye, lady. Your man asked me to guard you.'

It seemed from his tone that the old man did not particularly see a great deal of merit in this task. He spat on the ground in disgust and settled down on his haunches not far away in the bushes. Madselin crept to her allotted hideaway.

It seemed like hours before the tension was broken by a wild shouting and screaming as if all the spirits of the forest had converged on them. Madselin closed her eyes and prayed hard before realising that was probably a very foolish thing to do. Clutching her knife close to her breast, she almost stabbed herself with it. Saer moved closer as the noise grew louder.

Swords clashed and sparked against each other and inhuman cries rent the air. Madselin sank further into the bushes, terrified. Suddenly, she became aware of a different sound, and she doubted very much that it was human. Frantically she looked around, but Saer was nowhere in sight. Her heart was beating so fast she thought it might burst. The noise, a rustling, rooting sort of sound, was growing closer. Somehow she doubted it was a wolf since she had the impression of a much larger animal. Could it be a boar?

Suddenly the animal bayed. It was a cry born of hunger and hatred and her heart almost stopped. Never had she heard anything like it. A vague memory floated through her mind. 'Hound from hell'. Bronwen had once told her that her husband had been torn to pieces by Henry Orvell's favourite hunting dog. She closed her eyes and prayed, having no desire to stare death in the face.

The stench of wet animal hair and the rank smell of death was accompanied by a snarling fury that made Madselin cower into a tiny ball. The fetid breath turned her stomach over and she gagged behind her tightly clenched fist. Nothing happened.

A quietly evil laugh erupted by her ear, causing Madselin to risk peeping between her hands. Torch aloft, a familiar red-bearded brute of a soldier leered down at her.

It was the man who had tried to kill Edwin in the ambush.

At his feet, within a jaws-length of her face, lay the most monstrous creature she had ever seen.

Chapter Thirteen

'Well, well, Ballor. It would seem the forest has provided you with your next meal after all.'

Even in the torchlight, Madselin could see that her captor was a hard-bitten soldier with ice running through his veins. The dog, presumably Ballor, did not take his eyes from her and had clearly understood those words. Although he was held on a tight leash, it would not have taken much for him to break free.

Once the first shock had worn off, Madselin realised how very alone she was. Saer had disappeared and Edwin's men sounded some way off. She pursed her lips tightly together to stop her lips from chattering with fear.

The soldier hunkered down before her and jabbed the torch into the soft earth beside her. His thick arm lunged forward to grip her chin in a jaw-breaking clench.

'Nice soft skin,' he commented as his calloused thumb scraped over her cheek. Madselin gritted her teeth and tried to slide back, but the soldier just jerked her towards him in a bone-crushing grip. The stench of male sweat invaded every pore of her body and she squeezed her eyes shut in denial.

'Now, I wonder why a juicy morsel like you is hiding in the forest at this time of early morning?' He pulled her white face closer to the torch for an inspection. 'No peasant, are you, girl?' His lips pulled back in a snarl of a smile. 'You're not worn enough to be a camp follower, though.'

Madselin was too terrified to speak, but it was dawning on her that the dagger was still firmly in her grip and, as yet, hidden in the folds of her cloak. As the soldier's bug eyes stared at her, Madselin knew that the second she made her move if the man didn't kill her the slavering dog would. It still lay there, motionless, but had not taken its eyes from her.

She gulped. The dagger would be best hidden for now. Trying hard not to make any sudden moves, her hand slipped the dagger to the belt at her back. It would be as safe there as anywhere.

'Come with me, woman.' The man grabbed her arm and pulled her roughly to her feet. Picking up the torch and pulling at the dog's leash, he jerked his head towards the clearing.

Tripping and stumbling with fear, Madselin moved forward. Bodies lay strewn around and she could see a knot of men still fighting for their lives. Swords clashed against swords and shields, horses and men screamed and danced in the swirling darkness of the forest clearing. Strangely detached from reality, Madselin watched in fascination as men lived and died as fate decreed.

'So, what have we here?' Henry Orvell's gentle voice broke her trance. A tall figure stepped out from the undergrowth. He was almost invisible since she knew he was garbed in his customary black. Her guard lifted the torch to shine a light over her. All she could see of Orvell was the shine of his pearly white teeth in the dark beyond. 'Lady de Breuville? An unexpected pleasure.'

Swallowing, Madselin managed to utter a mannered reply which caused Orvell to chuckle softly. 'Guy was really quite a fool, I think.'

Madselin stared at him. 'Don't even mention his name, you traitor.'

Her strangled threat earned her no more than a raised brow as Orvell stepped into the circle of light. 'You still sorrow for him, I take it?' he said eventually after examining her cut face.

'He was a good man,' she spat at him. 'I'm glad he never knew what an evil man you are.'

A fist shot out and connected with the side of her face. She crumpled to the ground, dazed and in terrible pain.

'Enough, Fletcher. This is a lady, not one of the whores you're used to dealing with.' Despite the warning sound in his voice, Orvell did nothing more. Madselin could almost feel the smile on his face. The man enjoyed seeing her in pain. Swallowing hard, she fought back the tears.

He offered her his hand, but Madselin ignored it and stumbled proudly to her feet. She wobbled violently but concentrated her mind on remaining vertical.

'I take it you found the servant girl? Pity, but it can't be helped.' He paused. 'She seemed to think that you and the Englishman were. . .close.' His handsome face gazed down at her as his long fingers traced the line of her jaw. Madselin averted her head, dropping her gaze to the ground. 'Hmm. Hard to believe, but perhaps I'll put it to the test since the girl was so insistent.'

Madselin found herself grabbed from behind by her violent guard and pushed towards the fight. Uncertain as to her fate, she held her head as high and proud as she was able. Not far ahead she could see Edwin at last and she stifled a cry of relief. He wasn't dead yet.

As she watched him lunge, jab and rip, Madselin was filled with renewed respect and something else. Pride? He was truly magnificent in a fight. Quick and deadly, the man's strength was relentless in his grim task.

'Call him!' Orvell murmured at her side.

'No,' she hissed.

Orvell sighed and made a sign at her guard. He knelt to unleash the huge dog who was baring its teeth and drooling with hunger. 'Ballor has not been fed for days. I allowed him to bite the girl a little and he's keen to taste blood again. He likes to rip a victim's throat, you know, and yours,' he added softly, 'is a very pretty throat.'

Sick to her stomach, Madselin knew she had failed. 'Edwin!' she shouted hoarsely. 'Edwin.'

She was not at all sure that he had heard so thin a cry, but he looked over in her direction. Deftly sliding his sword through the stomach of one of Orvell's men, he uttered a few unintelligible words and moved forward towards the group.

He did not look at Madselin then, but all the same she wished the ground would open up and swallow her.

'Let her go, Orvell. She has brought me to you, so you have no further need of her.' His harsh voice cracked the tension.

Sighing heavily, Orvell smiled across at his foe. 'I don't actually think that is true, to be honest. I am, of course, most grateful for her interference,' and here he paused to bow in Madselin's direction. 'But the lady may serve another...ah...useful function in a short while. Much depends on your co-operation, Englishman.' The words were spoken as if between two old friends, but the threat was there.

He waved his hand at Edwin's blood-smeared sword.

'I think I would feel much more comfortable if that dangerous weapon were elsewhere.'

Frowning, Edwin stabbed it, point down, into the earth before him. It was the only outward sign of his intense frustration and anger. He stood back and waited. The guard leapt forward and searched him for any other weapons. Finding none, he tied Edwin's hands behind his back.

Madselin watched as he submitted silently to the rough handling of the soldier. He had suffered the same fate under her command, too, and she groaned inwardly. The man had been ill-used by Normans and he still stood proudly. If they ever got out of this alive, Madselin made a promise to God that she would make it up to him.

'Get her tied, too, Fletcher. She may be a Norman but I trust her not.' Turning sharply to Madselin, his eyes glittered down at her. 'You will be tasting my hospitality a little earlier than planned, Lady de Breuville. Unfortunately, the surroundings will be a little less comfortable than my own keep but. . .I must entertain some visitors who prefer to remain unseen.'

The guard took hold of her hands and yanked them behind her. The twine he used to tie her with cut hard into her skin and she winced. Gritting her jaw, she stamped hard on his toes and knew a certain satisfaction in hearing him gasp.

'Not yet, Fletcher!' Orvell's cool voice prevented her guard's immediate retaliation. 'You'll have plenty of time for that later. Get the Scots.'

Orvell had signalled for his horse and mounted whilst the soldier had disappeared into the undergrowth. He reappeared a few minutes later with five men of unkempt and somewhat frightening appearance.

Silently, the party retreated from the scene of the fighting and headed towards the north-east, deeper into the forest. Orvell's leaving did not seem to have made much difference to the ferocity of the fighting, so Madselin could only assume that he and the men who now accompanied them had not taken part in the foray.

She puzzled over it for a while as she did her best to keep up with the men and the horses, but lack of sleep and fear were beginning to catch up with her.

They numbered fifteen in all, plus the dog, Ballor. Orvell and the Scots had horses, whilst his guards, like Madselin and Edwin, had to travel on foot. The trees and undergrowth prevented any real pace and she was very glad since her strength was ebbing with the day.

For a while she had been able to concentrate on watching Edwin, who strode just ahead of her. If she could maintain his rhythm, she decided she could just about keep up. Tiredness stole through her body and it became harder and harder to concentrate. Finally, her eyelids drooped and she suddenly found herself floundering in the mud.

Edwin was immediately by her side, his grey eyes anxiously examining her. It was the first time he had even acknowledged her existence since their capture, and Madselin offered him a shaky smile.

'I'll be all right,' she murmured. 'I just tripped.'

The red-haired guard pulled her roughly to her feet.

'She's tired, Orvell. You know she'll only hold you up.' Edwin's tone was quiet but authoritative and his eyes stared levelly at his captor.

Orvell pulled his horse around to face him. After a moment or two he glanced down at Madselin. 'If she can't keep up, then I'll leave her for the wolves.' His voice was harsh and uncompromising now.

'Let me carry her.'

Madselin jerked her head up and stared at Edwin. 'No!' she gasped. 'You'd not last long.'

He gave a short, bitter laugh. 'I don't think I have much longer left anyway.'

Orvell shrugged. 'Have it your own way.' He gestured to the guard to cut her hands loose so that Madselin could grip Edwin's shoulders.

At first her embarrassment was acute. Her legs gripped his waist and her arms wrapped carefully about his neck. Pressing her body close over his back, Madselin could feel the rapid beat of his heart and smell his male scent. She squeezed her eyes closed and whispered gently into his ear that she was sorry. Edwin said nothing.

Dusk was filtering through the trees when they finally came to a halt. The forest had thinned out considerably and the ground was beginning to rise steeply. The higher they went, the more rock they encountered. Edwin's body was labouring under his extra burden and he allowed Madselin to jump down before collapsing in a perspiring heap at her feet.

'He needs some water,' she called to the guard imperiously. The soldier stared at her for a minute before leering at her. Picking up the water skin, he drank deeply of it before tossing it back over his shoulder.

Madselin turned back to Edwin. 'I'm sorry,' she said quietly.

Edwin eyed her almost blankly and shrugged. Closing his eyes, he lay back on the ground and took the chance to rest while he could. She sat down silently at his side. It was a very bleak moment as she realised that Orvell really did mean to kill them.

'Get a move on,' grumbled the guard as he sauntered towards them. He jabbed his toe at Edwin's leg but the Englishman only sighed before hauling himself to his feet.

'Can you walk now?' His grey eyes looked at her steadily as if trying to give her strength.

'Aye,' she replied with a weak smile. 'I'm sure I can.'

It soon became clear that they were headed for a rocky outcrop near the top of the hill. Madselin was grateful for the use of her hands since the guard had not retied them. Edwin was not so lucky. He fell and stumbled frequently on the slippy pebbles underfoot. Henry Orvell, now on foot himself, would stand and gloat as the Englishman fell.

Madselin was prevented from helping him by Orvell himself. 'For every hand you give him, Lady de Breuville,' he explained, 'he will be rewarded by Fletcher's fist. You understand, I take it?'

It was very clear to Madselin exactly how much the man enjoyed humiliating people and hurting them. It made her wonder—just a little—about Guy. Had he really not known about Henry Orvell? She would never know the answer since she had seen so little of Guy before their wedding.

He had spent only a few weeks in Normandy and although he was not far from her, there had been many things he had to take care of. Madselin remembered then how his lack of attention had hurt, but she had brushed it aside at the time. After all, they would have a long time together to become re-acquainted. Alice had goaded her about that, too.

Finally, they reached their destination. Behind the rocky overhang were two large caves. They were well hidden and invisible to the naked eye from below. Over the centuries, the caves would have provided welcome shelter for many people since they were large and relatively dry. For the time being, they were to accommodate Madselin and Edwin too.

The guard shoved them into the smaller cave and they landed in a heap on the floor. Two other guards remained with him, whilst the others were ordered into the next one. Orvell stared down at the two of them coldly. 'You will stay here until my friends and I have made our plans. When they have gone I will then be able to devote my entire attention to you.' He smiled then as if remembering something pleasant.

'I think,' he said slowly, savouring the sound of his own rich voice, 'a manhunt would be a good start to the day.' His eyes darted to his prisoners, relishing Madselin's look of absolute terror.

'She's a Norman,' Edwin spat. 'Why kill her? She's comely enough, if a bit stupid. Surely you have other uses for her?'

Orvell laughed. 'For her?' He looked at her and then inclined his head in thought. 'Well, it's just possible the Scots might be interested. . .'

Madselin pulled herself to her feet and glared at him. 'I'd rather take my chances on the manhunt,' she ground out. There didn't seem to be a lot of difference between those Scots and the dog, but at least there was only one of Ballor.

Edwin gritted his jaw but said nothing.

Orvell's face did not show what he was thinking. His expression was bland, almost mask-like. He reached out to lift her jaw with his gloved hand. 'Don't worry, Lady de Breuville,' came the soft, menacing voice. 'I shall have something suitable planned for you. In the meantime, however, I suggest you rest well.'

Jerking his head round at the guards, he barked out his orders before stalking from the cave. The three guards huddled sullenly round the entrance, leaving the two of them in the gloom. Edwin shuffled backwards until he was sitting with his back against the cave wall. Madselin turned on him.

'So,' she began quietly. 'You think I'm quite stupid, do you?'

Edwin stared up at her. 'No,' he replied finally. 'I think you are very stupid.'

'Oh?'

'Aye. If you were clever, you wouldn't be here.'

She couldn't fault that logic. 'I was trying to help.' Her voice had risen a little with fatigue and fear.

'Well, you didn't. You encouraged him.' His voice rang out cold and angry. 'Every time I suggested he didn't kill you, you interrupt and practically offer yourself on a plate. If I didn't have both of my hands tied, I'd be trying to throttle you myself.'

A huge lump had formed in her mouth, and to her horror, Madselin found she couldn't speak. Huge tears splashed down her cheeks. Edwin, she noticed through her tears, simply rolled his eyes to heaven and then sighed. 'Sit down here, by me.' It was a definite order and Madselin no longer had the strength or the will to resist. At least Edwin looked warm and comfortable. Hesitantly she sat down next to him.

'Sit between my legs and lean back. It'll be warmer.'

It was. And she had been right about him being comfortable. Her head relaxed back against his chest until finally, in a haze of fatigue and terror about the next day to come, she could no longer hold back the tears.

Turning away to hide her face, Madselin felt Edwin lean forward as if to gather her to him. As his arms were still tied behind his back, he couldn't manage that, but he wrapped as much of him around her as he could. His face brushed gently against hers. Rocking backwards and forward, he murmured soft words in his strange language into her hair.

She surrendered totally to her fear and her hurt for a while, weeping until she thought her heart would break. Slowly, very slowly, the tears stopped and she calmed down. 'I'm s-s-sorry,' she stammered into his chest. 'I didn't mean to wet you.'

He laughed softly at that. 'I think that's the least of our worries now, woman.'

'Did you know he killed Blanche?' Her tear-stained eyes blinked up at him. It was best that he knew.

Edwin shook his head silently and then lowered it, deep in thought.

Madselin pushed herself away from him a little. 'What will happen, do you think?'

He let out his breath and leaned back against the wall. 'Orvell is meeting with the Scots and some of the other barons from along the border. Once they have established a plan of action, the Scots and the barons will leave. Orvell will then concentrate on us.'

His honesty was welcome, if nothing else, but the truth certainly hurt. 'Will he kill us, then?' she whispered.

Edwin looked down at her and trailed his lips gently along the top of her head. 'Aye, he cannot afford to let us live. We know too much.'

She gulped. 'Is there nothing we can do?'

He looked over at the three soldiers who were now playing a game of dice by the entrance of the cave. 'Nay.' He looked at her then, his grey eyes soft. 'Best sleep a while.'

'I'm not sure I can,' she said in a quiet voice, but already she could feel her eyes drooping. 'But you're very warm, Edwin. Did you know that?'

His lips had dropped to the highly sensitive part of her skin just below her ear. 'It has been said once or twice,' he murmured wryly.

His voice sent shivers down her spine and she stretched herself against him in response. In truth, he felt a lot more than relaxed and she was glad that they were in a dark spot so he would not be able to see her blush. 'What are you thinking?' she asked, feeling his heart beat begin to throb a little harder.

After a few seconds pause, she felt him shrug. 'About kissing you,' came the muffled reply.

She smiled and fell asleep, wondering if it was true that Edwin did indeed find her quite comely.

'Madselin!' His voice hissed in her ear. 'Madselin!'

Slowly she opened her eyes, half-hoping to find that the whole thing had been a dream. Her stiff, cold body reminded her that it was all horribly true. Edwin's stubble rasped strongly against her cheek as she turned to look up at him.

'Unless you are badly deformed, I cannot imagine what is sticking into my stomach. What is it?' His tone was rather grumpy for someone who had been telling her not long before that he wanted to kiss her.

'The knife!' Her eyes opened wide as they stared at each other. How could she have forgotten? Slowly they turned to look at the guards. One was slumped back against the entrance whilst the other two were taking turns to swig from a skin. It smelled very strongly of rough wine.

Carefully, Madselin edged forward and slipped her hands behind her back to retrieve the knife. Once it was firmly within her grip, her hand stole behind Edwin's back to try to cut the twine at his wrists. It was not easy since he was a big man to reach round, but eventually they did manage. From the amount of blood on her hands, Madselin could tell that it was not only the twine that was cut.

She held her breath for a moment or two. 'Now what?'

Edwin didn't move. 'You'll have to distract the two guards,' he whispered eventually.

They both stared at the two men who were still

drinking and dicing. Edwin then eyed Madselin with a withering look. 'You're a woman. These things are supposed to come naturally.'

'That might be true of Englishwomen, but for us Normans, things are different.' She tossed her hair back over her shoulder in disgust.

Edwin shook his head in disbelief. Then he stopped. Inclining his head towards her, he gazed at her speculatively. 'They might just be drunk enough to make it work.'

'Make what work?' She looked at him suspiciously, her heart rate speeding up.

He sat up then, pushing himself hard against her, his chin resting on her shoulder. 'The young one, with the dark hair. He keeps looking at you. Go up to him and smile. Get him to kiss you and whilst you're doing that, I'll deal with the one watching. Try to get him to sit with his back to me.'

'I can't do any of that,' she breathed.

'Madselin,' he whispered urgently, 'if you don't, we'll die for certain and time is running out.' A large hand stole around her hips and patted them appreciatively. 'Take my word for it. He won't be able to resist. Do you remember what I taught you with the knife?'

She nodded silently, realising that everything depended on her. It would also have to be quiet so that Fletcher didn't wake up.

Madselin rose somewhat unsteadily and made her way to the front of the cave. The fumes from the wine were very strong, enough to make her stomach curdle, at least. Four bleary, bloodshot eyes stared up at her. The young one, blinked, his soft mouth slack from drink.

'Well, well. Decided to join us, lady?' His voice was thick and not a little slurred. Edwin had been right.

Chancing a smile, Madselin stepped forward towards the front of the cave.

'I thought a little fresh air might wake me up.' She stretched slowly and languorously, knowing full well that the men were watching her. Dropping her eyes to the younger one, who did possess a certain dark attraction, she smiled again.

His blue eyes glinted up at her and his mouth formed a most unbecoming leer. 'I can think of a few ways of waking you up, lady,' came the coarse reply. His companion merely grunted like a boar and reached for the wineskin.

'Can't think Orvell will bother much if you've tasted the goods,' he said amiably. 'She'll be dead soon anyway. I'll not mention it and what Fletcher there doesn't see, he won't know. He's drunk enough to sleep through anything.'

Madselin gulped in fear. Her suitor, however, appeared to be warming to the idea. Tossing back the last of the wine, he rose rather unsteadily to his feet and wiped his hands on his hauberk. Slowly with his eyes riveted on Madselin's breasts, he unbuckled his swordbelt and let it drop at his feet.

'Got a fancy for a real man, lady?' he sneered, and reached out to pull her tight to his chest. 'Them knights haven't a clue what to do with it, I'll be bound.' He wiped his dribbling mouth with his filthy sleeve and Madselin thought she was going to vomit all over him.

'Well—' she managed with what she hoped was a seductive smile '—you're very handsome and strong.' Her fingers lifted to touch his greasy black hair. 'If I'm to die, then I might as well die happy.' Her lips parted a little and she licked them with the tip of her tongue.

The soldier found this all too much. He pulled back her cloak and covered her breasts with his large hands. Madselin stepped back so that she was facing the inside of the cave with a good view of Edwin. The Englishman had not moved and, in fact, appeared to be asleep.

As if on cue, the other soldier glanced over his shoulder. Satisfied that he was asleep, he hunched up over the wineskin and eyed his partner's activities with barely concealed relish. 'If she's any good, I might try her myself,' he murmured.

The young soldier's hands were now busy pulling up her skirts and pushing her close to the cave wall. They fell in a heap of legs and skirts. Winded under the weight of the man, Madselin took a few moments to get her breath back. Uncertain as to whether she was supposed to be encouraging him or not, she decided that her Norman partner seemed completely oblivious to her needs. Slowly her hand crept up behind her and dislodged the knife.

The soldier was fumbling with his own clothing when Madselin looked up to see the other soldier lurch to his feet, presumably for a better view. Terrified that he would see what she was doing, she began to struggle. That earned her a winey compliment in the ear from her partner. 'I like it when you fight back, lady.'

She was just about to fight in earnest when she saw a shadow move stealthily behind their audience. A huge brown hand gagged his mouth and she saw his thick body tense, jerk and then sag. Moaning loudly in what she hoped was an enthusiastic response to her partner's bone-jarring grinding of her hips, she pulled the knife from behind her back.

Before she could do anything more, however, the soldier was heaved away from her and subjected to the same treatment as his friend. Madselin saw his eyes open wide in shock and disbelief before death relaxed its grip and they saw for the last time.

Madselin blinked and lay stockstill. Edwin had killed

him for her. Never in all her life had she been so close to death.

'Come. We must leave.'

She heard his soft words and dragged herself from her torpor. He heaved the soldier off her and laid him so that he looked to be asleep. Wordlessly he pulled her skirts down and offered her his hand. He felt warm and solid to touch.

'You did well, Madselin.' He turned her to him and pulled her hard against him. She breathed his scent and put her arms around him before pushing herself back. He was right. They had to go.

Silently they stepped past the sleeping Fletcher and into the daylight.

Chapter Fourteen

They managed to slip silently from their cave and beyond the rocky outcrop without being seen by the other guards. Neither of them exhaled until they had reached the cover of some bushes. Shaking, Madselin looked over Edwin's broad shoulders. Fletcher still slept.

'Will we make it?'

'I doubt it,' came the humourless response. 'But we're going to try.'

Minutes seemed like hours as they made their way down the steep and dangerous hill. Every time they slipped or dislodged a stone, they froze until the moment of danger passed. When they finally reached the bottom of the hill, Edwin looked up at the overcast sky.

'It's still early, but Orvell won't want to be about in daylight. My guess is that he'll be returning to the caves soon to hide the Scots until the light fades.' He looked around, assessing the potential dangers before turning to Madselin. 'This time, woman, you're to obey me. Do you understand?' He grabbed her arms and shook her a little.

She nodded. This was no game. They were no longer

Norman and English, just two people trying to survive. Her cold fingers stole over his and squeezed gently. 'I promise.'

He grinned at her, his teeth white against his brown skin. 'Takes quite a bit to put you in order, doesn't it?' Without warning, he crushed her to his chest and subjected her to a kiss that left her blood flowing a lot warmer than it had been. 'Much better,' he murmured against her ear. 'Now, woman. Let's go.'

'Which way are we going? Back to the keep?'

He shook his head. 'They'll expect us to head in that direction. There's a stream a bit further on which heads south-east which we could follow. It runs through the deep part of the forest and out towards the hills. It's dangerous but it might slow Orvell down. If we make it that far, there are several farms in the hills.'

'It sounds quicker to head back for the keep,' she said a little sceptically. 'We might get quite some distance before they discover us missing. Wouldn't it be better to try, at least?'

Her eyes settled on Edwin's dirty, scratched and impossibly handsome face. His stubble seemed to have grown into hedgehog bristles and she rubbed her chin gingerly.

He reached out and touched the raw skin. Before he could say anything, a wild, terrible baying cracked the morning silence of the forest. Its echo seemed to reverberate for minutes. There was no mistaking the cause of it.

'Ballor,' she whispered. Wherever that animal was, it didn't sound far enough away for her liking.

Edwin nodded and grabbed her hand.

For a man who had not slept in over a day, who'd fought for his life against a band of bloodthirsty savages, carried a woman on his back for miles uphill and killed two men, Edwin's energy was very impressive.

He pulled Madselin along with him, dragging her when she begged him to stop and almost carrying her when her feet refused to go any further.

They had covered quite a lot of ground before she heard the steady thudding of hooves. It was no longer an escape. This was a manhunt.

Terror coursed through her veins as they sped through the undergrowth and low-hanging trees. She saw nothing but a flash of greens and browns and the blue of Edwin's tunic as he ran before her. Fear made her stumble and fall. Neither spoke.

Suddenly the wild baying erupted right behind her and Madselin was certain she could smell the hound's breath as it hurled through the forest almost at her heels. Edwin stopped and turned, launching himself at the furious beast even as it leapt at her.

Dog and man fell in rolling, biting, tearing bundle. Despite his size, Edwin was finding it hard to contain the animal. It was nothing more than a heaving mass of anger and hatred, tearing at Edwin's clothes, ripping at his brown flesh.

'Run!' he grunted as they writhed on the ground. 'Now!'

She couldn't leave him. She could not.

'Stand back.' A voice behind her made her jump a mile.

'Saer!'

'This creature is mine. I've been waiting for my chance for years.' The old man brandished a wicked-looking knife and he glared at the wild dog doing its best to kill Edwin. 'He killed my son, Owain. Now it's my turn. No one will ever call me coward again. Tell Bronwen.' The tired eyes blazed with fervour as he watched the struggle. 'Run, now. Orvell isn't far behind.'

She didn't wait to be told again. Tired though they

were, her legs carried her faster than she had ever run before. She could hear a crashing behind her and the thudding of a large, heavy body in pursuit. Gulping for air, she headed for the sound of water just ahead. Without thinking, she launched herself into the stream, spraying water everywhere as she ran.

A blood-freezing scream tore through the air. Neither human nor animal, Madselin had no idea what uttered it and hoped to God it wasn't Edwin. She stopped dead and turned.

Edwin was running towards her, his arm motioning her to go on and hide. Dripping wet, her speed was severely hampered. It was not long before Edwin caught up with her. He was gripping his left arm and she could see from the blood seeping through his fingers that he was injured.

'Saer?' she asked breathlessly.

He shook his head in response and pulled her with him. 'At least he killed the dog before he died. Come on,' he whispered. 'They're almost on us.'

Ahead of them, the stream widened and Edwin pulled her towards the deepest part. Bullrushes grew in profusion and it was hard to walk at all. 'Sink down and hold on to me.'

That was easier said than done. Her cloak and skirts billowed up around her as the icy water flooded over her. Edwin pulled them down and wrapped himself around her. They floated out until they lay under the shade of a large, overhanging tree and just waited.

Orvell's was the first voice she heard. 'They can't have gone far. Use the spears.'

Edwin pulled her closer to the tree. 'Hold on tight. We'll have to go under soon.'

She nodded and drew her body as close as she could to his. The water was bitterly cold and had taken her breath away. If they stayed here for much longer, they would surely die of the cold. Clinging to him, Madselin looked into his eyes. 'I'm sorry,' she whispered. 'For everything.'

He did no more than smile and draw his arms around her tight. 'If we survive this, Lady de Breuville, rest assured I shall make you pay in kind.'

His expression was so wicked that she could not prevent a smile cracking her cold lips.

'Boasting, Angle?'

His eyes held hers in a solemn promise before they sank below the surface.

Horses surged through the water and spears rammed down towards the stream's murky bed.

Edwin pushed her further under the roots of the tree, protecting her with his own body. The blades of swords and spears whipped the surface of the water into stirring foam so that Madselin was certain they would be cut to shreds.

Every so often the need to breathe made them rise slowly and take in great gulps of air, but what they saw made them sink quickly. The place appeared to be swarming with Orvell's brutal men, intent on hunting out their prey.

A curious numbness enveloped her body, allowing her to feel nothing other than a desire just to close her eyes and float away. Suddenly Edwin stiffened. She could tell from the way the water was churning that someone on horseback was close by.

With a fierceness borne of self-preservation, Madselin gripped Edwin until she could squeeze no more strength from her arms. Way above her, she could hear the jingle of a harness and a loud, rough voice bellowing out to an unseen companion. A sword slashed powerfully through the water before its owner turned the horse back to the centre of the stream.

Slowly, very slowly, they floated up the surface.

Riders and guards alike were moving on up the stream, leaving the churning mud and broken bullrushes behind them like a scene of devastation.

'Don't move yet,' hissed a voice in her ear. 'It's too soon.'

They stayed immobile for what seemed like hours and their blood, Madselin was convinced, had frozen in their veins. Finally Edwin roused her from her cold stupor and indicated they could get out. That was not so easy as it seemed. Nothing would move. It wasn't until they had managed to rub each other's limbs vigorously that they could move their legs at all.

They dragged themselves through the rushes and squelched heavily to the banks. Madselin attempted to squeeze some of the water from her cloak and skirts, but it was impossible. Edwin pulled his boots off and emptied them. Neither of them said a word, but there was really no need.

Orvell and his men headed towards the de Vaillant keep, as Edwin had guessed they would, whilst Edwin and Madselin made for the hills to the south-east. The next few hours passed in a haze of cold, numb terror. At least that was true for Madselin. It was hard to see what Edwin thought since his face showed no emotion at all. His expression was set, but she doubted it was just because of the chill in his bones.

'If we do manage to get to the farms, what will happen?' she asked eventually when they sat hidden under some thick bushes. They were huddled together for warmth since Edwin would not even consider making a fire.

Edwin turned his grey, assessing eyes on her. 'I'll try to send word to Mallet about the Scots in the caves and Orvell. With luck they might take them all.'

'And will Mallet have them killed, do you think?' She picked up a stick and scraped it along the earth.

'No.' His reply was fierce and immediate. 'I'll kill Orvell.'

'You?' Madselin jerked her head up to stare at him.

'Aye. I'll offer him combat. Orvell will take it.' His jaw was tight and a pulse throbbed steadily at his neck.

Madselin's jaw opened. 'He'll kill you.' She held his eyes, not letting him turn away from her. His were filled with hate and anger.

'Most likely.' His eyes dropped to the ground and his fingers idly pulled at the grass. 'It doesn't matter.'

But it did matter. 'It matters to me, you foolish Angle.' There was no trace of a smile in her voice. Just sincere regret.

He looked up at her then, the anger gone, replaced by something much warmer. 'Aye. I'll miss you too.' The words were spoken so softly that she could barely make them out. 'But he is my fate.'

Their progress was slow but sure as they trudged towards the higher ground that would offer them safety. At every moment Madselin had expected to hear Orvell and his men return for the kill, but as the day wore on their chances of survival increased

Grey storm clouds gathered overhead, causing her to amend her assessment of their situation. If they did not find cover soon, they would die of cold, exhaustion and exposure. She had also noticed that Edwin's injured arm had begun to bleed again. Stopping briefly to examine it, she tore a long strip of wool from her cloak and bound it carefully.

As she finished tying the ends together, Madselin was aware of his gaze on her.

'I said I'd make an Englishwoman of you,' he said with a hint of amusement. He winced a little as he flexed his arm. 'You seem perfectly at home here in the cold and wet.' He reached out to push strands of her wet hair from her face. 'You look like a drowned rat, though.'

Madselin glared at him. 'That makes me feel so much better,' she replied with asperity, shaking his hand away. 'And if we don't find shelter soon, I suspect that this will be my permanent resting place.'

The forest fell away as they climbed higher. Whilst Edwin appeared to be able to take such effort in his stride, Madselin was finding it very hard to keep up. Breathlessly, she collapsed in a heap behind a large crop of rocks.

'Do you want me to carry you?' Edwin stood before her, his expression perfectly serious.

'No.' she snapped irritably. 'I want to get rid of these cold wet clothes and sleep.'

His eyes left her to gaze over the horizon. 'If I remember correctly, there's a small farmholding over the brow of the next hill. Do you think you can make it that far?'

She looked but could see nothing. 'If you are lying to me, Angle, I will be your fate.' Taking his outstretched hand, she pulled herself wearily to her feet. 'Be warned.'

Edwin hesitated a moment before turning to her. 'I think it might be a good idea if we told these people we're married.'

She remained stockstill. 'Oh? And why should we tell them that?'

He pushed back her hair and pulled a few stray weeds from her tattered cloak. 'Well, for one thing, farmers always regard strangers suspiciously, especially Norman strangers.' The emphasis he placed on 'Norman' lingered in the air between them. 'And for another, you have a somewhat dishevelled appearance that might give them the. . .ah. . .wrong impression.'

Placing her hands on her hips, Madselin narrowed

her eyes. 'You don't appear completely wholesome either, Edwin Elwardson.'

'No, that's true,' he replied carefully. 'But it might stop the men trying to. . .er. . .find out for certain about your status.' Satisfied that he had tidied her as much as he could, he placed a filthy finger under her chin and forced her to look up at him. 'Nor do I want to spend the next few hours worrying about you. You'll stay where I can see you.'

She had no intention of arguing with him. The thought of fighting off the attentions of several foreign farmers was the last thing she wanted to do. Staying with Edwin was a small price to pay for peace and sleep. 'Whatever you think best,' she replied quietly.

Somewhat taken aback by her acquiescence, Edwin continued to stare at her. Then he smiled and placed a heavy arm round her shoulders. 'Good.'

Edwin had not been lying. There was indeed a farming community, living in a collection of homesteads about an hour's walk away. Five or six low wooden buildings lay together within the protection of a stockade and to Madselin's unpractised eye, the village looked very welcoming.

They were greeted at the open gate by a giant of a man who made even Edwin look small. Wild blond hair massed over his shoulders and two faded-blue eyes stared at them suspiciously. Madselin could not help but feel apprehensive as she assessed his ponderous bulk. He and Ulf could have been brothers. From the way he was looking at her, Madselin was very glad she had agreed to Edwin's plan and moved closer to her new 'husband'.

As if they had been married for years, Edwin slung his good arm over her shoulders and gave her a comforting squeeze. The farmer's gaze returned to Edwin, clearly satisfied as to her status.

The two men talked for several minutes in a language that made little sense to her at all. Eventually, the farmer stood back and indicated that they could enter the stockade. Behind them the gates slammed shut and Madselin felt faint with relief. They were safe.

Several curious faces peeped out from doors and windows to examine the newcomers. Most were children and women, dressed in brightly coloured woollen tunics and cloaks.

At the farmer's impatient bidding, Edwin and Madselin followed him to a large farmhouse in the centre of the village. A tall, well-built woman in her forties stood outside the doorway, her blue eyes fastened carefully on the couple. The man and woman exchanged words before the woman stood aside and beckoned them in.

The warmth hit them immediately. A huge fire burned in a stone grate at the far end of the long, very comfortable room. Dried herbs and smoked meats hung from the low wooden rafters and bright woollen hangings covered the walls. Rugs and sheepskin pelts were piled together to form beds and seats close to the fire.

Wonderful smells emanated from an iron pot bubbling by the fire and Madselin could feel her mouth watering. The woman must have guessed as much, since she gently took her arm and lead her to the fire. Edwin was engaged in a serious conversation with the farmer and Madselin guessed that he must have been explaining about Orvell and his men.

Grateful for the warmth, Madselin smiled her thanks at the farmer's wife who waved away her words with the flap of a plump hand. Within minutes of being wrapped in a thick warm blanket, Madselin found a bowl of hot, wholesome pottage thrust into her hands. Edwin sat down next to her, his mouth full of bread.

'What's happening?' she asked quietly, sipping at the food. It tasted heavenly.

'He's sending two men to Mallet to warn him. They lost their horses in a raid by the Scots in the summer, so it will take a while for them to get there. We may as well lie back and rest for a while.'

'Does he believe you?' Her eyes flickered up at the farmer and his wife who were talking in low tones by the doorway. Whatever was said seemed to have satisfied the wife, since she returned with a beaming smile and some cups of warm ale.

'About Orvell? Aye.' Edwin gulped down his pottage with a look of deep satisfaction on his face. Such praise earned him a wink from the farmer's wife, causing Madselin to assess her hostess a little more carefully.

The woman was perhaps more voluptuous in the way of the large-boned Danes, rather than fat. Close to, she was fine-skinned and attractive with soft silvery hair and dancing blue eyes. It would seem that Edwin had taken her fancy. Madselin smiled to herself at that unlikely thought.

'Osric has no love for Orvell, apparently, and welcomes anyone who wishes to see justice done,' continued Edwin, oblivious to Madselin's train of thought. Tossing back his ale, he placed the cup on the table and wiped his mouth on his sleeve. The farmer's wife grabbed the cup and refilled it in seconds.

'If I didn't know better, I'd say she was trying to get you drunk,' she observed tartly. Her mouth twitched as she saw his stunned expression. On cue, the farmer's wife, whose name was Frieda, bore down on the hapless Angle and encouraged him to drink up so that she could give him more. Too taken aback to resist, Edwin could only nod and drink. Madselin took pity on him.

Rising gracefully, she went to stand behind Edwin and placed her hands firmly on his shoulders in a proprietary manner. Using very obvious gestures, she managed to convey to Frieda that they were both in great need of a bath and some sleep. Frieda eyed her somewhat warily, but Edwin seemed to have regained his speech and added something that caused a broad smile to split her face. She left the room in a flurry of skirts and hair.

'What did you say?' Madselin enquired, coming to sit at his side.

'I said that we had only just married and you were most keen to display your wifely devotion.' He carried on chewing at the bread, avoiding her eyes.

'I see.' Her heart started beating faster at the thought of what might be expected of them.

Any further discussion was interrupted by the arrival of a huge wooden bath tub and several brawny boys with steaming buckets of hot water. They all returned on several occasions until Frieda was entirely satisfied that all was well. Clean, dry clothes and blankets were placed carefully on the table and then everyone was ushered out quietly and efficiently. Frieda herself left with a few softly spoken words on her lips.

'What did she say?'

Edwin grinned. 'That the tub is big enough for the two of them, so we can enjoy ourselves.'

Her cheeks burned at the very thought. 'You can leave right now!' she commanded, pulling her tattered clothes more tightly about her.

'We're married!' he protested, smiling at her discomfort. 'It wouldn't be right if you threw me out now.'

He was enjoying this, but Madselin knew he was right. 'Well, you'll have to turn around until I'm done.'

'Couldn't we just try it? Together?' The world had gone silent as he spoke the words. There was no mock amusement in his voice, just a quiet entreaty. The fire crackled and shifted.

Madselin was stunned to find herself considering the consequences of such wildly abandoned behaviour. No one need ever know that they had spent a few hours together as man and wife. It was very likely that Edwin would be killed in the morning and it was that thought that stayed with her as she looked at him then.

This Englishman had protected her with his life and made no protest about it all being her fault. She had never met anyone like him before and was unlikely to ever do so again. Marriage to Hugh would be... predictable. She could never envisage life with Edwin being any such thing.

She lowered her head and closed her eyes, not wishing to see the look on his face. 'Do you truly wish to?' This was no sudden impulse or whim. It went far, far deeper.

After a stunned silence, gentle fingers slipped around her jaw and turned her face towards him.

'Look at me, Madselin.'

Shyly she opened her eyes. His face was still and yet intense. 'Aye, I truly wish to. It's only a bath after all. No more than that.'

Slowly, very slowly, she moved her face closer to his and their lips met in a soft kiss.

He pulled her to her feet and removed her blankets and cloak. 'We'd best not let the water get cold then.'

Each removed their own clothes with fumbling, nervous fingers, but it was at least a relief to be rid of the damp things. With her clothes in a puddle at her feet, Madselin turned to Edwin, her face blazing. As she stared at his naked chest, she caught her breath. On a leather thong around his neck lay her gold ring.

'You kept it,' she whispered, her fingers reaching out to touch it. His skin was silky soft and burnished copper in the glow of the firelight. In fact, all of his skin was like that. Edwin was beautiful.

As she drew her fingertips over his chest, he shuddered and stopped her with his own hand.

'If you carry on doing that, you foolish Norman, you are not likely to have a bath at all.'

It was impossible for him to hide the effect that she was having on him, but still he did not move. Touched by his gentleness, Madselin took his hand and pulled him into the tub.

Frieda was right. There was plenty of room for two. The dirt and grime of the day was gently soaped away with their fear. Gradually they relaxed and leaned against each other, quiet and peaceful in the firelight. As the water cooled, they stepped out of the tub and dried themselves. Madselin pulled on a short chemise before climbing onto a pile of lambswool fleeces and blankets. Edwin crawled in beside her and drew her close. As sleep claimed them, he kissed her damp hair and breathed in her scent. She felt blissfully happy.

Chapter Fifteen

They did not stir until night had fallen and delicious smells from the cooking pot permeated their dreams. At first, Madselin had no idea where she was but the sound of unfamiliar breathing behind her focused her thoughts.

She was pulled hard against him, with Edwin's large body cradling hers. His arm was draped protectively about her and she had absolutely no desire to remove it. Feeling deliciously sinful, Madselin stretched gently and was rewarded with an appreciative squeeze.

Edwin struggled to prop himself up on his elbow and gazed down at her. 'You're very comfortable for a Norman,' he murmured, his voice a little husky.

She smiled at that and reached to push back a lock of hair. 'Comfortable? And just how many Normans have you shared a bed with?' It was very easy to flirt with him like this.

He met her uplifted brow with his steady gaze. 'None that I recall.'

She shifted round to look up at him properly. 'I thought you were a man of great experience?'

'Aye, well, I always thought you were a bit impulsive.' He began to trace a path downwards from the top of her arm to her elbow. Even through the soft material of the chemise, Madselin could feel the heat of his fingers.

Facing death together, bathing and sleeping together certainly engendered a sense of intimacy, and Madselin could feel the attraction between them pulling tight. She ran her fingers through his tousled hair. There was a shyness between them as well as a mounting sense of anticipation.

Edwin fixed his grey eyes on her. 'Do you remember my threat?' His finger continued its slow path up and down her arm as he spoke. His very touch heated her blood and she was sure he could feel her shudder in response.

Her lips twitched into a smile. 'As I recall, you have issued several threats recently. Which particular one did you have in mind?' Madselin turned in towards him so that they were practically touching from chest to toes.

Lowering his head so that his temple brushed her cheek, Edwin breathed gently by her ear. Every hair on her body seemed to stand on end, straining towards him. 'I said I would make you pay in kind for using me so abominably.'

His words did not seem at all like a threat to Madselin. In fact they were having a very different effect on her body. Every inch of her skin suddenly seemed to crave his touch. 'Have you decided on the form this payment should take?' Her voice sounded slightly hoarse.

'Aye.' His fingers moved to untie the lace at her neck. Pushing the fabric aside, his lips brushed her skin. Soft and insistent, they sent shivers of desire shooting down her spine. Lower and lower they moved until they reached the full curve of her breast. His mouth closed over her nipple, drawing from her a sharp intake of breath.

Unable to hold back her response, Madselin reached out to pull his head closer to her breasts. She didn't want him to stop.

A loud clattering at the door made them spring guiltily apart. Frieda bustled in, apparently unaware of disturbing them, although Madselin was certain that those blue eyes missed nothing. She had brought warm ale and told them firmly that as soon as they were ready, the rest of the villagers would be pleased to meet them.

Picking up their damp, discarded clothes, the farmer's wife winked broadly at Edwin and then fled into the darkness.

Left alone in the silence, Madselin and Edwin eyed each other warily and then burst into self-conscious laughter.

'I think she came in on purpose,' said Madselin, pulling the blanket up over her exposed breasts. 'Frieda clearly has doubts as to the validity of our marriage.'

Edwin sat up and ran his fingers through his tangled hair. 'You don't look obedient enough to be a wife,' he muttered rather grumpily. 'Not enough proper respect.'

She smiled and sat up, clutching the blanket. 'Obedience and respect, is it? You drive a very hard bargain, Angle.'

He fixed her with glittering eyes and a very seductive smile. 'Tonight then, we shall discuss a proper price for my troubles.' That seemed to be more of a promise than a threat.

After a few moments of awkwardness, they dressed themselves in the clothes provided by Frieda. Bright and a little on the large side, they were nevertheless comfortable, warm and dry. Madselin tugged the long skirts up and frowned. 'Why do I get the impression that Frieda doesn't like me?'

Edwin glanced up at her as he pulled on a huge pair of leather boots. 'You're a Norman,' he replied in surprise. 'What do you expect?' Standing up to try out his footwear he came to stand in front of her. 'Not all the natives are as long-suffering and patient as me.'

Her narrowed eyes met his innocent, wide-eyed gaze. 'There are some natives who don't appear to know their place,' she said darkly. Tossing her thick, black hair over her shoulders, she stood squarely in front of him.

Edwin bent down suddenly to place a kiss on her forehead. 'Aye, well, some of us are very slow learners. Are you ready?'

She smiled up at him and slipped her hand around his proffered arm. 'I'm not sure this is a good idea, but I am hungry.'

He shook his head regretfully as they reached the door. 'As someone who has hauled you over mountains, woman, I'm not sure this is a good idea either.'

They followed their noses. The delicious smell of roasting pig and an assortment of other indefinable dishes came from another home close by the gate. It was similar in design to Frieda and Osric's house except that it was perhaps smaller. The inhabitants of the settlement had clearly been awaiting their arrival for a while and several of the men grinned with relief as they tentatively stepped through the door.

Altogether there were about five married couples, five unmarried men and three young girls. Numerous children bobbed around the trestle table, but it was impossible to place any one of them to a family. They all looked very similar. Tall and rangy in build, the villagers sported thick blond hair and blue eyes. Their skin was soft but tanned and they spoke with an odd lilt that Madselin found very difficult to understand.

'Danes,' whispered Edwin in response to her confusion. 'There are several such settlements hereabouts. No one interferes with them much and they prefer to keep it that way. They're very fierce when roused,' he added gravely.

The food was delicious. For all that Edwin had complained about her weight, he was very attentive to her needs. Her trencher was never empty and he offered her several tempting morsels from his own.

'If I didn't know any better, Angle, I'd think you were trying very hard to please me.' Her eyes stared at him speculatively.

He placed his hand over his heart as if wounded. 'You have a very suspicious nature, woman.'

'It would seem I'm not the only one.' Madselin glanced over in Frieda's direction to find a pair of blue eyes boring into them. Flushing with embarrassment and indignation, Madselin took another sip of the ale. Strong and yet quite sweet, she found it helped her feel more relaxed.

Edwin's hand came to rest gently on top of hers. 'Unless you plan to spend the entire night and most of tomorrow in oblivion, I suggest you drink less of the ale. It takes some time to accustom yourself to it.'

'Well, it makes me feel less. . .conspicuous,' she observed quietly, reaching for some bread. It was most disconcerting to eat with several pairs of eyes trained on your every move and Madselin was beginning to feel very uncomfortable.

Taking pity on her distress, Edwin patted her hand and then directed a blistering smile at Frieda. They conducted a brief conversation under the suspicious eye of Osric, but the latter seemed to relax a little as some of their neighbours joined in. Madselin was pleased to be ignored for the time being, watching these people carefully for the first signs of anger.

The other women, mainly younger than Frieda although perhaps not quite so attractive, vied with each other to engage Edwin in conversation of sorts. Every so often she would find his eyes flicker towards her and give her thigh a gentle squeeze. She found the whole thing a very enlightening experience.

Far from being the surly peasant she had always accused him of being, Edwin was clearly the possessor of a quick wit and a fair amount of charm. The women and girls would stammer and blush the moment he turned his eyes on them. Even the men laughed at some of the things he said.

After the meal, the villagers cleared the table from the middle of the floor so that the dancing could begin. It was a custom with these people to entertain visitors in such a manner and they all appeared to relish the prospect. With mixed feelings, Madselin realised that she would have to partner Edwin once again but she was given no time to dwell on it.

It was not, however, Edwin who stood up to be her first partner. The huge form of Osric lumbered up to her and gravely held out his hand. Conversation being out of the question, Madselin nodded quickly and found herself propelled to the centre of the floor. Edwin had been captured by Frieda, who was all but dragging him along behind her. The two couples were joined by an assortment of villagers and children.

As the pipes fluted out tunes that set feet tapping, Madselin found herself surprised into enjoying herself. Osric was light on his feet for such a huge man and he manoeuvred her about the floor with astonishing expertise.

The villagers plunged into the dancing with an unrestrained joy that was infectious, hurling each other across the floor with enthusiasm. What they lacked in finesse, they made up in sheer exuberance. Every so often Madselin would catch sight of a red-faced Edwin being whirled around by a determined Frieda.

Once Osric had fulfilled his duty, Madselin found herself in great demand by the other men, and she assumed this was also the case with Edwin and the women. After several very enjoyable but highly exhausting dances, Madselin retired to a quiet corner to catch her breath.

Glowing with the heat, she leaned back on a cool wall to watch the proceedings. This was the second time she had enjoyed herself like this. Here she was just another visitor and, despite her origins, the people accepted her presence for what it was. They had extended their protection to her as well as to Edwin and she found it a sobering thought.

Having spent eight years hating the English, she realised that her anger had been misplaced. For the most part they were just ordinary people trying to survive. Who knows, she thought bleakly, exactly what Guy had done? She knew first hand what Henry Orvell was capable of doing.

She watched Edwin escape from the clutches of another bright-eyed villager and collapse by her side against the wall.

'Escaping? Surely not?' Her gaze of wide-eyed innocence met his eyes.

'We warriors are no match for Danish women,' he replied ruefully. 'I'm thinking of asking Frieda and her sisters to join up with my men.' He closed his eyes briefly and took some deep breaths. 'The Scots wouldn't stand a chance.'

They had tacitly refrained from mentioning anything about the Scots or Orvell until now, but it seemed natural to continue. 'Are you still planning to fight

Orvell?' she asked somewhat hesitantly. His skin was glowing amber in the torchlight and there was a faint sheen of perspiration on his brow.

'Do you think Frieda might do better, then?' he asked drily.

She pursed her lips at this deliberate avoidance of her question. 'You are tired and injured,' she snapped, staring straight ahead of her. 'Orvell is neither.'

'Don't tell me you are worried about me, you foolish Norman?' His voice held a note of amusement.

'I am not being foolish. I am being perfectly serious.' She folded her arms and refused to look at him. 'Why can't you leave Orvell to the King?'

He stared silently across the room at the dancers before finally turning to look at her. 'I vowed to avenge my family, and I will.'

'Even if he kills you, too?'

'He probably will,' Edwin replied soberly. 'Orvell is a better swordsman than I am.'

There was nothing more she could say to him. His mind was clearly made up. 'So this could be your last night alive?' The thought was utterly numbing, but it might at least shock the man into rethinking his position.

Strong fingers reached to grasp her wrist and she could feel the heat from his body flood into hers. It seeped into her veins. 'You are tired, Madselin,' he said softly. 'Rest will make you feel better.'

Madselin looked at him then. 'I doubt it, but I don't think I can stay here much longer. Will they be offended if we leave?'

He smiled gently and shook his head. 'Wait there and I'll explain.'

It was a relief to have left the heat and the noise behind. In contrast, the night was cool and quiet and acted like a soothing balm on her shattered nerves.

Edwin walked silently at her side, his expression unreadable.

'You were enjoying yourself,' she said apologetically. 'You should have stayed. I don't mind if you go back.'

He grimaced convincingly. 'I think I feel safer with you.'

There were several torches burning to light the way. Beyond the wooden palisade, the thickness of the night was overwhelmingly frightening. Madselin imagined Orvell and his men searching for them and shivered.

Edwin put his arm about her shoulders and pulled her close to him as they walked back to Osric's house. 'We're safe here. Mallet and his men will find us in the morning.' He gave her a small squeeze that made her smile up at him. 'Then you'll be able to give the poor man one of your famous tongue-lashings for being so tardy.'

'Famous tongue-lashings?' Madselin stopped and shook off his arm, hands on hips. 'What do you mean?' she demanded in an outraged tone.

Edwin raised his brows and stared down at her, his eyes glinting in the torchlight. 'You know very well what I mean, woman. There isn't a man amongst us who hasn't been subjected to your icy glares and scathing retorts and most of us count ourselves lucky to emerge from the skirmish in one whole piece.'

'Oh.' She was very glad that he could not see the deep flush to her cheeks. Was that how she truly seemed to them? 'Well. . .' she lifted her eyes almost defiantly to his '. . .you all deserved it.'

'No doubt,' came the dry retort. 'Come on,' he urged, tugging gently at her arm. 'It's been a long day.'

Osric and Frieda had apparently given up their home for the night to offer quiet and privacy to their unexpected visitors. Frieda had thoughtfully left ale, bread and some cheese and despite their recent meal,

Madselin and Edwin found that they were really quite hungry.

As they brushed the crumbs from their clothes, Madselin glanced over at Edwin. The playful, intimate mood that had gripped them before had been replaced by one that was altogether more reflective and sub-dued. His mouth was set in a determined line as he stared into the fire.

'Are you thinking about tomorrow?' she asked, pulling her hair from its tight braid. Picking up Frieda's comb, Madselin dragged it slowly through her hair.

'Aye.' His head turned briefly in her direction and watched her as she fussed at a tangle. 'It's a strange thing,' he continued, his gaze returning to the fire. 'I've imagined this moment for so long that it hardly seems real.'

His words stilled her. It didn't seem real to her either. Edwin was here, with her, alive and strong. They had survived Orvell and his men for now, but he could be dead by tomorrow. Her eyes roved over the familiar planes of his handsome face. She would miss him. More than that. It would be as if she had lost one of her own limbs.

Swallowing hard to remove the growing lump in her throat, Madselin put down the comb. 'If you win, what will happen?' she asked.

He rubbed involuntarily at his arm. 'An old woman I used to know once told me I would die fighting my greatest enemy. I have no reason to doubt her.'

'You plan to do this because of an old woman's prophecy?' she asked incredulously. 'Even if it were true, it could mean any number of things.' She reached over to him and placed a hand on his arm. 'Don't do it, Edwin. I beg of you.'

The atmosphere in the room was suddenly charged with an emotion and a tension she could not identify.

Edwin blinked slowly and then took a deep breath as if preparing himself for an unpleasant duty.

'Madselin, I think I ought to tell you something about myself that you. . .'

'I do not wish to hear anything more,' she interrupted quickly, placing a forefinger on his lips.

'But you must listen to. . .'

'No.' As she spoke, Madselin knew without a doubt that she had no desire to hear anything more of his past. It would make no difference. 'But I have something to say to you.' Madselin drew in a deep breath. It would be the hardest thing she had ever said, but it could not keep. Not when he might die in the morning.

'I have had few choices in my life,' she began, measuring the words carefully. 'But I have one this night. For tonight, I am no one's sister, aunt or chatelaine. I am myself.'

Edwin watched her face, his body still, waiting.

'I choose to spend the night in your arms, Edwin Elwardson. If you'll have me.' She could not bear to look at him, so great was her embarrassment. The silence in the room was punctuated only by the crackling of the wood burning in the fire.

'Why?' His voice echoed in the silence between them. Gently he took her hand and pulled it to his heart. 'The truth.'

Slowly, she raised her eyes to his and smiled tentatively. Edwin was looking far more nervous and apprehensive than she was. 'I want you,' she said simply.

Without a word, Edwin stood and drew her to her feet. Pulling her hard against him, he framed her face with his fingers. She could feel his heart beating rapidly in time with her own and knew that this was right. 'You have a betrothed,' he reminded her, his grey eyes searching her face. 'He will expect you to be innocent. There might be a child.'

Madselin did not look away. 'I am not yet betrothed.' The prospect of having Edwin's child made her heart leap. 'I would be proud to bear your child, Angle.'

Edwin smiled at that, but as he gazed down at her the smile faded. Slowly, very slowly, he lowered his lips to hers and closed his eyes. This kiss was a promise.

'I've wanted you since the moment I laid eyes on you, woman.' His voice was barely a whisper. 'I have no idea why it is like this between us, but I cannot help myself any longer.'

This time his kiss was hard and demanding. His hands moved from her face, down over her arms and rested for a moment on her hips. As their passion deepened, he pulled her to him hard. She could not have known how it would affect her.

Edwin wanted her for herself. His body did not lie. That knowledge was an aphrodisiac in itself. Looping her arms around his neck, Madselin pushed herself against him harder. Groaning softly, he pushed her from him until she stood at arm's length.

'Are you sure, Madselin? I mean. . .I don't think I can be gentle and I don't want to hurt you.'

'Edwin,' she muttered with a smile. 'Be quiet and kiss me again.'

That elicited from him the heartstopping smile that made her weak at the knees. He sighed softly and reached for her. 'You're a very demanding woman.'

They stood together, before the fire, just looking at each other, memorising every feature, every contour. For an experienced man, Edwin's fingers fumbled nervously at her laces as he began to undress her. Madselin watched in fascination as the flush on his cheeks deepened. At last her gown slithered to the ground, leaving Madselin in her chemise. His eyes glowed with suppressed passion as he reached out to touch her hair.

'It's like silk,' he whispered, almost shyly. Half closing his eyes, he buried his face in her long tresses and breathed in the soft scent of lavender.

Her fingers found the clasp on his belt and it slithered onto her discarded gown. Pushing Edwin gently back, Madselin went to work on his laces. Never having even attempted such garments before, it took a great deal longer than she expected. Laughing, they finally accomplished the task together. He stepped out of his large boots and pulled off his breeches.

Naked, Edwin was even more beautiful than she could ever have imagined. His skin was soft and glowing in the firelight. Holding her breath, Madselin ran a shaking hand down from the pulse at his throat and across his chest. Edwin was absolutely still, hardly breathing either, as she then pulled her chemise over her head.

The first touch of skin against skin was intensely thrilling and very arousing. Unable to stop herself, Madselin moved her palms slowly over his chest, wondering at his hard strength. 'Magnificent,' she breathed, placing a soft kiss at the base of his throat.

Any further words she might have uttered were stifled by his lips coming down hard on her own. His hands drew her to his body and they fused, flesh to flesh, as his tongue invaded her mouth.

Suddenly, he lifted her in his arms and carried her to the bed. His face was flushed and his eyes bright with passion. Had she done that to him? He laid her carefully down, sitting back to stare at her.

'Dear God, woman, but you're beautiful. I tried to imagine so many times. . .'

That caught her by surprise. Madselin raised herself onto one elbow and reached out to touch the thick bristles on his chin. 'Oh?' she queried, raising an eyebrow in amusement. 'And I was certain that all you ever thought about was escaping from my venomous tongue?' she teased gently.

Edwin had the grace to blush, but pulled her beneath him. 'Well, Lady de Breuville, you erred in your supposition. Perhaps I had better show you exactly what I thought of.'

He lowered his mouth to her breast and she arched to him. 'I think you'd better,' she gasped, her eyes closed.

Madselin could not have imagined how it would feel to have him touch her, to have him want her with such powerful urgency. There was not a part of her he did not stroke or kiss, until he burned away every bit of her modesty and her inhibition. Finally, she yielded to his embrace with abandon, returning his kisses with a passion that made him burn.

'Now,' he whispered thickly in her ear. 'I can wait no longer, Madselin.'

Eagerly she opened herself to him. 'Don't stop,' she urged him.

He speared her to the root with a single thrust that caused her to moan aloud as pain mingled with a strange satisfaction. Edwin searched her face as he waited for her to catch her breath. His jaw tightened with the effort of holding back, until he could stand it no longer.

'You are mine for tonight, Madselin, and I do not intend to let you forget me. Ever.' His words were softly spoken as he pressed her deep into the bed. Taking her wrists, he pinned them above her head before thrusting into her again and again.

Pain and discomfort were quickly replaced by an echoing response that was wild and almost pagan in its sinfulness. This act could never have been sanctioned by her church, she was sure. This was born of the gods of this barbaric land and she welcomed it joyfully.

Every inch of her body tingled and shivered as Edwin lowered his head to suckle at her swollen breasts. Pushing herself hard against him, Madselin rose to meet his every thrust. Suddenly, without warning, a feeling of exquisite pleasure burst forth deep within her and exploded into every part of her body. Hearing her cry out, Edwin pushed himself into her very depths again and again until her moans mingled with his own sigh of release.

The last thing Madselin remembered as they collapsed against each other was the furious music of the pipes and the heat of Edwin's soft skin.

Chapter Sixteen

It wasn't the music that woke Madselin again. It was the heavy pounding of Edwin's heart close to her ear. Still fused together, they had not moved.

Sensing a change in her breathing, Edwin shifted to pull her close to his chest, his arms locking around her. Madselin sighed faintly.

'Did I hurt you?' he murmured into her ear.

She opened her eyes and looked up into his still flushed face. He smiled at her somewhat ruefully.

Madselin made a quick mental inventory of her body. 'Not too much,' she said, snuggling closer to him and breathing in his faint, musky smell. She felt his lips brush gentle kisses close to her ear and her skin tingled in immediate response.

'That's good,' came the muffled reply, as he lowered his lips to the sensitive part of her neck.

Madselin gasped in surprise. 'What are you doing, Edwin?' she managed. A large hand moved slowly up her body, lingering over her breast.

'What I've been longing to do since you fell asleep on me,' he informed her.

'You want to do it again?' she asked, pulling herself up to a sitting position. Edwin merely nodded, seemingly bewitched by the sight of her naked body in the firelight.

'This time,' he said quietly and persuasively, 'I'll be very gentle.'

Any tiredness or discomfort disappeared as she saw the desire in his eyes. Her nipples hardened under his gaze and laughed softly. 'It doesn't take much to persuade you, woman.'

Madselin eyed him speculatively and then reached for him under the blankets. His laugh vanished immediately, to be replaced by a quickly indrawn breath.

'Nor you, it would seem.'

Neither spoke for some time.

'Edwin?'

'Mmm?'

'Is it always like this?' Gently, Madselin traced the line of an old scar which ran from his breastbone down to his navel.

He took so long to answer that she thought he had fallen asleep. 'No,' he said finally. 'With other women, all I generally wanted to do was leave or sleep. I'm not sure why it is, but with you, all I want to do is to hear you cry out beneath me. The minute I stop, I just ache to love you again.'

She stilled then and looked up at him. 'Again?' Narrowing her eyes in mock suspicion, Madselin reached for his ale cup and sniffed it. 'Frieda might have given you a potion of some sort.'

Grinning, he pulled her to him and kissed her until she was breathless. 'Aye, she might. Shall we put it to the test?'

It was Frieda's cheery greeting that woke them shortly after dawn. If she felt any rancour about wasting a love potion on Edwin, she gave no sign of it. Madselin and

Edwin struggled to sit up as she busied herself with the fire. The delicious smell of freshly baking bread wafted towards them, reminding the pair how hungry they were.

Uncertain as to the etiquette demanded by such a situation, Madselin gripped the blankets tightly to her and focused her eyes on a spot at the far end of the room. Several huge war axes hung menacingly on the wall. They reminded her of Edwin's future and she found her eyes welling suddenly with tears. A large, solid body enveloped her from behind and a pair of soft lips kissed her gently on her shoulder.

'Regrets, Madselin?' Edwin's tone was bland but it did not fool Madselin.

She shook her head. 'Only that we had just one night.' Willing away the lump in her throat, she turned to look at him. In the soft morning light, with his thick stubble and his tousled hair, Edwin Elwardson was still magnificent. 'You might. . .?' Her hopeful question was cut short by a long finger on her lips.

'Nay. Don't think it. My death is prophesied. Besides,' he added more slowly, 'if you knew what I had done, you might not want to spend another night with me.'

Madselin sighed. 'Whatever it is, Edwin, I cannot believe it to be so awful that I could refuse you that.'

They were disturbed by Frieda bringing their pile of dried clothes and dumping them somewhat pointedly on the bed. She and Edwin exchanged a few words before Frieda smiled knowingly and made a hurried exit.

The moment the door banged shut, Edwin dragged Madselin down so that she lay beneath him, pinned down by his weight. His face was no longer smiling and amused. 'Mallet is on his way. We have but a short time until he arrives and I must not let him find you like this.'

He kissed her with a growing urgency. Placing his forehead on hers, he closed his eyes and held her tight. 'You are a part of my soul and have been for years, Madselin. Our fates were bound from the start and I regret only that I have caused you such pain.'

'But you have not. . .'

'Hear me out,' he interrupted. 'We haven't much time and I won't have your reputation compromised.'

His fingers stroked back her hair from her face and his eyes tried to memorise her features. 'When I die, know that you hold my heart forever.'

Their tears mingled as he kissed her fiercely. He took her then, urgently, stamping his mark on her as she had heard other men did to their women before riding to meet their deaths. No words were spoken, but they cried out loud as their pleasure swept them away to another world.

Minutes later, Edwin stood up and pulled his clothes on hurriedly. He left without another word, picking up a loaf on his way out.

Madselin closed her eyes and tried to will away the inexorable passing of time. Feeling more than a little bruised and battered, but at peace none the less, she determined that whatever happened, she would be with him. Edwin was hers. He had told her so himself.

Clutching that thought to herself, Madselin forced herself from their bed. She washed and dressed with care, wondering if indeed she still looked the same person. Could anyone tell that she was no longer a maid?

Just as she was debating whether or not she could take one of the loaves of bread, Frieda bustled in, her skin flushed with the morning chill. Madselin jumped away from the bread a little guiltily, but Frieda just laughed. A large, warm loaf was shoved into her lap.

Not long after she had eaten her bread, the silence of the early morning was broken by the loud blare of a hunting horn. Frieda wiped her hands on a cloth before rushing to the door, summoning Madselin by gestures and a rapid volley of words.

Albert Mallet was approaching with about twenty guards. The rivets on their hauberks glittered in the early morning sun as they rode steadily towards the village. All the villagers had stopped their chores to watch them from doors or windows. Edwin was standing at the gates with Osric.

Once at the gates, Albert Mallet dismounted hurriedly and clapped Edwin on his back in the manner of friends. As Madselin approached, he stepped forward to greet her with relief etched all over his handsome face.

'My lady. We were pleased to hear of your safe escape from Orvell's men.'

She smiled at him. 'My thanks, sir. We have been well looked after by Oscic and his villagers. I hope that we shall be able to repay their kindness in some way.'

Mallet inclined his head. 'I shall see to it, lady, but my first concern is to return you to the Lady d'Aveyron. She has been most anxious these past few days.'

'And Orvell?' Madselin could not contain the question any longer. 'What of him?'

A shadow passed over his blue eyes. 'Safe in the de Vaillant dungeon. We caught him close by here late yesterday. He was not far behind you.'

Madselin glanced nervously up at Edwin, but he was simply frowning at the ground.

'What of the Scots?' he demanded. 'Did you get any of them?'

Albert Mallet shook his head in regret. 'Nay, but at least we might get something out of Orvell.'

'I doubt it,' muttered Edwin, pushing back his unbound hair. He looked at her then. 'Come, my lady. You're in need of rest.'

The journey back to the de Vaillant keep was arduous because of the need to travel slowly through the forest. Despite the clement weather, Madselin felt cold. Edwin had been as good as his word and had largely ignored her since they left the village. She very much doubted if any of the men could have guessed just how much her reputation had been compromised.

That brought a secret smile to her lips. Aye, and it had been wonderful. Madselin allowed her mind to wander back over their very difficult first meeting. She had thought him a barbaric poacher and all he had wanted to do was kiss her! His expression, if she remembered aright, had not given her that impression though. She could have been forgiven if she had thought murder a more likely possibility.

It was noon before they passed through the gates of the de Vaillant keep. Anxious faces greeted them and the bailey was unnaturally quiet, despite the gathering of many familiar faces. Emma rushed forward, her round, plain face bright with relief.

'Oh, my lady. I'm that glad you're back,' she cried, placing her hand on Madselin's leg. 'I thought I'd never see you alive again.'

'Well,' Madselin smiled down at her, 'you've Edwin to thank for that. He saved me.'

The recipient of her approbation appeared at that moment to lift her from her horse. His hands gripped her waist tightly and she could feel her skin glow where he touched her. Neither spoke, but as her feet met the ground, their eyes held for no more than a few seconds.

She could stand the silence between them no longer.

'What will you do first?' she asked, her hand resting on his arm. 'You will rest.'

Edwin sighed and looked across at Albert Mallet, who was directing the soldiers with significant energy. 'Aye. I'll rest. Nothing will happen for a while. Much has yet to be done.'

'Send me word,' she urged anxiously.

After a moment, he nodded curtly before turning to make his way towards the hall.

Emma shook her head as she watched his retreating form. 'I'd never have thought it would be him as saved you, him hating us Normans as he does.'

'Some Normans,' Madselin corrected, allowing herself a wry smile. 'Come. I'm in need of a hot bath and a strong cup of wine.'

'Aye, you'll be needing to look your best.'

Madselin cast Emma a puzzled look. 'Why?'

'There's to be a trial, here at the keep.'

The news stunned Madselin. 'A trial? But I thought it would just be between Edwin and Orvell.'

Emma shook her head most knowledgeably. 'Nay, my lady. It's all got to be done right. There's five barons going to listen to his story and they decide what's to be done with him.'

Her heart fluttered with anxiety. Perhaps that would mean that Edwin would not have to fight him. 'Come, then. We have much to do.'

Emma stared at Madselin's bedraggled appearance and sighed.

Three notches of the thick candle had burned away by the time she heard the hunting horn calling everyone to the hall. Bathed, rested and freshly dressed, Madselin now felt able to face Orvell. Calmly, she made her way to the great hall, where the trial of Henry Orvell was to take place.

Despite the late afternoon sun, hundreds of candles were needed to provide enough light for the proceedings to take place. A space in the centre of the hall had been cleared for Orvell, whilst the barons sitting in judgement on him sat at the top table. The lower tables had been pushed back against the walls to allow everyone else to view the trial. A huge fire burned in the grate.

Madselin sat close to the door, which allowed her a good view of Orvell, the barons and, hopefully, Edwin.

She had seen nothing of him since parting with him in the bailey, but he had sent her a small, leather-wrapped package in his stead. It was a tiny, circular brooch of polished silver fashioned in the ancient Angle style. Fastened securely to her cloak, the brooch glistened in the candle light. It was exquisite and she was very proud to display her acceptance of so beautiful a gift.

By the time the barons entered the hall, the villagers had crowded onto the benches and spilled over on to the floor rushes. The hall was hot and smoky and she found it difficult to breathe. Tension was mounting.

Albert Mallet was the only one of the five that Madselin recognised. Clearly he was to represent Richard d'Aveyron. The other four were a surly-looking quartet who did not seem at all pleased to be administering justice in the de Vaillant hall. With a flourish of his hand, Mallet gestured to the guard to have Orvell brought in.

All heads turned to the door to watch Henry Orvell walk slowly to the clearing in the centre of the hall. He came to a halt before the top table and eyed his judges with a bored expression. He did not look his normal, immaculate self. His dark breeches and tunic were covered in dirt and dust, his boots coated in mud and his cloak badly torn. He did not look like a man prepared to face death.

Looking beyond Orvell, Madselin craned her neck to see if she could catch sight of Edwin. She had not seen him, but knew he must be there. On the opposite side of the hall, half-hidden in the shadows, stood the Angle. His blond head towered over the rest of the people about him, but his eyes were riveted on his enemy. There was no doubt in his mind that this was the man who had butchered his family and destroyed his life.

Her attention was then caught by Albert Mallet, rising to address the assembly.

'Henry Orvell is accused of treason and my Lords FitzNeville, de Montmorency, Vernon and Stanlegh are to dispense justice on behalf of the King.' A faint murmur whispered through the crowd, but Orvell remained impassive.

Mallet's handsome face stared stonily at the accused. 'What say you to this charge, Orvell?'

A smile curved his lips and Henry Orvell shook his head in disbelief. 'You know as well as I that I am innocent of all charges.' His soft, persuasive voice carried across the hall. 'I believe, in fact, that I am the victim in this sorry tale.'

The five judges viewed this strange accusation with hard-faced disbelief and the tension in Madselin eased a little. These men did not have a sympathetic air about them and it seemed most unlikely that they would spend much time agonising over sending Orvell to his death. Few barons cared much beyond their own lands and position. Ridding the land of another was in their own best interests.

'Explain yourself,' drawled the smallest of the judges. His fat jowls quivered as his pudgy fingers rubbed over a stubbly chin. Dark, beady eyes glared out at the

prisoner from beneath bushy brows, but Orvell seemed
unconcerned. He merely inclined his head in graceful
acceptance.

'I have always been a loyal servant to the King—
both Kings—and have been duly rewarded for my
services,' he replied, eyeing his accuser boldly. Sweeping his cloak over his shoulder, Orvell then turned to
stare at another of his judges. 'I came here with William
of Normandy, as did you, Vernon. Times were hard
then, were they not?'

The man he addressed nodded reluctantly. Vernon
sniffed loudly and wiped his nose on a rather grubby
sleeve. 'Men change in twenty years, Orvell,' he muttered somewhat incoherently before drinking deep of
the wine cup.

'Maybe so. I was young then, perhaps more foolhardy, but a good commander all the same. We held
our ground and kept the Englishmen down. It was dirty
work but I followed the King's orders.' Orvell turned
his eyes to another of the men before him. 'De
Montmorency can vouch for that. We joined forces on
occasion.'

All eyes fastened then on the tallest of the five, and
the eldest. Spare and harsh, de Montmorency's
expression was one of complete indifference. Wisps of
grey hair clung to his shiny scalp as he scratched at
them. 'Aye. The King was pleased with your results.
He described the methods you used as very...
"thorough".'

'He gave me lands which required a harsh and
trustworthy master in return,' replied Orvell sourly.
'The Scots have been hammering at my door ever since
and it would be foolish indeed to betray the King's
trust.'

'Aye, foolish indeed,' echoed de Montmorency. 'But
lucrative.'

Orvell shrugged his shoulders carelessly at that. 'True. However, I may be many things, but stupid is not one of them.'

Madselin noticed that he glanced in Edwin's direction but could not see Orvell's expression. Edwin just stared unblinkingly at him.

'Get on with it, Orvell,' growled Vernon, his coarse, bulbous features somehow thickening in the torchlight.

'When the Conqueror died and Rufus became King, the Scots grew more restless. They became bolder and sent more raiding parties to cross my land. It was hard to keep them back since we are so scattered here.' Orvell raised his brows as if demanding an answer to a question.

Only de Montmorency replied by way of a grunt. The rest continued to glare at Orvell with growing distaste. Although she felt no pity for Orvell, Madselin was glad it was not her before these harsh men.

Orvell sighed. 'It was clear that more devious methods would be required to defeat the Scots, so I offered them peace at a price.'

The barons shuffled in their seats at this and looked at each other with self-satisfied smirks. 'A lucrative one?' asked Vernon with a sneer.

'To find out their plans only,' came the stiff reply. 'Killing off a few Scots every day achieves little, but the King would be pleased to capture a few of their leaders. Or a prince?'

The silence in the hall was deafening. There was no doubt in anyone's mind that William Rufus would indeed be most keen to get his hand on a Scottish prince. Certainly one that was organising raids on his lands. The barons lost their sneers then, and stared at Orvell with renewed interest.

Madselin realised she had been holding her breath

and slowly breathed in again. It was too clever and Orvell was too devious. They could not believe him.

'Apparently,' continued Orvell, 'I was not the first to try to make a pact with them. They were very wary of my intentions, but over a period of time I gained ground.'

'And why did you not mention these plans to d'Aveyron?' Vernon eyed him suspiciously.

'Too dangerous. The Scots had already indicated that another was already in their pay and I did not want to kindle suspicion. It had to be kept secret.'

'Convenient,' muttered the smaller baron with the dark eyes.

Ignoring that gibe, Orvell turned to look at Mallet. 'D'Aveyron's suspicions about me were helpful to my cause. The Scots heard the rumours and began to trust me. I was close to discovering who was behind the raiding when d'Aveyron made his mistake.'

Albert Mallet inhaled loudly. 'Richard d'Aveyron is no fool, Orvell. He never trusted you.'

Orvell merely shook his head. 'He was mistaken. He trusted the wrong man.'

Those words caused a buzz of murmuring around the room. Madselin shifted on the bench, her stomach churning. A loud bang from the top table silenced them all.

'So the accused becomes the accuser?' De Montmorency's eyes stared at Orvell harshly. 'And who is this man?'

Madselin held her breath as Orvell swivelled on his heels and pointed directly at Edwin Elwardson. 'That Englishman is the true traitor.'

A spontaneous outburst of chattering amongst the crowd forced another bang on the table from Albert Mallet. 'Silence,' he ordered loudly. Edwin did not move nor change his expression. He continued to stare woodenly at Orvell, clearly unsurprised by his accusation.

'Richard d'Aveyron is a shrewd judge of character,' Mallet's icy words echoed around the hall. 'He trusted Edwin Elwardson with good reason. He may be an Englishman, but he is loyal, trustworthy and honest.'

Orvell's face remained impassive in the face of this support. 'Aye, to d'Aveyron, and have you ever wondered why?'

Madselin suddenly looked up at Edwin and found his eyes pinned on her. There was longing and sorrow burning almost from the very depths of his soul and it was awful to behold.

'Edwin Elwardson killed a Norman noble, in revenge for the death of his family. Richard d'Aveyron has shielded him ever since.'

Madselin could feel her throat constrict as she stared over at Edwin. His eyes were closed.

'Who was this Norman?' asked de Montmorency.

'Guy de Chambertin. He campaigned with me in the north of England. Elwardson sought him out and murdered him on his wedding day.'

The blood drained from Madselin's face. She had never guessed for a minute that Edwin had killed Guy. '*You* killed him?' she whispered. 'You killed Guy?'

Edwin did nothing more than nod, guilt set deep in his eyes. That was the last thing she saw before the buzzing in her head exploded and Madselin slipped into the welcoming dark of oblivion.

Chapter Seventeen

'Wake up, my lady!'

Emma's pleading suffused her consciousness and Madselin opened her eyes. She was no longer in the hall but lying on the bed in her own room.

'Did he really kill Guy?' Madselin remembered her last coherent thought before she had fainted.

Another face appeared next to Emma's. Edwin loomed large and frowning far above her. The silence between them lengthened until Emma tutted loudly.

'No doubt the pair of you have much to say to each other, so I'll leave you be for a while. And no upsetting her further, Angle,' she admonished Edwin with a wag of her finger.

Edwin did no more than nod curtly. It was not until Emma had left the room that he sat down lightly at her side.

'Did you?' she repeated, knowing the answer but needing to hear it from his lips anyway.

'Aye.'

He said nothing more in explanation but just sat and waited for her questions. Madselin struggled to sit up. 'Why did you not tell me yourself? You must have known.'

Taking a deep breath, Edwin nodded. 'Aye, I've known since that day at the beach when you told me his name. I tried to tell you last night, but you would not allow me to. Although,' he admitted with a shrug, 'I did not try too hard.'

Madselin said nothing but stared at him, willing him to continue.

'I did not try hard enough since I knew you would hate me then. God forgive me, Madselin, but I could not bear to see you hate me. It was wrong, I know, but I just wanted to spend one night of happiness with you and take it to my death.'

She shook her head, unwilling to believe that the man she had come to know as honest and trustworthy had not only butchered her betrothed, but had not told her the truth. His deception speared her to the core.

'I could forgive you many things, Edwin Elwardson, but I cannot forgive you for this. Had you told me and allowed me the choice, I might have been able to love you anyway. As it is, you took from me by deception what was given to you freely in love.'

Edwin bent his head. 'Aye.' Then he looked up at her and gazed at her fiercely. 'But I regret not one moment of it, Madselin de Breuville. For one night we loved each other. It was all we could ever have and although I regret the deception, I cannot ever regret what happened.'

He stood up quickly 'I will not stay to hurt you further.' His grey eyes lingered over her face, softening a little, and her heart felt as though it would burst with the pain. 'I love you,' he murmured before turning quickly and leaving.

The empty room felt cold and Madselin flopped back against the bolster. 'I loved you too,' she whispered after him, 'but I cannot forgive you this.' Yet what did it matter? Edwin planned to die anyway and he had snatched at the only straw offered him. Groaning, she turned into the bolster and wept bitterly until there were no more tears.

Oblivious to the passing of time, Madselin stared into the flames of the fire. She had no idea how long Edwin had been gone. It could have been hours or minutes, but it felt like years. She would never see him again and her heart was breaking, just as it had eight years before. And yet this time, everything seemed even worse.

In truth, she had known Guy little, other than as this handsome knight who was charming and so very amusing. When he died, she had mourned the life she thought they might have had as much as the man himself. But Edwin was very different. They had argued, clashed and stalked their way through the past weeks. They had loved for one night. She thought she had known him.

A lump formed in her throat and tears began to spill onto the blanket as Father Padraig suddenly appeared before her.

'I'm s-s-sorry,' she managed. 'I-I-I didn't h-hear you.'

'No,' came the soft reply. 'It doesn't surprise me.'

Madselin sniffed loudly in an attempt to stop crying, but it didn't work. The priest offered her a clean-looking rag and sat down at the bottom of the bed. 'So?' he began firmly. 'Have you anything you want to talk to me about?' His dark eyes watched her carefully as she wiped her eyes and blew her nose.

Madselin looked at him rather warily. 'In what capacity? As a priest, do you mean?'

'In any capacity at all,' he replied. 'It can help to talk to someone. I may be more understanding of life than you expect.'

There was a catch to his voice that made Madselin

look at him more carefully. Maybe she had been wrong to judge the priest so quickly. Her mind flitted back to her rather cutting comments over his interest in Morwenna, and she winced ruefully.

'He killed Guy,' she said quietly. 'And ruined my life.'

Father Padraig nodded, his mouth pursed tightly. 'That would be very hard to forgive. Did he tell you why?'

'He believed Guy to have been one of the Normans who butchered his family.'

The priest sighed heavily and looked at her. 'That would be very hard to forgive too, don't you think?'

Madselin's fingers began to fiddle with the edging of the blanket. 'But he waited years to do it. And then killed him on the morning of our wedding.'

'And now?' he prompted gently.

'Now? Now I find I'm in love with the man that killed my betrothed and yet I can't help hating him, too. It makes no sense.' Madselin screwed up her fingers tight and fought back another bout of tears.

'Human nature is a strange thing,' said Father Padraig. 'In my experience, people do tend to want most those things they can't have. The reality is usually somewhat different.'

Frowning, Madselin looked up at him for enlightenment. Now he was making no sense.

'How well did you know your betrothed?' he asked patiently.

'Since I was a child although, as Guy was much older than me, I did not see much of him. He was away in England a great deal.'

'Would you have been happy with this man, do you think?' The dark eyes pierced her with their intensity.

Madselin shrugged. 'I shall never know.'

'I see. And this man you are hoping to marry on
your return to the Vexin? What of him?'

'Hugh?' She had forgotten about him completely.
Well? What about Hugh? These past few weeks, she
had rarely thought of him at all. Compared to Edwin,
Madselin realised that he was good-natured but shallow, and she knew deep down that she would not be at
all happy with him. 'I'm not sure. But I doubt he has
ever lied to me.'

'If he had told you the truth, would you have forgiven
Edwin, do you think?'

And that was the nub of the matter. He had killed
Guy and she had hated the man that had done that for
the last eight years. Closing her eyes, she shook her
head. 'God forgive me, Father, for I don't know.' Had
Edwin not used that very same plea not long before?

Father Padraig smiled at her wanly. 'I had best tell
you, then, that Orvell has been found guilty. Edwin
offered him trial by sword. They fight at the lake
shortly.'

'How long is left?' Madselin asked, the blood drain-
ing from her again. Despite the fact that she could not
forgive him, and should by rights hate him, the thought
of his death struck her to the core.

'Half a candle notch, no more,' he replied. 'Do you
wish to go?'

Her heart was thudding heavily as she drew back the
blankets. 'Will you take me?'

Torches were staked around the lakeside, just as they
had been on All Hallows Eve. The flames leapt and
danced in the breeze coming in from the sea, lending a
very eerie quality to the assembled crowd. Streaks of
pink mingled with the grey of the sky, announcing that
night was on its way.

Pulling her cloak tightly to her, Madselin stumbled

on the uneven ground as she made her way to the edge of the sacred lake. Father Padraig guided her firmly towards the front where she could see what was happening.

The five judges were stood solemnly before the sacred stones, watching the two combatants prepare themselves for their duel. If Orvell was fearful, he did not show it. In fact, thought Madselin, he appeared much relieved. He had pushed back his cloak and was brandishing a broadsword of particularly evil appearance. Edwin remained as still as one of the sacred stones, his face grim with concentration.

At Mallet's command the fighting began. Someone in the crowd began a haunting melody on the pipes as the two men launched at each other with their weapons. The tune, she knew, was supposed to summon the spirits of the sacred lake and chase away the foreign oppressor.

Edwin began well, thrusting his great sword down and then slashing across as she had seen him do so often in practice. Orvell was agile and knew what was coming. Smaller in build and lighter than Edwin, his cunning and expertise had not been exaggerated.

Instinctively concentrating on Edwin's weakened arm. Orvell pressed home his advantage remorselessly. Dodging and moving, Orvell thrust and lunged with a determination that was as unexpected as it was effective.

Despite her anger at Edwin's betrayal, Madselin could not help but watch Orvell's every move like a hawk. The man was fighting like a demon and Edwin was not doing much to stop him. He looked as if he were more determined to die.

His last words echoed in her head. 'I will not stay to hurt you further,' he had said. 'I love you.' At that moment, Orvell parried a heavy thrust from Edwin and then spun round to slash deep across the Englishman's chest.

Knocked back by the strength of the sally and the pain, Edwin stumbled to his knees. The crowd drew in its collective breath as Orvell swept his sword down. Whether or not it was the spirits of the lake or just good fortune, the music faltered and Madselin's gasp of his name carried across to Edwin.

Almost as if he heard her, he glanced across and his expression changed. He lifted his sword with renewed strength and stopped the Norman's sword from taking his head. In a fluid movement, Edwin jumped to his feet and bore down on the smaller Norman with a vigour that had been missing before.

Madselin's heart was in her mouth. Whatever she felt for the Englishman, she did not want him to die. Nor, it seemed, did the spirits of the lake.

Edwin was fighting the Norman so that Orvell was forced towards the reeds at the edge of the lake. Orvell still knew no fear. Sweat ran down his brow as he kept the Englishman's sword from drawing blood, but he, too, was tiring.

Whether it was the reeds or the Norman's clumsy foothold, Orvell suddenly faltered and fell to his knees. If they were expecting instant death, the crowd was to be disappointed. Edwin stood back to wait for his enemy to rise.

That gesture of chivalry was lost on no one, least of all Orvell. 'Your father did exactly the same, Englishman. It cost him his life,' hissed the Norman with vicious intent. Those words did what nothing else could. Edwin launched himself at Orvell, his face wreathed in hatred and anger. It was exactly what the Norman wanted. Stepping neatly aside, Orvell caught Edwin on his weak arm and the blood welled instantly.

Madselin gasped audibly as Edwin groaned, his arm

hanging limply at his side. Grinning from ear to ear, Orvell raised his arms in a death blow. As he stepped forward, however, his feet must have caught in some reeds and he tripped heavily. Falling headlong before the Englishman, Orvell sank below the surface of the lake.

Despite the water reaching no higher than their knees, the Norman did not rise. Edwin stood back, but made no move to kill him.

Albert Mallet rushed forward and pulled Orvell from the water. The side of his head was smashed into a bloody pulp. He had hit his head against a jagged stone lying just below the surface.

'Henry Orvell was guilty. God has decided.'

From the murmurs around her, Madselin could tell that the villagers thought differently. 'The gods decided and took him for their own,' came the whisper. 'The lake claimed his black soul.' Madselin closed her eyes, both in relief and pain. Aye, he had survived Orvell's sword but she could never be with him even though he lived. The pain was wrenching her heart in two.

Almost as if he could hear her agony, Edwin lifted his eyes to hers. A faint smile crossed his lips before he turned to leave. Madselin watched him. She could not do it. She could not call to him. The feelings were too raw.

Caring arms wrapped around her as her tears splashed to the cold earth.

Chapter Eighteen

'Well, Madselin? Are you ready?' Beatrice's gentle voice roused her from her contemplation of the wild land beyond the palisade. The deep snows of Yuletide had melted with the coming of the spring and Madselin could almost smell the new life beginning to emerge. She smiled, remembering how much she had hated this barbaric land at first.

'Aye. I'll see him.' She drew back from the open shutters in Beatrice's solar and turned to look at her friend. 'Is Richard in a good mood?'

'As much as he ever is these days,' came the rueful reply. Beatrice looked up from her sewing and raised her brows in despair. 'I've hardly seen him myself since he returned.'

Richard and his men had ridden through the gates of the keep towards the middle of January and over the two weeks since then had spent most of it visiting his vassals. William Rufus, concerned about the treachery of Orvell, had ordered all his barons to be vigilant in patrolling the northern borderlands.

Richard had been anxious to comply with his King's orders and had returned from one such visit only the night before, with a request to see Madselin that morning.

Under Beatrice's careful watch, Madselin had recovered from her ordeals. The scars that were left were hidden deep within and Madselin doubted that those would ever heal. She would not allow herself to think of Edwin. Yuletide had passed quietly, Madselin having relinquished the de Vaillant keep to Ivo's eldest son.

Alain de Vaillant had returned to find his mother dead and his father still away with his lord, but accepted his lot with a resignation that reminded her greatly of Ivo himself. Madselin's immediate usefulness clearly at an end, Beatrice had insisted that she keep her company instead. Now that Richard was back, he would decide whether or not she would be able to marry Hugh.

Her kinsman was waiting for her in a small room off the great hall. Two chairs stood before a bright fire. whilst Richard paced the room.

'Madselin!' He greeted her with an affectionate kiss on her cheek. 'It pleases me to see you looking so well. I had thought you found our land somewhat. . .tedious.'

His dark eyes watched her carefully as though looking for some special sign.

She smiled at him. 'I admit to finding your land far more hospitable than I could ever have imagined. And far more. . .adventurous.'

Richard laughed. 'I am greatly cheered that your humour at least is restored.' As if his own words reminded him of something far more serious, Richard gestured at the chairs, inviting her to sit.

'You did not ask me here to talk about my humour, I take it?' she asked softly.

Pursing his lips tightly, Richard shook his head. He sighed heavily. 'There's no easy way of telling you this

and perhaps I should have done so before, but I believe
I owe you the truth.'

Frowning, Madselin looked at him. 'I have no idea
what you are talking about. Pray explain.'

He rubbed his thick black stubble with his fingers.
'Had I told you all this years ago, I might have saved
you much heartache and unpleasantness. Things might
have turned out differently for you but I believed I was
right in holding my tongue eight years ago.

'I never liked Guy de Chambertin,' he began somewhat hesitantly. 'He was. . .cruel and I was not happy
at the prospect of your wedding him. Your father was
adamant though, since it was a good match.'

Madselin stared at him. This was something she had
never expected to hear from Richard. 'Go on,' she said
faintly.

'Did you know he had made Alice his mistress not
long before your wedding?'

Ice swept through her veins. 'Alice?' she repeated
dumbly. 'Alice, my sister-in-marriage?'

'Aye. She was but sixteen and very determined to
have her own way.'

Madselin remained silent, so he continued. 'I saw
what happened to Guy on the morning of your wedding
day. He had spent the night with Alice and was late. I
have no doubt,' he said with distaste, 'that this was
done expressly. I think Alice believed he would change
his mind about marrying you even then. As he was
slipping back through the bailey, Edwin stopped him.'

Madselin placed her hand over her open mouth but
made no sound.

'He asked him if he was the de Chambertin who had
raped and butchered his sister. Guy just laughed and
told him exactly what he had done to her—and many
others like her—and enjoyed it. There were so many
apparently, that he had no idea who Edwin's sister

really was, but he did not deny it.' Richard shook his head in disbelief.

Sickness washed over her. This could not be Guy. It could not. 'Why would you say such a thing?' she whispered. 'Guy was good and kind.'

'Nay,' said Richard adamantly. 'He was not. He had always been cruel and liked to hurt people. Especially women. If you want proof, I have no doubt there would be many from his estate who would tell you his true character.' He sighed, raking his hair with his fingers.

'Edwin challenged him and Guy accepted. There was no butchery. Edwin won the fight and killed him fairly. I knew what would happen if Edwin was arrested, so I hid him and brought him back to England with me.'

'So you knew all the time? Then why did you let me go with him to the de Vaillant keep?' She stared at him in confusion.

'I thought you would have forgotten Guy, what with wanting to marry Hugh. How could I know anything like this would happen?'

'Did you know of Henry Orvell's part in all this?' Madselin gripped the chair until her fingers went white.

'Only that I believed him a spy. Edwin could not prove that Orvell was the man he had been searching for all these years.'

For several minutes they remained silent together. Finally, Madselin looked at him: 'I thank you for telling me the truth. At least I can put those false memories of Guy behind me and begin a new life.' There was no reason for her to doubt Richard's words. Indeed, they confirmed several strange memories that had nagged her over the years. Especially concerning Alice. Was that why she had always hated Madselin? Because of Guy?

As for Edwin, how did she feel about him now? Perhaps he had withheld the truth from her to save her misery? She had often thought over the past weeks how loyal he had been to his family, if nothing else.

Now that she knew the truth about Guy, her unhappiness deepened. She had treated Edwin badly, preferring to believe in a Norman she knew little of rather than an Angle she respected and loved. It would be better for all of them if she returned to the Vexin and made her marriage with Hugh.

'Tell me, Richard. Have you decided about my marriage to Hugh yet?'

'Ah.' Richard heaved himself to his feet and stood before the fire warming his hands. Finally he turned to face her. 'William Rufus was pleased with Edwin's part in Orvell's capture and offered him a reward.'

'I'm sorry,' began Madselin, 'but I don't see what this has to do with me?'

'He asked only that you be given a choice in the matter of your husband.'

Her hand floated to her temple in disbelief. He could have asked for anything, but he had thought only of her. Despite her lack of trust in him, he wanted still to make her happy. Madselin fought back the lump in her throat.

'The King was impressed by his gesture, so much so that he granted the request and gave Edwin Orvell's keep anyway.'

'Edwin is up here? I thought he had gone. . .' Her voice trailed away. She had thought him gone back to Cheshire, perhaps to see his old love. Knowing that he was close by was hard to bear.

'Aye. This happened a few weeks ago. Edwin is at the de Vaillant keep, helping Ivo and Alain with the border patrols. I will knight him there two days hence.' He paused to peer carefully at Madselin's white face. 'Rufus sent for Hugh.'

Madselin sat up with a jolt. 'Hugh? Hugh is here?'

Richard shook his head. 'We expect him any day now. I thought you would prefer to be...prepared. You might wish to think things over in the light of what I have told you.'

Madselin lowered her head. 'What do you mean by that?'

Richard turned his head away, clearly embarrassed by what he was about to say. 'I have no idea what went on between you and Edwin, but whatever it was certainly had a deep effect on him. He is not himself.' Richard glanced at Madselin. 'He is a good man and were you to think of accepting him, I—as head of the family—would welcome the match. So would Rufus, I daresay.'

After a moment's pause, he continued. 'You are both sensible adults, for all I have said on that subject, and were there to be...er...consequences of your time together, I am certain that Edwin would be more than happy to bear responsibility.'

Madselin's cheeks burned. 'No. That will not be necessary.' How could she even consider asking for Edwin? He would never forgive her for her lack of trust and she could not blame him. He was a proud man and she was not worthy of him.

Richard came to her then and took her hand. 'Then think about it carefully, Madselin. Even if you cannot take Edwin, there are others here if you wish to stay. You have a choice now.'

'You mean you wish me to reconsider marrying Hugh?' She raised her brow in question.

Richard kissed her hand lightly. 'Aye.'

If Emma missed Ulf, she had given no sign of it. On occasions Madselin would find her staring into the distance with a dreamy look in her eyes, but would leap into action the minute she thought anyone was watching her.

'Do you look forward to returning home, Emma?' she had asked her once.

'My home is with you, my lady.' Emma's plain face would smile at her gently. 'That is my choice.'

Had the woman made more fuss about leaving the de Vaillant keep, or even the country, Madselin would have understood. As it was, knowing that she would perhaps be depriving Emma of happiness, was far more upsetting.

'You know that you only have to say, Emma. If you wish to stay here, I will understand. Don't feel you have to return with me.'

Emma had pursed her lips tightly and remained quiet for a moment or two. 'It's no good, my lady. I could never leave you. Ulf knows how I feel and we have said our goodbyes. I think it best this way.'

Nothing more had been said between them, but Emma was noticeably subdued. Madselin determined she would speak to Beatrice about the problem. Her decision, however, was delayed by the arrival of a large party the next afternoon.

'Madselin!' Beatrice huffed as she ran up the stone steps that lead to the solar. 'He's here!'

Jerking her head up, Madselin's fingers froze mid-stitch. 'Hugh?' Her heart began to pound until she was sure everyone could hear it. 'He's really here?' Despite the fact that she had thought of nothing else since Richard had told her, it was still a shock to know he was finally here. A lump formed in her throat and her hands suddenly became unusually clammy.

'Aye.' Beatrice's face was pink with the unaccustomed effort. 'But I don't think he's alone.'

Beatrice's prediction turned out to be accurate. No doubt overwhelmed by a potential family member being summoned by Rufus, Robert and Alice had taken it upon themselves to accompany Hugh. Madselin's heart sank when she saw Alice's graceful figure alight from the litter. Hugh remained doggedly at her side, allowing Alice to clutch at his sleeve and simper blatantly.

Something inside of Madselin died at that moment, seeing them together and knowing how it would be. Had she really thought it possible to be happy? The larger figure of her brother stalked up to Alice and snatched away her hand, placing it firmly on his own arm. He then lead her towards the steps, with Hugh trailing somewhat aimlessly behind.

Madselin stepped forward. 'Robert. Alice. This is a very unexpected pleasure.' She bent forward to kiss each of them on the cheek. Robert managed a rueful grin and pulled her to him in an awkward embrace. It had been years since he'd tried it, after all. 'Aye. It's good to see you again, Madselin.' Stepping back from her, he smiled broadly. 'This barbaric land seems to suit you.'

Alice's cold green eyes swept over her. 'You do indeed look most at home.' Despite the bitter chill of the wind, Alice's nose and cheeks looked prettily pink and glowing. Her pale beauty was enchanting and she was well aware of it. 'But we have missed you greatly,' came the soft rebuke. 'It is to be hoped you will return with us immediately.' There was no mistaking the deeper irritation in Alice's voice.

Madselin's jaw tightened but she smiled stiffly, her eyes going beyond Robert and Alice. Hugh. Smaller than she remembered, he was still handsome. A little ostentatious, perhaps, in a rich red cloak lined with coney skins, but it suited his dark colouring. His hair fell in soft waves about his face and shining, brown eyes swept over her with a proprietorial air that she had never noticed before.

She had the feeling he did not approve of her plain but eminently practical gown of dark blue wool. Aware that the cold weather did not enhance her own looks, she smiled at him nervously.

'My Lady de Breuville. I am most glad to see you once more.' His fingers were white, Madselin realised quite irrelevantly. Long, white and delicate, they reached for her own and carried them to his lips for a brief kiss.

'Hugh. I cannot tell you how pleased I am to see you.' Somehow everything was just so awkward, so wrong, that Madselin wanted to run away. Perhaps all they needed was some time to themselves, but they were surrounded by people who expected far more than they were able to give at that moment. 'Come meet my kinsman.'

Once the introductions were completed, Madselin accompanied Alice to her room whilst Robert and Hugh were ushered away by Albert Mallet.

Alice swept through the door of the room and gave the plain walls and prettily embroidered bed linen scant attention. Throwing her gloves carelessly on to the bed, she turned to face Madselin. All traces of pretence were gone.

'So. You have what you want, finally.' Her voice was harsh and contrasted most strangely with her soft prettiness.

Madselin frowned. 'I'm not sure I know what you mean, Alice. Do you mean Hugh?'

Irritation flickered across the younger woman's face. 'Hugh? Do you think you could ever hold a man like Hugh?' She gave Madselin's sensible gown a dismissive glance before walking to the embrasure to watch her baggage being unpacked. 'He is very. . .accommodating, to be sure. But,' she smiled sweetly at Madselin over her shoulder, 'that was not what I meant.'

Pushing the shutter to, Alice strolled around the room until she stood once more before Madselin. 'You have the attention of the King.'

'The King?' echoed Madselin in confusion. 'I have never wished for that.' Had Alice gone deranged in her absence? The woman was making no sense at all.

Alice shook her head slowly. 'Your innocent acts never fooled me for a moment, Madselin. I knew you sought power and riches. At home you would be the pious sister, all welcoming, kind, organised and efficient, but I saw the way you tried to attract the eyes of the men. Once you had lost Guy, all you ever wanted was to find another rich husband.'

'You err greatly in your supposition, Alice. Perhaps a drink might restore your wits?' Madselin took a step back, but was prevented by Alice's strong grip on her wrist.

'I loved Guy, you know.' Her eyes were shining in the firelight. 'He hated you. He knew you only wanted him for his estate.'

Shaking her hand free of Alice, Madselin gave Alice a pitying look. 'Guy hated all women, Alice. That much I have learned.'

'Guy loved me. He spent the night before your wedding with me and he was late because he tarried with me. I would have been his mistress even after your marriage. He promised me that.'

Madselin shook her head. 'I have no idea why you are telling me this, Alice. I know about you and Guy. Is that not enough?'

Alice stared at her with barely concealed hatred. 'You always looked down on me, always treated me as if I were no more than dirt underfoot. He would have married you because your family connections were better, but he chose me to warm his bed, not you.'

She turned to flop down on the bed. 'And when I married Robert, I had the perfect opportunity to show you how it felt to always be second. Yet even then, you were able to make me feel stupid and silly.'

'So that was why you tried to marry me off to the old man?'

Alice eyed her with dislike. 'Yes,' she hissed. 'It made me feel better to think of you bedding with that disgusting old man. He only wanted you for your paltry manor.'

Only the sound of the fire crackling disturbed the silence.

'And now you can have Hugh, too. Except that he is already mine.' Alice's bitterness welled up from deep within as her pretty face drew itself into a mask of hatred. 'He loves me as I loved Guy. I shall make you pay a high price for this marriage since his only wish is to be near me. You, at least, can offer him that.'

Madselin stepped back. Her mind was reeling from such an outpouring of hatred. Never had she suspected Alice of such deep emotions. Whatever she was about to say was interrupted by Robert stepping into the room.

'Well,' she managed, walking towards the door, 'I am sure you will need to rest and refresh yourselves after such a tiring journey. We will meet again at dinner.'

If Robert had overheard any of their conversation, he gave no indication of it. 'I admit to being in need of some time alone with my wife,' he responded lightly. 'We have had little privacy over the past few weeks.'

'If you have all you need, then I shall leave you.' Madselin had taken no more than two steps, when Robert reached out to grab her arm.

'You'll find Hugh in the hall. He is hoping to see you before dinner, I think.' Robert's blue eyes studied his sister carefully before turning to stare at the pale face of his wife.

Shutting the door quietly, Madselin heard Robert's softly menacing voice. 'Up to your nasty games again, my dear? Do you know what I shall do if I find you once more with that ambitious little upstart?' Was that how Robert viewed Hugh? Did everyone know about Alice and Hugh? Not wishing to hear any more of Robert's opinions on Hugh, she shivered and made her way along the cold stone corridor.

Madselin was not at all sure that she wanted to see Hugh. She thought she had. Hugh had seemed so safe, so kind, so uncomplicated. There would be no cause for worry with him. She doubted they would argue much since Hugh—as Alice had so clearly pointed out—was a most accommodating man. It would seem, however, that she had misjudged him too.

Bracing herself, Madselin decided that she would have to face the man, nevertheless. Alice might well have lied; there would be nothing new in that, after all. With her resolve strengthened, Madselin made her way to the great hall.

Hugh was sitting before the fire, a cup of wine in his hand. Stretched out almost full length, he looked very much at ease and Madselin felt some of her own tension dissipate. There were few servants about at this time and to all intents and purposes, they were on their own.

'Would you like to take a turn in the garden, Hugh?' she asked quietly as she came to his side.

He looked up, his dark eyes soft and bright. 'Most gladly, my lady.'

My lady. How many times had she heard those two particular words from the mouth of another lover— spoken in very different tones? Harsh, full of sarcasm, amused. Madselin conjured Edwin's face and her composure nearly deserted her. Only a slight gasp escaped her lips. Forgetting Edwin Elwardson was not going to be easy at all.

Hugh stood up and took her arm gently in his. He smiled at the slight tremor that ran through her body. Together they made their way to Beatrice's walled garden. The sun was dying and the air was cold, but at least they had some privacy.

'My lady,' Hugh began rather nervously. 'Madselin. You must know why I have come here?'

She indicated that they sit on the bench. 'Aye. I sought leave from my kinsman for our marriage. I have that choice now from the King.'

He nodded, his brown curls bouncing in the wind. Edwin, she reminded herself, had always braided his blond hair, which was far more practical. 'And I would consider myself a fortunate man if you still wished for our marriage to take place. I have been patient these many years.'

Madselin smiled in acknowledgement, but wondered at the lack of emotion she felt in hearing him say these words. 'Do you truly wish this, Hugh?' Perhaps they were in need of getting to know each other again. Talking might help a little.

He shrugged his shoulders dismissively and peered at her curiously. 'Do you question it, then? I had thought you wished it too, my lady.' His handsome face mirrored his hurt. 'On the whole we deal well together and would make a comfortable match.' Wounded dark eyes stared at her reprovingly. Madselin was reminded of one of Alice's small dogs that forever yapped around her ankles.

Had she expected anything different? His face looked very young and very innocent, although he was only a few years younger than she was. Alice had found in him an easy target. 'And what of Alice?' she asked quietly. 'Where does she fit in to this "comfortable" match?'

Unaccustomed to such forthright questions, Hugh seemed genuinely taken aback. 'How do you know about her? Did your brother tell you?'

At least he did not hide the truth. 'Alice told me. She expects to remain as your mistress.'

Hugh had the grace to flush. 'Well, we might be able to come to a sensible arrangement,' he said eventually, unable to look her in the eye.

'Sensible?' she queried, wondering at her ability to remain so calm.

He shrugged again in that careless way that was beginning to irritate her. His eyes were fixed on a piece of ground by his feet. For all his protestations about their companionship, Hugh did not seem at all comfortable in her company. Shifting slightly on the bench, his mouth formed a tight smile. 'Well. Something. This is hardly important, Madselin.'

She remembered how he had liked Alice's simpering and girlish laughter. Was that really what he wanted in a woman? 'I see,' she said abruptly. Aye, she did see. Very well. Madselin withdrew her hand from his arm. 'The hour grows late. We should go in, I think.'

He pulled her to him quickly as she rose to go. 'Well? Is the marriage to take place? I would leave this accursed land as soon as possible.' It was a fair question, but not one that suggested a man newly reunited with his lover. Nor could she fault his logic for wishing to leave so quickly since Madselin had felt much the same not four months before. Not now, however.

Madselin hesitated, her eyes studying him carefully. 'I need some time to think,' she said quietly. 'There are other things, that need to be taken care of.' She searched wildly for a good reason. 'My maid, Emma, has formed an attachment.'

'Your maid?' Hugh's dark eyes stared at her uncomprehendingly. 'Why concern yourself over her affairs? She'll get over it.' Gently he reached out his long white fingers and drew her face to his. His kiss was soft and gentle.

Pulling back, Madselin found her cheeks had flushed and not simply because of his kiss. 'I had better go.' Turning quickly, she fled to the sanctuary of her own room.

Dinner that night was a trite affair with everyone's eyes turned constantly to Madselin and Hugh. Together they were awkward, their speech stilted and their smiles tight and forced. Had they always been this way? By contrast, whenever Hugh spoke to Alice his eyes shone and his boldness returned, although Madselin could not help but think it shallow.

Alice had been remarkably subdued since coming to the hall. Dressed magnificently in a beautiful silk gown of pale blue, she put all the other women to the shade. However, as she did not wear a cloak, Madselin surmised that the woman must have been feeling very cold. This was, after all, a place where beauty took second place to practicality.

She was beginning to feel some pity for Alice, since all she had to rely on were her looks and a younger lover of little consequence.

Beatrice had said very little either. Every so often, Madselin would notice her eyes flicker in Alice's direction and then towards her husband.

For his part, Richard appeared unmoved by Alice's unexpected appearance in his life. Most of the time, he engaged Robert in discussions concerning the family. If Alice made any contribution, Richard would merely smile politely and then continue. Hardly the actions of a jealous man. Clearly Beatrice also came to the same conclusions and allowed herself to relax a little.

Beatrice had organised music and dancing to celebrate their reunion, but Madselin could have told her that she would not be expected to join in. When the dancing began, Madselin could see Hugh stiffen visibly. She doubted even Beatrice's feelings would override his views.

Beyond the top table, Madselin could not help but notice the cheerful banter of the lower orders and her heart gave a lurch. Normans mixed with Angles and Saxons, much as they had at the de Vaillant keep. Every so often she would catch sight of a blond head or hear a deep laugh that caused her heart to skip a beat.

Conversation with Hugh had become desultory, bordering on difficult and all she longed for was to leave them all. No matter how much she admonished herself, Madselin could not be happy. Was this not what she had wanted but four months ago?

As the dancing became rowdier, Alice suggested that she and Madselin retire. She caught Hugh's look of approval and knew that they could never be happy. Despite the fact that a love of dancing was such a foolish thing, it perhaps went to the heart of a person. Madselin withdrew in silence, glad to be alone.

Madselin blinked up into the warm sunshine and then closed her eyes. The morning was clear and fresh and she had taken the chance to escape into Beatrice's garden to think. She had spent the previous night trying to convince herself that the sensible course of action would be to marry Hugh and return to the Vexin with him.

The truth was that she did not want to leave this

land. Nor did she really wish to marry Hugh. There was no alternative though. She could not remain here married to another whilst Edwin was so close. Nor did she wish to retire to a convent. No, perhaps Hugh would learn to love her. Maybe, though, she could help Emma find happiness.

Later on that morning, the whole party would be leaving for the de Vaillant keep to witness Edwin's knighthood and she was very apprehensive. Had there been any way of getting out of this, she would. Richard, however, had insisted and naturally Robert, Alice and Hugh wished to attend as well.

She missed Edwin, damn him. For all his lack of truth, she longed to see him, to touch him, to kiss him. Aye, she admitted wryly, even dance with him. When Hugh had kissed her yesterday, she had known deep down that she could never love him. It had meant nothing to her.

'It's good that the sun shines on so special a day.' Beatrice sat down beside her and Madselin opened one eye to greet her.

'How so special?'

Beatrice turned to sit back and push her pale face towards the sun. 'Did you not know what today is?'

'You speak in riddles again, Beatrice,' she replied irritably. 'Truly the damp has addled your wits.'

Laughing, Beatrice tugged at Madselin's demure braid for such irreverence. 'You foreigners.' She sighed. 'Today is the one day of the year when the young women of this land may choose their husband. It marks the coming of spring and the beginning of life. Had you not noticed how many of the servants were giggling and wearing special ribbons?'

'No,' admitted Madselin. She had been too preoccupied to notice much. 'What happens?' Her interest was piqued all the same.

A slow smile curved Beatrice's lips. 'The girl entices her chosen partner to a quiet place and then captures him. She binds his wrists with her ribbon and then takes him to the priest. They are then wed according to the custom. Such marriages are supposed to be very favoured.'

'Just as well you have a husband already.'

'Ah! But you do not, Madselin. Do you not wish to try it out on Hugh?'

Madselin glanced somewhat warily at Beatrice, but she was sitting with her eyes firmly closed.

'No. I think not.'

That caught Beatrice's attention. She sat up quickly and opened her eyes. 'Do you mean that?'

Grimacing, Madselin nodded. 'Aye. But I will marry him. There is nothing else for me.'

For a moment or two there was silence. 'He told you about Alice, then?'

'Alice told me herself, and Hugh did not deny it,' Madselin replied. Pulling the ribbon from her braid, she began to fiddle with her hair. 'Do you remember you once told me that you wished to be loved by Richard with such a passion that it made him lose control. . .?'

A faint blush tinged Beatrice's cheeks. 'Aye, I did.'

'Well, I found out how that can be.'

'Ah,' said Beatrice, before closing her eyes and sitting back in the sun once more. 'Perhaps I should lend you some new ribbon.'

Madselin managed a weak smile. 'Edwin would not have me now. My future lies with Hugh.' After a brief pause she took Beatrice's hand. 'I think Emma might be glad of your ribbon though.'

'Ah. I had wondered about that.' Beatrice smiled at her friend kindly. 'She will not wish to leave you. Is there no way you can stay? We shall all miss you.'

Madselin shook her head. 'I truly cannot, Beatrice. There is, however, one thing that would ease my heart, Beatrice. It concerns my niece, Mathilde.' Madselin tugged at a loose thread on her gown.

'Could you ask Richard to take her in to your keep when she is seven? I know that Alice is already considering Mathilde's betrothal and I do not want to see her married off to some old lecher because of Alice's avarice. I know you would love the child for herself, Beatrice.'

Beatrice thought for a moment. 'It is too early to consider a match between your niece and Jordan,' she said slowly. 'But I am sure that Richard would be willing to foster Mathilde.' She smiled at Madselin and patted her hand. 'I will see what I can do.'

Madselin returned the smile. 'You are good, Beatrice. At least now I can be certain of saving Mathilde from Alice's poison,' she muttered bitterly.

The de Vaillant keep stood dark and proud against the late afternoon sky as Madselin drew her horse to a halt. They had reached the top of the last rise, just as they had done only four months before. This time she felt very different. Her heart gave a leap of excitement as she caught the salty tang of the sea wind in her throat. It was wonderful to see the place again.

'God's teeth,' murmured Alice. 'I wonder if they've discovered the wheel yet?' She pulled her cloak closer to her shivering body and pouted sullenly. It had been a long, muddy journey and Alice had been very vexed that Richard had refused to allow a litter to carry her. Robert had been forced to ride at her side and neither of them were consequently in a cheerful frame of mind.

'Not very inspiring,' added Hugh, frowning down at his mud-spattered clothes. 'Perhaps it's just as well I didn't choose to wear something more elegant. Such clothes would have been wasted here, I daresay.'

Madselin listened to the pair of them bemoan their fate and was secretly quite pleased that they felt uncomfortable. For the first time in weeks, she smiled as though she truly meant it.

This time, their approach to the keep gates was unimpeded by attack and the party thundered into the bailey with relief etched on their faces. A cheerful crowd had gathered to meet the visitors and Madselin's face lit up with pleasure. Her heart, nevertheless, was thudding unaccountably as she looked about. Edwin was not in sight.

Ivo de Vaillant stepped forward, his face almost hidden by a swathe of black hair. He greeted them all cheerfully enough, although Madselin thought him thinner. Bronwen smiled radiantly two paces behind him, baby Maude clutched possessively to her chest. Madselin fancied Bronwen looked almost cheerful, but dismissed this as a trick of the light.

Alain, his elder son, was still out on patrol but would be back for the ceremony. With no more than a few brief words from Ivo, servants came running to assist his guests dismount and they all headed for the hall.

As she picked up her skirts to avoid the ever-present puddles and dung patches, Madselin was stopped by the grip of a hand.

'Well, my lady. You look much recovered.'

She looked up to find Father Padraig standing beside her. His kindly face was beaming with pleasure.

'Aye. I thank you, Father. It's good to see you all again.' It was true.

'We are all very pleased that you have come back, my lady. Very pleased indeed.' He raised his brows and moved a little closer to speak in confidence. 'It has at least stopped Edwin from biting all our heads off.'

At the mention of Edwin's name, Madselin could feel the blush steal over her cheeks. 'I'm sure Edwin has far more to think about than that.'

Father Padraig took hold of her elbow and guided her towards the hall as he spoke. 'Perhaps its just the spring. The men are apt to be a bit awkward about now,' he sighed.

A huge bellow from the gate caused them to stop in their tracks and turn to see what the commotion was about. Ulf had spotted Emma, bedecked now in colourful ribbons, and was pounding across the bailey to pull her into his arms. Despite the shaking of his head, Father Padraig smiled. 'And he's another one who's been hard to please of late.'

Joanna and Gyrth waved at her from a distance. It was good to see all these people again and even their strange tongue was a most welcome sound. Madselin had not appreciated just how much she had come to care for them and how important they had all become. The thought of leaving them for the Vexin plunged her into depression. This was where her heart belonged.

Robert, Alice and Hugh appeared to think the surroundings fell considerably short of their expectations.

'My dear Madselin. Pray do not tell me you left your home to live here?' Robert stared around at the simple hall with a scandalised expression on his face. 'It must have been hard to bear.'

Madselin smiled 'Well, no. I. . .'

Alice gripped her arm to interrupt. 'I cannot believe you liked it here. Why, the land is cold, wet and dismal beyond belief. The people are even worse, what with their dreadful language and coarse ways.'

'Actually, I found it most pleasant here,' Madselin said with more force than she had intended and her voice carried. Several heads turned in their direction and she felt very uncomfortable. Hugh, she noticed, was watching some of the women servants with great interest. Was it him who had changed or her?

When everyone was assembled, Richard went to stand by Ivo. Alain had rushed in from his patrol not minutes before still spattered with mud, but no one save Alice and Hugh appeared to notice. After a short speech by Ivo and Richard, Edwin was lead to the space in the centre of the hall. It was over two months since Henry Orvell had done the same thing, but today's events would have a very different outcome.

Edwin's appearance caused Madselin's heart to beat faster. He looked truly magnificent in a new linen shirt, clean dark breeches and mud-free boots. His hair was braided neatly and someone had taken great care to barber him well. Despite the fact that he had spent the night on the church floor, he looked remarkably good. Cool grey eyes swept around the room and alighted on Madselin. For a moment, neither of them moved or breathed.

In a gesture that only Edwin noticed, her hand touched the silver brooch that adorned her cloak before smiling at him. His glance flickered over Hugh and then he turned to Richard.

Without more ado, Richard d'Aveyron knighted Edwin with his own sword. Still kneeling, Edwin gave his oath to the King and to Richard. Every eye in the hall was on him, but he remained calm and patient. His voice carried loud and clear to the lofty rafters above and Madselin felt absurdly proud. When he rose, Richard handed him his silver spurs. It was done. Edwin was a knight with his own lands.

The feeling in the hall was one of united friendship, except perhaps amongst Madselin's own family and Hugh. They had taken little interest in the proceedings but few had noticed them. Wine and ale were hurriedly distributed, and Richard called a toast to his newest vassal.

'To Edwin Elwardson, a loyal and trustworthy man. A knight of the kingdom.'

The whole hall burst into loud congratulations as Edwin made his way to the villagers at the back of the room. There he was surrounded by his friends who thumped him heartily on his back and shouted out coarse suggestions as to what the new lord of the manor could do. Madselin was glad that Hugh could not speak the language.

The heat in the hall was stifling and the smoke from the huge fire was causing Madselin's head to ache. As the music began, the villagers surged forward, determined to dance and drink as much as they could.

'If I promise to be gentle, will you dance with me?' Madselin whirled round to find her nose almost pressed against Edwin's chest. She gulped down the lump in her throat as she looked up at his face.

'My betrothed does not dance,' interrupted Hugh, eyeing the Angle with extreme suspicion. He moved closer to Madselin and took hold of her elbow with a great deal more possessiveness than he had displayed thus far.

Edwin ignored Hugh and continued to watch Madselin's face. 'Lady de Breuville is entitled to decide for herself,' he responded abruptly.

'I would be honoured,' replied Madselin equally gravely, ignoring Hugh's quietly indrawn breath. She placed her hand in Edwin's and allowed him to pull her into the centre of the hall. Hugh forgotten, they whirled around the hall, body pressed tightly against body, skin glowing.

'You improve each time, my lady. Been practising?' His grey eyes twinkled down at her.

The tension within her melted away. Nothing had

changed between them at all. She smiled. 'You presume too much, Angle. Norman ladies do not dance.'

She breathed in his soft musky forest smell and closed her eyes. How could she ever bear to live without him? A memory of the last time she had been with him drifted through her mind and she felt like flinging her arms about him. The derision from her countrymen would not matter but she had no desire to shame Edwin. His sense of honour would not allow her to bear it alone either.

It would be far better for Edwin if she left as soon as possible. He deserved a better woman than her. No doubt he would have women queueing to marry him now that he was a favoured knight.

'Are you not well, Madselin?' Edwin had drawn her to the side of the hall as the jig came to an end and was looking down at her with concerned eyes.

Determined to remain strong, Madselin blinked back the tears but could not bring herself to look at him. 'Of course. It's just the heat and the smoke. I had perhaps best return to Hugh.'

At the mention of Hugh, Edwin stepped back and she could feel him withdraw from her. Wordlessly he took her back to the safety of her family and with no more than a curt nod, left.

They did not speak again. Madselin savoured the brief moment before Hugh descended on her.

'I do not approve of you dancing with such peasants, Madselin.' His dark eyes bore a stamp of superiority she had never noticed before.

'Edwin is not a peasant. He's a knight,' she replied wearily. 'Besides, he asked me.'

'When we marry, Madselin, you will look to me for permission. Dancing at all, let alone with uncouth barbarians, is not very acceptable.' Hugh's lips were tight and uncompromising and he had folded his arms belligerently across his chest.

Angered at his tone, Madselin glared at him. 'I will dance with whomever I choose, before or after we are married.' Her tone was sharp and did not disguise her irritation.

'I think you have had too much freedom allowed you, Lady de Breuville,' came his haughty reply. 'Marriage requires women to be obedient to their husbands and to defer any such decision to a sharper mind. You are clearly not aware of the implications of such actions.'

'What do you mean?' she asked curiously.

Hugh lifted his chin and stared down at her gravely.

'You mixing with such ruffians reflects directly on my own reputation and I have no wish for it to be sullied so. . .frivolously.'

Madselin could tell from his tone that he was very serious. She wanted to laugh at such pomposity and arrogance, but managed to keep a straight face. 'Your. . .liaison with Alice, however, does not reflect on me?'

'That is an entirely different matter, but I do not wish to discuss the matter now.' He took a step back and turned to see where Alice was.

Furious at his high-handed attitude, Madselin glared at him before storming out of the hall. If anyone wondered at her actions, they said nothing.

She had to leave. The only thing on her mind was escaping. Here was the man she loved, the place she loved. These were the people she wanted to be with. But they were no longer hers to have.

Her mount, a quiet grey mare, snickered a greeting as Madselin charged into the stables. The stable boy stood up, startled at the noise and the speed of her, but said nothing as Madselin ordered him to saddle her up.

Within minutes she was plunging back through the de Vaillant gates into the wilderness beyond.

The wind was strong and cold, but it did not deter her from galloping towards the beach. The fresh air revived her spirits a little as she jumped down from her horse and tethered her to a loose branch. Madselin yanked off her shoes and her stockings before marching onto the sand. The freedom felt marvellous and she smiled. Deep within, she felt at home.

Her feet were freezing as they squelched over the wet sand towards the grey waves. It was hard to breathe as the wind powered in from the sea. There was nothing else to be heard except the crashing of the waves and the screaming of the gulls.

In complete exultation, Madselin whirled herself around and around like a child. Buffeted by the wind, her hair was wrenched loose from their braids and flew in wild skeins about her. Anyone who saw her would think her mad. Nonetheless, the weight of her troubles had fled her shoulders for a few brief minutes.

She loved Edwin. Closing her eyes, Madselin allowed the salty sea air to collide against her until she could take no more. Marriage to Hugh would be impossible. Better to remain unmarried than to wed a man who would seek to dominate her at every turn. Feeling better that she had made a decision, Madselin opened her eyes at last.

Edwin stood but thirty paces away, his bow aimed directly at her. Madselin's heart shuddered to a halt. Slowly, he took aim and pulled the string back until it strained with the force. Everything then seemed to happen in slow motion.

With practised ease, Edwin let the vicious arrow fly and it sped through the air with unerring aim. Frozen, she shut her eyes, not believing that he wished to kill her. From the expression on his face though, that was clearly Edwin's intent. He did not waver in his determination.

The arrow swooped past her shoulder as Edwin started running towards her, shouting something she could not hear. Turning suddenly behind her, Madselin almost jumped out of her skin.

No more than a few paces away from her stood Orvell's vicious bodyguard with the red beard. He was brandishing a fierce-looking sword and an expression of anger and pain. Despite Edwin's arrow lodged deep in his shoulder, the man was hurling himself rapidly towards her.

'Dear God,' she whispered feverishly and backed away. Frantically Madselin felt for the knife she still wore behind her kirtle and pulled it quickly from its sheath.

The soldier's eyes were cold and deathly as he lifted his sword for the death blow. She did not wait to find out if his aim was good. Launching herself at him, they landed with a heavy thud on the sand. The blade of the knife sank quickly between the soldier's ribs and he gave a terrible choking sound, as if he were drowning.

Suddenly, Madselin was yanked from the man's body and hurled across several feet of sand. Edwin kicked the sword from the soldier's limp grip before approaching the still body.

'He's dead.' Kneeling at the man's side, he pulled the arrow from his shoulder and then the knife from his chest. Raising his eyes to hers, Edwin nodded briefly. 'You learnt well, Lady de Breuville.'

Madselin stood on shaking legs and brushed the sand from her gown and cloak. The blood had drained from her and she thought she might just faint. 'I. . .er. . .had a good tutor.' Unable to look at the inert body of the soldier, Madselin turned to look at the sea. Warm, brown hands slid over her shoulders and she was pulled into a hard chest.

Turning thankfully into him, Madselin wrapped her arms around him and buried herself in his strength. 'I. . .thought you were truly trying to pin me down,' she muttered, her teeth beginning to chatter.

'I tried to warn you, but you couldn't hear,' he explained, his large hand gently stroking down her wild hair. 'There was no time for me to get any closer.'

'Thank you, Edwin,' came her muffled voice.

'Nay. You did well, woman.' His arms pulled her tight against him and he held her there for a minute.

'For a Norman?' she managed with a wobbly smile.

'No Norman lady I know would carry a knife and stab a soldier through the heart.' He lay his head over hers as if to protect her.

She could feel his heart hammering away beneath her cheek. 'Why did you come?' she asked, pulling back a little to look up at him.

His smile disappeared, to be replaced by a familiar frown. 'It's dangerous here. There are many of Orvell's men still in the forest, so I came to take you back. By force, if necessary.'

'It was most fortunate that you did come.'

'Had you not been so reckless, none of this need have happened. I see that time has not curbed your impulses.' Edwin watched her with narrowed eyes.

Had she imagined the mingled look of fear and tenderness before? 'Then it is lucky that I shall be returning to my own lands before I do any more harm.' She turned away, hoping he would not see her tears and her hurt.

'Do you mean to marry him, then, Madselin?' His voice was soft but the tone was unutterably sad.

She shook her head quickly. 'I cannot. It would not work well.'

Her admission was met with silence. Eventually Madselin looked up at him, wiping her eyes on her cloak. 'And what of you? You'll be wanting a wife for your new keep. There must be many young girls waiting in line?' She tried to keep her voice normal, but it sounded very squeaky.

He said nothing, but just bent to pick up Beatrice's new ribbon that had come loose from her braids. Holding it out to her, Edwin raised his brows, almost in question. 'I'm not sure that a young girl would suit me, Lady de Breuville. Do you not think I might find such a wife overly wearing?'

Madselin's lips twitched a little in amusement. 'Older women can be notoriously choosy.' She plucked the ribbon from his hands.

He sighed heavily. 'Aye, but I had thought I might have been lucky today with so many new ribbons about. There must be some poor woman in need of a husband with an empty keep.'

He looked so serious that Madselin could not help but laugh out loud. 'Edwin Elwardson, I do believe you are trying to make me marry you out of pity.'

He held out his hands silently and her smile vanished. Her heart was almost thundering and she was certain he could hear it. Between them the silence grew. Swallowing hard, Madselin slowly wrapped the ribbon around his wrists.

'I would choose you, if you'll have me,' she whispered.

'Only if you promise to obey me.'

She frowned. 'I'm not at all sure that will be possible, if I am to be honest.'

He sighed heavily in resignation before shrugging his acceptance. 'I doubt I shall ever know another moment's peace.'

Despite the lightness of their words, Madselin could

not quite understand why he still wished to marry her. 'You do not have to do this, Edwin. I will understand if you would rather find another... I mean, I have treated you badly and...'

'Shut up, woman. Just kiss me.' His arms lifted over her shoulders and drew her close. There was nothing soft or sweet about his kiss, just controlled passion. 'I think it was perhaps just as well that I asked Father Padraig to be ready by the church doors.' Edwin's cheeks were flushed as he put her gently from him.

'You asked him to be ready?' Her frown cleared. 'So that's why you followed me?'

He pushed back more of her wayward hair. 'It seemed a lot easier than kidnapping you on your way back.'

Madselin stared at him open-mouthed. 'You had planned that? You could have been killed!'

'Aye. But I'd have died a happy man.'

He kissed her again, their passion deepening.

'I think I'd better make an honest man of you very soon, Edwin Elwardson,' Madselin murmured somewhat breathlessly. 'Are you sure this is what you want?'

He smiled down at her softly. 'I chose you the moment I first laid eyes on you. It's you I've been waiting for, woman.'

Madselin's eyes sparkled as she tugged at the ribbon round his wrists. 'Didn't I have you tied up then, too?'

'Aye, but at least this time we both know what we're doing.'

Edwin bent his head to kiss her again and Madselin had no desire to disagree with him at all.

Historical Romance™

Coming next month

RAKE'S REFORM
Marie-Louise Hall

Mr Jonathan Lindsay was most surprised when he was
confronted by the passionate Radical, Miss Janey Hilton.
Upon learning that he was an MP she begged him to
release a young boy who was to be hanged for a crime he
did not commit. Taken aback by her astonishing beauty
and forceful ways, he agreed to help. But he also had an
ulterior motive—he had made a bet with a friend that he
could seduce Janey! He knew he could do it but then the
unthinkable happened—the rakish Jonathan fell in love!
He knew he had to call off the wager. But would it be a
case of too much, too late, when Janey discovered his
horrendous deception?

THE YOUNGEST MISS ASHE
Paula Marshall

Sir Simon Darrow had known and liked Meg Ashe since
she was a child, and, secure in his acceptability, his blunt
proposal totally lacked romance—he was stunned when
Meg refused him, and went instead to her aunt in Paris.

Eight years later, as the widowed and very wealthy
Comtesse de Mortaine, Meg returned, trailing an
apparently slightly soiled reputation—to find Simon still
unmarried and not prepared to accept Meg's decision
never to marry again...despite his misgivings!